BAD HABITS

Sarah Evans

First published by Clan Destine Press in 2021

Clan Destine Press
PO Box 121, Bittern
Victoria, 3918 Australia

National Library of Australia Cataloguing-In-Publication data:

Sarah Evans

Bad Habits

PB ISBN: 978-0-6450426-4-1
EB ISBN: 978-0-6450426-5-8

Cover artwork by © Willsin Rowe

Design & Typesetting by ClanDestine Press

www.clandestinepress.net

ABOUT THE AUTHOR

Sarah Evans, an English ex-pat journalist and former home-schooling mum, is the author of a lifestyle/recipe book *Seasons and Seasonings in a Teapot*, romance and crime novels, novellas, short stories and poetry.

She gives author talks and teaches memoir, creative writing, poetry and song-writing. She lives on a 20-acre hobby farm in rural Western Australia with her family and a menagerie of fur and feather and has added granny duties to her repertoire.

'Well, I'll try. But no promises.'

'I collected *Wild Thing* today.'

And the air began to throb. Or was it my lusting heart?

'That's nice.' I smiled a smile.

He smiled a smile too.

'Hell, let's go. I've lost my appetite,' said Quinn, still holding my hand. 'We've better things to do than eat.'

Oh good.

Bring it on!

To all those with bad habits...

1

IT WAS CHRISTMAS CRACKERS AND CONFESSION TIME AT THE ROCKS' abode and I wanted none of it. I'd had enough explosions these past few days – my heart, my house, my car – without adding to the list.

Sister Immaculata, my mother, was staring at me, suspicious and expectant, as was my daughter, Chastity.

Father Fox grinned: I think he was enjoying my discomfort.

My chest suffered a savage twist. I glared at him. How dare he stand there with that dangerous smile on his face? This was no smiling matter. This was serious, life-changing stuff.

Tall, broad, tanned and fit, Quinn Fox was deadlier than usual. His habitually tousled, sun-bleached hair was tamed into a pony tail to reveal the small jet stud in his ear. His sky blue shirt was sharp, as were his black jeans. Even the sling supporting his recently injured shoulder was hospital neat, unlike my haphazard affair with its cack-handed knot.

I looked at him. He raised his brows: his expression brokered no deal. 'Tell them, Red,' he said.

Heck, I didn't stand a chance.

I took a deep breath. It was confession time.

Or was it?

Because this man was no priest, licensed to give me absolution. Oh no – he was a cop.

Just like me.

I'm Detective Inspector Eve Rock, a single mum to a 16-year-old daughter and, until a few days ago, a proud owner of a house, a car, a to-die-for vintage flying jacket – *Italian, brown leather, silk lined and sexy* – and a mane of long curly red hair.

I'd had some trouble; my prized possessions had been blown sky high and my hair had been singed so badly I'd had to shave it off so that now I resembled an orange bog brush.

The golden hunk standing opposite me was DI Quinn Fox and he'd been part of the trouble.

We had matching job-related injuries. I'd been grazed by a bullet; he'd been shot in the shoulder. I had a tonne of facial scratches and bruises, including a black eye. So did he. Mine weren't pretty; I looked as if I'd survived an encounter with an angry possum by the skin of my teeth. But Quinn's had morphed him into a swashbuckling buccaneer. It was so unfair. Why couldn't I look gorgeous and heroic for once?

But we didn't just share injuries; we shared explosive history. His boat had been blasted to smithereens, hot on the heels of my own fire-bombed home and car, and there were other explosions, too, which I didn't want to talk about. But suffice to say, it had been a helluva of a couple of weeks. Along with the bombings, I'd been stalked by a creepy Santa, got involved in a drug bust, and had solved murder and kidnapping cases.

I'd also come face-to-face with my past: aka Quinn.

And so, here we were, two pig-headed cops, both adept at prising confessions out of people; except this time I was in the hot seat. I felt a twinge of empathy for all the crooks I'd arrested and interrogated over the years.

I squirmed. Quinn wanted me to announce to the world – or at least to my immediate family – that he was Chastity's dad.

And I didn't want to. At least not until after Christmas. Candy canes and confessions just didn't mix in my opinion, especially when an emotional teenage daughter was in the potent cocktail.

There was only one thing for it; I needed to take control.

Or escape.

I smoothed down my little turquoise sun-dress – it was the only item of clothing to survive my bombed house – and took a deep breath.

'I've got to check the potatoes,' I said. After all, someone had to take charge of Christmas lunch and no one else was in a hurry to hang out in the kitchen. 'We don't want them burning.'

At least two people in the room snorted in disbelief.

We were gathered in the common room of St Immaculata's School for Girls, an exclusive establishment in the leafy Nedlands suburb of Perth, which was acting as my temporary home for the duration. I emphasise the temporary. Back in the day it had actually been my home, when my former hooker mum had swapped her dozen-men-a-night habit for a nun's and had re-invented herself as a doyenne of respectability. The place wasn't homely then and it wasn't now and I couldn't wait to shake the dust from my heels and get right on out of there.

We were an uneasy, awkward bunch of people. There was Chastity, Sister Immaculata, my long lost father, Henry Talbot, my hunky cop colleague and almost-lover, Adam Fox, and, of course, Fox Senior, who also fitted that last description.

In retrospect, I shouldn't have invited Henry. He had taken himself off to the far end of the common room with a painful, hunted expression. There, he hunkered down on a hard-backed plastic chair next to the spindly Christmas tree Chastity and I had decorated with red and gold tinsel and yellow fairy lights. He had the air of someone pretending that this was all a particularly nasty dream.

And then there were the Foxes. I shouldn't have asked them either, but lust had been a defining factor. What can I say? I fancied both of them.

But, hey, the damage was done. More importantly, I was out of here.

As I made for the door, Chastity said, 'Since when did you go all Nigella Lawson on us, Mum? You never care about food prep unless it's to order a curry takeaway.'

Okay, I do have a penchant for hot Indian takeaways. So? It wasn't a crime the last time I checked.

'You'd be surprised at her talents,' said Quinn with a wicked glimmer. 'She has so many.' The inference hung in the air like the aroma of a pungent tandoori.

I gave Quinn the evil eye. This wasn't the occasion to tease. Humour wasn't my family's forte and especially not today, when my mother had presumed I'd invited an Anglican priest as my date and hadn't delivered the promise. She was now puffed up like a belligerent bullfrog ready to explode, eyes popping and nostrils flared. She was brutal in her disappointment that he wasn't a man of the cloth but a cop. It was enough she disapproved of my career choice; she certainly didn't want another police officer in the fold. I had to be grateful she wasn't vocalising her annoyance, just doing it by osmosis. But it was awkward all the same.

'True. They're legendary,' chipped in Fox.

He was Quinn's cute son and my sergeant; a veritable angel in a flak jacket. He delivered one of his Raphaelian smiles that still got to me, even though I'd slept with his dad in another life and he was half-brother to my daughter. It wasn't a good situation.

It didn't help that I still lusted after both him and his dad, and that Chastity – who didn't know they were related – had the hots for him too. Hormones are tricky, especially in my family.

I steadfastly ignored his sweet smile. 'Yes, well, let's not go there, Adam,' I said, wanting to slap down both him and his dad.

'Which talents were you thinking of, Adam?' said Quinn. Was it my imagination, or was there an edge to his question?

'Probably the same ones as you, Dad,' said Fox and now imagination didn't come into it. There was a definite tension between them.

The men stood there, a double cliché: two blond, blue-eyed hotties in their crisp shirts and snug jeans.

Now, I'm like any other red-blooded woman who appreciates beauty on the hoof, but not today. I was struggling. My zing wasn't zinging. More flat-line twanging.

'Stop right there,' I said. 'Stop discussing me as if I'm a participant in a TV talent show. Let me check those spuds and prove my daughter wrong. I won't be long.'

I legged it into the kitchen and grabbed my mobile. It was time to ring for the cavalry and get out of here quick smart, hang the culinary duties, because I didn't want to explain to my family about Quinn.

And I didn't want to know what was going on between the two Foxes.

And I hated the toxic tension between my parents.

Silly me, I'd thought it good to get them together over Christmas. But no, another great idea dead in the water.

Henry had unexpectedly turned up in my life a week or so ago. I hadn't known he'd existed. My mother had barely mentioned him over the years. My knowledge of him and their relationship was scant. She'd fallen pregnant while on the game. Henry had apparently wanted to marry her but she'd refused. I don't know why.

But while Sister Immaculata didn't talk about him to me, she had kept in contact over the years and he knew all about us.

I liked the idea of trying to make us more of a family, but reconciling my parents at this particular moment was the least of my worries.

I took my phone outside and squatted down between the green wheelie bins. Before I could punch the number, I was eye-balled by an orange barrel on legs.

The cat was huge and battered, as though it had been in a fight. It had one-and-a-half ears and a mangled tail with matted dried blood. Apart from that, it looked awfully like Horace, my late neighbour's cat. But it couldn't be. He'd been taken to the cat haven after Margot's death.

'Scat,' I said.

He didn't, but rubbed up against my bare leg, friendly like, sharing his fleas. I elbowed him off with my good arm and then hit speed dial.

'Ely.'

'Boss.' My sergeant's one word vibrated suspicion.

'Hey.' And my *Hey* was very quiet. I didn't want anyone else overhearing my clandestine conversation. 'Merry Christmas and all that jazz.'

'Yeah, like you'd call to wish me the happy holidays. What d'ya want, boss?'

'I'm hurt.'

'Yeah, sure you are. What do you want? And why are you whispering? You suffering from laryngitis or something? Been caterwauling too many carols?'

I could hear the chink of glasses, the low murmur of happy voices, muted music, and it wasn't coming from my end. My Hark the Heralds was just a mangy mewling mog.

Ignoring his interrogation, I began one of my own. 'I thought you were at the office?'

'I am.'

'Really? Sounds more like a nightclub. You partying, sergeant?'

'No way. That's your suspicious mind.' He wasn't convincing. A party popper or champagne cork popped and a resounding cheer made him even less convincing.

'Yes, way. You enjoying hijinks among the filing cabinets?'

He sighed. 'Yeah. We're making the most of having to be on duty.'

'Excellent. Can I join in too?' It sounded pathetic even to my own ears.

'You're meant to be playing happy families for once.'

'I'm not cut out for it. It's giving me hives. Come and save me, Ely.'

'Hmm.'

'That's an order.'

'I don't know...'

'Please.'

'I suppose.'

'Good! Give me an official call in about...five minutes. Actually, make it three. Or two. One, even.'

'All right.' He wasn't impressed.

'You'll have to come and get me. My arm is still out of commission. I can't drive.'

'Anything else?' His long-suffering came over loud and clear.

'Yeah. Make the fake call-out a good one.'

'And that's it?'

I thought rapidly. I didn't want my 'boys' spending too much unsupervised time with my mum and daughter. There was no telling what might be discussed. What secrets divulged.

'No. I need you to call in the two Foxes, too.'

'Why? Quinn's on sick leave and it's Adam's day off. Leave them be. Let them enjoy Christmas, unlike the rest of us suckers.'

'Just do it.'

'But they're probably off playing on their boats or something. I might not be able to reach them.'

'Try, sergeant.'

'I can't see the point.'

'You don't need to, but get on to it. Time is of the essence.' I wasn't going to give him any extraneous info such as the Fox men were at St Immaculata's and meant to be spending Christmas with me.

'You don't ask for much.'

'I owe you.'

There was a high pitched screech from the kitchen.

'What the hell was that?' said Ely.

'My daughter. I gotta go.'

Back in the kitchen, the new potatoes had boiled dry. There was an acrid smell of burning and Chastity was squealing with outrage like only a teenage girl can.

'You said you'd check on the spuds!'

'I got waylaid.'

'They're ruined.'

'Harsh. I'm sure they can be salvaged.'

Chastity gave me a hard look. The two spots of angry colour on her cheeks matched her wild red hair. 'No! They! *Can't*!'

'I'll scrub some more.' My offer was half-hearted. I'd be out of here any moment now, Ely willing.

'One handed? I don't think so, Mum. I'll do it.' She slammed pans and spuds and anything else that got in her way. 'What on earth were you doing?'

'Feeding the cat,' I said promptly.

'We don't own a cat, Mum.'

'It's a stray.'

'You hate cats.'

'This one's kinda cute.'

'Show me.' She looked suspicious, which was understandable.

I took her outside. The chewed-eared marmalade was cleaning his crooked tail. I hadn't realised before but Horace had a nasty squint. He didn't look kind or cute. More evil and wicked.

'It's my good deed for Christmas.'

'It looks like Horace,' said Chastity.

'It's not.'

She squatted down and stroked the cat. 'Yes it is.'

'It's a stray.'

'It's Horace. Look, he knows his name.' And the cat loudly miaowed and insinuated himself under Chastity's elbow. 'Good old Horace. How amazing is that? He's found his way here all the way from Subiaco. Poor thing's hungry. No one's been looking after him since Margot died.'

'Don't jump to conclusions. He was given to the cat home and he looks more than well fed to me. In fact, he's obese.'

'We should keep him.'

'No we shouldn't.'

'Gran will be up for it.'

Hah, I doubted it. But before I could reply, my phone rang. 'Ely?' I injected surprise into my tone. 'What's up?'

'You tell me, boss. This is your baby.'

What? He wasn't going to give me an excuse? 'I'll be there straight away.'

'I thought I was picking you up?'

'I'll grab a lift.'

Chastity, who was now standing with fat Horace in her arms, was back to looking suspicious.

'What?' she said.

'I gotta go.'

She let out her long-suffering-daughter wail, startling the cat so he wriggled free. 'You can't. This is our first family Christmas in, like, forever.'

'I'm sorry. But you have the others here.'

For all of ten seconds.

'It won't be the same without you,' she said, retrieving an extremely reluctant Horace, who flexed his claws and yowled.

'It can't be helped, Chastity. Work takes priority. You know that. Careful with that cat.'

'But you're meant to be resting your arm.' She jiggled the cat, trying to avoid being feline swiped.

'I can still rest it while working. I'll get the guys to do any dirty work. It's my brain they need, not my brawn.'

She followed me back inside, complaining all the way, just like the cat.

In the family room, the erstwhiles were making awkward small talk. My mum was sitting ramrod straight, her expression icy. Henry had moved away from the Christmas tree and was now huddled close to a giant aspidistra in a black ceramic pot with his back to everyone as he stared out of the window. The two Foxes were perched, side by side, on a couch. No one looked comfortable.

On cue, Quinn's phone beeped. He made his apologies to Sister Immaculata and answered the call. He disconnected and then Fox's phone rang. Two pairs of electric baby blues fastened on me.

'Seems we've an emergency,' said Quinn, his voice drier than beef jerky. 'I'm sorry to break up the party, Sister.'

'Me too,' said Fox. 'A shame. I was looking forward to a real family Christmas.' And he gave me an ever-so slight smile, damn him.

Chastity's face fell. 'You don't have to go too, Adam?'

''Fraid so.'

'Mum, can't Adam stay at least? You're the boss. You can swing it.'

'Not this time, sweetheart. He's the only one who can drive. I'm presuming I can grab a lift with you guys?' I said and hoped, for once, that Fox wasn't driving his ultra-cool racing green Spitfire.

Being a compact two-seater, one of us would be walking and I didn't fancy my chances.

Quinn raised his brows. 'You're not coming, Eve. You're on sick leave.'

'So are you but they're short staffed.'

One eyebrow hitched higher but he didn't question me further. At least, not in front of my mum.

'You are one terrible liar,' said Quinn as we piled into his beat-up Holden with young Fox at the wheel. He twisted around from the front passenger seat to eyeball me. 'How did you wangle it?'

'I don't know what you mean, DI Fox.' I wrestled with my one good hand, trying to click on the seatbelt.

'Eve.' His tone was blatantly patient and I met his eyes. 'You know there were enough officers to cover the holiday break. And you and me, we're legitimately signed off. Why did you pull rank?'

'It was necessary.'

'Really?'

'You were hassling.' I struggled with the seatbelt again so I wouldn't have to look at him.

'Don't tell me this is about Chastity being my daughter?'

'No. Yes. I'm not comfortable sharing the details with all and sundry.'

'It needs to be said.'

'I've had 16 years without having to explain her parentage, so why now?' I lost patience with the old seatbelt and gave up. 'I don't see the point.'

'Because I want you to.'

'Leave it, Dad,' interrupted Fox who'd come around to my side to help with the seatbelt. He clicked it into place and briefly touched my shoulder. 'Eve will tell them when the time is right.'

Quinn ignored him. 'You were with family, not the frigging public. We're all connected.'

'That's the problem,' I said.

'You embarrassed about the past? You embarrassed about me? Jeez.'

'No.' But my colour rose.

'You've got issues, Red.'

'Stop getting at her,' said Fox, sliding into the driver's seat and firing up the car. 'We've all got issues. Confession time can wait.'

Quinn gave me a hardball stare. 'Not for long, it can't.'

2

THE PARTY WAS IN FULL SWING WHEN WE GOT TO THE STATION. ELY, MY young sergeant, was dancing with half a dozen other revellers. He was wearing a green and purple paper hat over his black crew-cut and his shirt was unbuttoned to reveal surprisingly impressive abs. I hadn't realised he possessed such fine muscles and wondered what else he'd kept under wraps in the six months we'd worked together.

The music abruptly stopped. Everyone ceased dancing as we entered the crew room. Ely fumbled to re-buttoned his shirt.

'Don't on my account,' I said.

'You're funny, boss,' said Ely. His dark eyes flicked to my companions. 'You all came together,' he stated. 'A bigger family affair than I thought.' He pulled off his hat, scrunched it into a ball and tossed it into a waste-paper bin.

I wondered what he knew or guessed. I wasn't good at keeping secrets from my colleagues. I spent far too much time with them. Family were much easier to hoodwink.

'Carry on with the dancing,' I said. 'We don't want to spoil the party.' Wasting no time, someone flicked the music back on.

'So now what?' said Quinn over the Jimmy Barnes din. He still didn't look happy.

'You can go home.' I gave him a half smile. 'Enjoy the rest of your day off.'

'And me?' said Fox.

'You can go too, Foxy.'

'What about you?'

'I'll just chill here until Christmas is over.' I reckoned that was the safest bet all round.

'So Adam and me have been done out of a slap up Christmas dinner because you're a coward,' said Quinn.

'Yep, that's about it. So sue me, Fox.'

I held his gaze with mine.

'Fine. So now I know where we stand.'

And Quinn walked away. Just like that. I had a horrible feeling I'd blown it. That things were over between us before they'd even got started.

The story of my life.

I kept my chin bravado-high. I didn't want to show any emotion. It wasn't my style.

'Oh dear,' said Fox. 'He's not happy.'

'Neither am I. You'd better go after him and make sure he's okay.'

'You don't want to come too?'

'Best not. Your dad and I need to sort out some things, but not today.'

'If that's what you want. It's your call.'

For a split second I thought he was going to kiss me, but my expression must have put him off. It wouldn't have been a good move, not in the office. Not anywhere, really.

He was out of bounds. I had to keep reminding myself, but it was hard to fight temptation on a daily basis. He was more delicious than chocolate.

'It's what I want,' I said and spun on my heel and headed for my office. I closed the door with a sad click. This wasn't the Christmas I'd imagined. Okay, so I hadn't imagined anything. I'd blocked the festive season from my mind. It'd never been my favourite time of year anyway. As a kid, they'd been soulless affairs with just my mum and me racketing around in a large, empty school, trying to avoid each other; and as an adult too, working the holiday because I hadn't wanted to be duty-pulled back to St Immaculata's.

To take my mind off things, such as Fox men, I looked at the crime reports for the previous day.

Christmas Eve was always a quirky one. It was as if the crooks were doing their last minute "shopping" by nicking any stuff they could lay their hands on. There had been a ram raid on a bottle shop, a jewellery theft from a Perth CBD store and a spate of burglaries. Nothing too major. Just same old, same old.

There was a tap on my door. Ely poked his head in. 'Want anything, boss?'

Another glimpse at his six pack? I guess that would be classed as unprofessional. I had enough trouble with the Foxes without tempting fate. So I said, 'A coffee wouldn't go astray, thanks, Ely.'

'I'm onto it.'

A few minutes later, Ely placed the plastic mug of coffee on the desk along with a paper plate sporting two party pies, Rocky Road and a slice of un-iced Christmas cake, courtesy of Lions. He perched on the edge of my desk and picked up the Rocky Road. 'You shouldn't be here and dressed like that.' He indicated my strappy dress. Usually I was a boring jeans and t-shirt girl.

'Well, I came here in a rush. You'll have to put up with it.'

'I'm not complaining,' he said. 'You're easy on the eye.'

'Ely!'

'Sorry, boss. That was out of order. Forget I said anything. Blame the season of goodwill. Or the booze.'

'You've been drinking?'

'No. 'Course not. But I needed an excuse.' He grinned.

I laughed. 'Behave.' Though it was nice to be appreciated, especially after my dud morning. 'Fill me in on yesterday. Did anything interesting happen?'

I blew on my coffee while Ely took a bite of the confectionery.

'Not really,' he said around his mouthful. 'A bunch of country kids smashed into the front of a bottle shop and took off with a load of beer.'

'How do you know they were from the country?'

'Hipsters would have gone for the boutique beers. This lot went for the common-or-garden brands.'

'They could have been bogans.'

'They weren't. Their ute was covered in mud and it had a roo bar and spotties.'

'Oh right, so they were caught.'

'Yeah. They got lost trying to find the freeway south. They were picked up by the traffic unit for doing an illegal U-ie. The traffic guys saw all the grog in the back and called it in.'

'Crime solved. Good. What about the jewellery robbery?'

Ely moved on to the fruit cake. He wouldn't keep his sculpted abs if he carried on eating my sugar treats, but at least it saved me from adding stature to my muffin top.

'We're waiting on the CCTV for that,' he said. 'But basically, some guy rocked up, pulled out a gun and made off with a handful of bling.'

'Not a lot then.'

'A million dollars' worth.'

'Ouch. I take it back. Was there a getaway car or anything?'

'No. The store was that fancy one in the mall. The man left on foot with the booty in a plastic supermarket shopping bag and, poof, disappeared into the Christmas crowd.'

'Don't you hate that? Any witnesses?'

'Not so far.'

We went through some of the other cases and then Ely mentioned Hugo Maine. 'You heard he's out?'

'No. Damn.' A shiver went through me. 'When?'

'Yesterday. Just in time for Christmas.'

Oh boy. I'd run foul of the financier and alleged drug baron while a guest at his Christmas party two weeks ago. Only moments before the drug raid, I'd turned down his dodgy invitation to join his payroll. Maine wasn't a good person to have as an enemy. After the drug bust, his security louts had been responsible for bombing my house and car. They'd also dumped a load of tiger snakes in my toilet.

Now their boss was free. It didn't give me any warm and fuzzies.

'All charges were dropped,' said Ely. 'He must have friends in high places.'

'I reckon. I wish I had friends like that.'

'Keep alert in case he tries to get even.'

'I'll sleep with my peepers pinned open and my gun in my one good hand. Is there anything else I should know about?'

'Not really. We were notified a few minutes back that a fire has started in the CBD. The emergency crews are onto it. It should be containable.'

It wasn't.

Fifteen minutes later, flames were shooting out of manhole covers as the gas mains caught fire. It was like an early Australia Day firework display: lots of flames, lots of bangs. Forrest Place, Hay Street Mall and the adjoining St George's Terrace, Wellington, William and Barrack streets had to be evacuated, but at least there weren't too many people to hustle out, with most of the retail outlets and businesses closed for the festive holiday.

I didn't get involved. That sort of shenanigans was the province of uniform and the fire fighters. Instead, I did paperwork, keying in the words one-handedly onto my computer. It was a painfully slow process but I had time on my side. After that, I tidied my desk and fielded any phone calls the party-goers didn't pick up.

One of the calls was from a guy who said he had inside information on some unusual art thefts and related illegal activity. He wouldn't give his name, just an address, and he refused to elaborate over the phone. As it didn't sound too urgent, I booked an appointment with him for the following day.

As the office party wound down, Ely and I decided it was time to the hit the road and return to our respective homes. I use the term for mine very loosely.

We left behind the air-conditioned comfort of the office and braved the sluggish heat of the baked city. A cyclone was gathering momentum in the north of the state and had left Perth so muggy you could wring water from the air. Heat from the car park's concrete burned through the soles of my thin sandals and I was glad to get into Ely's car. He cranked up the air-con along with the rap.

'You okay to drive by my old place before you drop me back?' I yelled over the music as we hit Hay Street.

'Sure, though why would you want to go there? There's nothing to see but devastation.'

'I want to take stock and ponder on what might have been.' And I wasn't ready to go back to St Immaculata's.

'I didn't have you down as a masochist.'

'I'm not, but I've got to work out what to do next. Rebuild, sell, I don't know. I'm still waiting on the insurance to see what they'll pay out.'

If.

The minion I'd spoken to had inferred the explosions were my fault and not an accident. He didn't sound hopeful I'd get anything. I could see my dream of residing in the buzzing heritage hub of Subiaco disappearing as fast as my cottage had done. I'd have to come up with a Plan B because staying at the school was not an option.

Ely parked on the opposite side of the road to my black crater. He turned down the rap so that you could still hear the staccato voice but not the bass bang beat in the middle of your brain and chest.

'Wait here,' I said. 'I shan't be long.'

He grunted and got out his phone. I left him scrolling through his messages while I wandered around the empty lot. There wasn't a great deal to see. Dom Ferrari, the builder who'd been renovating my house before it was obliterated, had been cleaning things up for me. There were piles of debris, bricks and wood along with a yellow skip bin of rubbish.

I scuffed through the ash and dirt, getting gritty sand lodged between my toes, and kicked up a piece of mottled green and gold dented tin. I picked it up, brushing off the ash. It was the lid of my Earl Grey tea caddy, the one I'd kept my bullets in for emergencies. That tin had been with me since I'd joined the Force. I clutched it tight, getting a hold on my stab of self pity. Now wasn't the time to go all maudlin. I wondered where the rest of the caddy was, including the ammo. I cast my eyes around. There was a fragment of my favourite blue wren coffee mug and some twisted metal that had once been my rusty Hills Hoist, otherwise nothing much. The place was desolate.

Though saying that, my old outside dunny, which now listed dangerously to one side, and my dented tin mailbox had surprisingly survived the blast.

Out of curiosity, I stood on tiptoe and peeked into the skip to see if there was anything else I could salvage along with the caddy lid. It didn't look promising; rubble, splintered planks, half a door – and a man.

A what?

I rocked back on my heels and then stretched up for another look. Yep, there was some big guy in a grey-pinstriped suit lying prone on top of my house detritus.

As it was the tail end of Christmas Day, I presumed drink had got the better of him. But why choose my skip bin to sleep off his excesses? Couldn't he have picked someone else's?

'Hey, wake up,' I called to the bloke. He didn't move so I called again.

'What's up?' Ely slammed his car door and sauntered over, shoving his phone in his back pocket.

'Some drunk's comatose in my bin.'

Ely came and stood next to me. He took a squiz. There was no need for him to stand on tippy-toe.

'I don't think he's drunk, boss.' He reached over and shook the guy's foot. 'More dead.'

'Oh, come on. Now is not the time for a sick joke, Ely.'

'I'm not joking.' He jostled the black-shod foot again to make sure. 'I'll call it in.'

'Honestly, what are the odds?' I said. 'Why my place?' I tried to get a look at the man's face to see if I recognised him, but I was too short to get a clear view. 'Why not pick on someone else? I'm already out of favour with my neighbours. This won't go down well.'

We stood in my sad, charred garden and waited for the troops.

I swiped at mosquitoes. They were having a field day, as my dress exposed far too much flesh. Ely texted his wife to say he'd be late.

'I'm sorry about that,' I said. 'You could have been home in time for the Queen's speech and Royal Variety Show.'

'Nah, that's okay. I get to miss the in-laws. There's always a silver lining.'

One of my neighbours came by with his fat black Scotty dog. He nodded hello.

'Merry Christmas,' I said.

'It hasn't been so far,' he retorted.

'Oh. I'm sorry to hear that.' But I didn't sound it. I hoped he would get the message that an evening chat about his disappointing Christmas wasn't going to happen. Mine had been dire too. I wasn't in the mood to compare notes.

But he was as thick as the Scotty.

'You working out what you're going to be doing with your place?' He stared at me hard from under his hairy brow. His dog snuffled about and cocked his leg against my once whitewashed mailbox.

'Something like that.'

'Not thinking of rebuilding are you?' He sounded accusatory, but perhaps I was imagining his combative tone, because what was it to him what I chose to do?

'I haven't got that far in my plans.'

'Good, because I think the neighbourhood association will have something to say about that. You should sell. Do us all a favour.' He walked purposefully off before I could answer, yanking his dog's lead so that the stumpy mutt bounced along on three legs, his fourth waving in the air, trying to finished his tiddle.

'Oh dear.' Ely gave me a sympathetic smile. 'Looks as though you aren't Miss Popular.'

'Tell me about it. Next they'll be signing a petition to banish me from the street.'

'The whole suburb, if they're smart.'

'Thank you, sergeant. I'll remember that in the future, when you're needing a good character reference for promotion and all.'

Ely laughed. 'I'll be sure not to ask you, then.'

It wasn't long before the forensic team turned up and sealed off the area. Once the dead man was fished out of the skip and cocooned in a body bag on the scorched grass, I took a closer look at his face. It was puce with eyes staring wide. He would have been in his late sixties, I suppose, and was well nourished, if his chins were anything to go by.

'Do you know him, boss?' said Ely.

'Nope. Can't say I do.'

Rachel Gath, the new pathologist, was there bustling around in her blue paper jumpsuit. She was a girl of robust assets that made both her jumpsuit and the eyes of any heterosexual men in the vicinity go pop.

'Any immediate indication as to cause of death?' I asked her as she finished zipping up the body bag.

She pulled off her face mask and shoved back her hood to reveal a thick plait of sweaty yellow hair. A pair of festive teddy bears earrings dangled from her earlobes. 'Not at this stage, DI Rock. See me tomorrow and I should be able to tell you.'

It was getting late and there wasn't much else we could do, so we left the team tidying up and Ely drove me back to my temporary digs at St Immaculata's.

St Immaculata's was a small boarding school in the better part of town. My ex-hooker mum had established it when I was a baby. With me in the equation, she'd hung up her fishnets and stilettos and done a rethink on her career, which obviously didn't factor in Henry and marriage. Henry had told me it was because he was a lowly artist. I doubt if that would have deterred her if she'd loved him enough. Or loved him at all.

Anyway, my ma had promptly done a 180 degree turn and left whoredom to become a nun. She'd then assembled a team of top-notch teachers and opened a school. How she'd managed it, I don't know. She wasn't wealthy or educated. But she'd lived up to her moniker of the Iron Nun, I guess, and crafted her new life with sheer steel and determination.

Or, of course, she'd had friends in high places.

Or she'd been a higher class tart than I'd realised.

Or she had blackmailed a client or three.

Or maybe I was being uncharitable and she was simply a very canny businesswoman.

Anyway, I doubted I'd ever know the truth. She never spoke of her past and she didn't invite confidences.

And, to be truthful, I never asked.

On request, Ely dropped me off at the back of the building so I could go in through the kitchen and slip up to my bedroom. I didn't want to use the front entrance. I didn't feel like socialising.

Best laid plans and all that. Chastity was in the kitchen. She was dressed in dinky floral shorts and a pink pastel crop-top with her long red hair caught up in a high ponytail. She was eating smashed avocado on toast, drinking tea and watching something on her laptop. She shut down the laptop as soon as I entered.

'Hey, Mum.'

'Hey, yourself.'

A china teapot, splashed with hand-painted poppies, sat near her on the counter, along with a matching poppy-patterned fine bone cup and saucer. My girl was a lot classier than me.

'Is there any tea left in the pot?' I asked, hefting it up to gauge the contents.

'It's stewed but help yourself.'

The milk wasn't out. That should have been a sign. I took the carton out of the fridge and splashed some milk into a thick white utilitarian mug and poured. I stared at it. The tea looked the colour of pee.

'What is it?' I sniffed the insipid, tepid liquid. It smelled rather like dirty socks.

She said some outlandish variety I didn't recognise. Going by the smell, I wasn't game to try so I poured the tea down the sink and turned on the kettle. I dunked a teabag of ordinary, double strength breakfast tea into the boiling water, added milk and then went over to the counter. I pulled up a stool and sat down, jiggling the bag until the tea was the colour of mahogany.

'Had a good day?' I said and immediately regretted the question.

Chastity shot me a what-do-you-think look and shrugged.

Uh-oh.

I squeezed out the teabag and steeled myself for a dicey mother-daughter talk.

'What did you think of Henry?' I asked cautiously. I couldn't bring myself to call him dad or granddad. It didn't feel right. I needed more time to get used to him. Even then I wasn't sure I'd be okay with it. Old habits die hard, I guess.

'Pops?'

Oh. So obviously Chastity had no such qualms.

'He's cool. He taught me how to play poker.'

Okay, then. I hadn't expected that. But I was grateful for anything that made Chastity's Christmas a smidge happier, even if it was learning to be a card sharp.

'But he was tired and went off to have an afternoon sleep. Gran did too and so I went and watched TV.' Her tone dipped. 'One rip-roaring Christmas once again. I shouldn't have anticipated anything different. I was setting myself up for disappointment.'

'I'm sorry, sweetheart.'

'No you're not.' She tossed her head, sending her red ringlets bouncing. 'You didn't want to hang around. I bet you orchestrated Sergeant Ely to call you. I can't work you out, Mum. You say you love us but you sabotage anything to do with family.'

'Not true.'

'Is so.'

I decided to grab the proverbial horns of the bull and come clean. 'Actually, Chastity, while we're on the subject of family... there's something important I need to tell you.'

'What, that you're not my mother? Thanks goodness for that.' She sounded as if she meant it. Which hurt.

'Hey!'

'No, *you* hey. I want a normal family life. Like other girls. I'm sick of being different.'

'You're like any other teenage girl.' Emotional, unreasonable, volatile, but I didn't specify. I valued my health.

'I am not. I have a Chaucer nun for a gran, a retro seventies cop for a mum and a boarding school for a home. Neither of you want to spend time with me and the school sucks.'

'Ouch.' Though I was touched with her opinion of me; Starsky had been one of my heroes back in the day. But I wasn't sure how extensive her knowledge was of Chaucer. His Canterbury Tales nun was no saint. I wondered if Chastity knew of her grandmother's previous life. I hadn't told her. Some things were best left unsaid. 'You're wrong. We do want to spend time with you.'

'Pah. I don't believe you.' Chastity pouted. 'I'm sick of everything. I want to go away.'

'Where to?'

'I don't know. Somewhere overseas. Anywhere but here.'

'Well you can once you've finished your exams.'

'That's another two years. Ages! I can't wait that long.'

'It'll go fast.'

'Not fast enough.'

'Look, sweetheart. I know how you feel. Don't forget that I was brought up at this school too. I had to live here *all* my formative years. You've only been here a few months. At least you had some experience of ordinary living.'

'In cruddy rentals.'

'They were all I could afford. Stop being a snob. There was no money. My promotion was the only reason I could afford to buy our house.' Out of nowhere a lump formed in my throat. My lovely little house. The renovations had almost been completed. It was about to be habitable and then – BOOM!

'But you bought the house and shoved me into boarding school.'

'I work long hours. It was for the best. Anyway, you're with your grandmother. It's hardly the same as sending you away to strangers.'

'More like you didn't want me cramping your style with those gorgeous cops.'

True, except my style was questionable.

'Rubbish, Chastity. Quinn and Adam weren't in the equation then.'

'There were probably other men you didn't tell me about.'

'No, there weren't. I don't have time for relationships. But while we're on the subject....' I took a deep breath to spill the beans on Quinn.

'What? Are you going to give me a lecture? Don't worry. I never go anywhere to meet anyone. I probably never will.' With that, she slammed out of the kitchen with her laptop under her arm.

I watched her go with mixed feelings. With her roller-coaster mood swings, I sometimes – most times – felt inadequate as a mother. Then I shrugged. I was used to feeling out of my maternal depth. There wasn't much I could do about it. I hadn't had the best role model. I suppose Chastity hadn't either. Such was life.

I drank my tea and my tummy rumbled.

I needed food.

Unfortunately, the only bread I could find was gluten free, my least favourite, but it was almost tolerable toasted and thickly spread with butter and chunky, three-fruit marmalade. I washed it down with another mug of extra strong tea before going up to my room.

I retrieved the caddy lid from my shoulder bag and placed it on the study table as a reminder of what might have been. I allowed myself a minute to wallow in regret and then had a blissfully cool shower and washed away the black sand from between my toes. I slathered lavender oil over my insect bites and then lay naked on my hard single bed. I'd taken over one of the vacant Year 12 student rooms. It was small and compact, which was ideal as I had barely any possessions since my house had died. It was also comfortingly familiar, as it was a mirror image of my old bedroom. My mum hadn't set aside cosy living quarters for us when I was growing up. We had lived liked the boarders. I never thought I would be grateful for my lack of expectation, but I was at this particular moment.

The window was open but hardly any breeze stirred the torpid heat of the room. I turned on the desk fan full bore and, after a few minutes of thinking I wouldn't, I fell into a deep, deep sleep.

I awoke with a start to hysterical laughter.

A kookaburra was perched in the jacaranda tree right outside my window. The fan was still roaring like a jet engine and my body was cold and stiff from hours of relentless air blasting.

Jerking like a clockwork puppet, I clumsily rolled out of bed and turned off the fan. Still naked, I stretched to limber up my sluggish body and winced as my injured arm and stiff muscles complained. My injuries were healing but not as fast as I wanted. Still, it could have been worse: I could be dead.

I finished my minuscule session of exercises and wondered what to do next? It was Boxing Day. Mmm. How to spend it? Definitely not at the sales. I was allergic to shopping and bargain-hunting crowds.

And then I remembered the body in my skip bin. Well, that would be as good a starting point as any.

Then I remembered something else; I didn't have a car.

Regardless of that, my arm was still too sore to drive.

Really, there was only one thing to do. Oh dear. *Temptation.* I punched in a number.

'Hey,' I said.

'Red.'

Eek! I nearly dropped the phone. What was he doing answering Fox's mobile!

'Quinn! I didn't expect you pick up. Where's Adam?'

'In the shower. What do you want with him, Eve?' The question sounded as loaded as a bikie's sawn-off shotgun.

I could have supplied him with a list but I didn't want to go there. I wanted lot of things from the gorgeous Adam Fox but they weren't going to happen, *not if I kept my integrity*. In another life I could have been his step-mum for heaven's sake. So I kept it simple. 'A lift into work.'

'Yeah, of course you do. You're not working, remember?'

'I am,' I said with indignation. 'And so is he. I want him to drive me in.'

'It's not right, you know, hounding him like a bitch on heat.'

I held on to my temper. I was sure he was being snitchy because he was jealous, so, I don't know why, I decided to goad him. 'Well, I'm not getting it anywhere else. Because you seemed to have gone cold on me and there's no one else in the equation that isn't in jail or a suspect.'

His voice softened in a twinkling. 'That could change.'

'What, are you talking of kissing and making up, then?' I said, experiencing a sudden flair of hope in my otherwise dark blue existence.

'No.'

'Aw, come on. I'm sorry I ticked you off yesterday. I *will* tell Chastity about you. It just hasn't been the right time.'

'Will it ever be?' Again, there was that edge.

'Yes. Soon.' Maybe. 'Look, I even tried last night.'

'Sure you did.'

'I did! She walked out on me.'

'Try harder.'

'I will. Next time.'

'Anyway, I wasn't suggesting we talk.'

'What were you suggesting then?'

'I want action, Red.'

I had a hot flash and a double nipple pop.

'Sounds interesting,' I said and I grinned, feeling smug that he still fancied me even when I annoyed him.

'It'll be more than that.'

And I laughed, now buoyant after yesterday's deflation.

'So why don't we spend the day together?'

'Ah. Sorry. I can't.' *Dammit.* 'I need to go into the station and talk to Rachel Gath.'

'Because?'

'I found a body.'

'Of course you did.' I could imagine him shaking his head in exasperation.

'It was in the rubbish skip outside my house yesterday.'

There was a deep silence.

'You don't have a house, babe.'

'Okay, so my bomb-crater bit of dirt. Better?'

'Who is it?'

'No idea.'

'Eve's found a body,' I heard Quinn say, presumably to Fox. 'She wants a lift to the station and I'm coming too.' He then spoke to me. 'We'll pick you up in half an hour.' He hung up.

I didn't have to think too hard about what to wear, as my minimal wardrobe consisted, along with yesterday's itsy-bitsy dress, of a couple of pairs of skinny jeans, t-shirts and a denim jacket, all newly purchased since the bombing.

I had to admit, I missed the gravitas of my old leather jacket. I mourned it like a long lost friend. We'd been together for years. Without it, my street cred wasn't the same. Not that I'd had a lot. But this new blue denim just didn't cut it for me. I was a leather junky through and through.

I couldn't do a lot I about my afro hair. I gave it a quick brush, which fired up its electric bounce. I tried flattening it, but the short curls wouldn't stay down. I gave up and concentrated on my face. I debated whether or not to wear make-up. My black eye was turning purple-green and the scratches were beginning to fade but not much. I didn't think mascara would make much difference in the scheme of things and I didn't have any concealer. That made it easy. The natural look would be just fine.

On my way out, I swung past Chastity's room. The door was firmly shut. I didn't want to wake her, so I left a note saying where I'd be and that I'd see her later. I slid it under her door and tiptoed away.

I grabbed a glass of water in the kitchen before I left. The red and white carnations Adam Fox had given me the day before were on the draining board. They'd been unceremoniously shoved into a chipped white enamel jug with no attempt at style.

I buried my nose in the flowers. Disappointingly, they had no scent. Still, I didn't often get flowers. They deserved better than an old jug. I rummaged around and found a glass vase at the back of one of the cupboards. I washed off the dust and cockroach muck before arranging the carnations and asparagus fern to my satisfaction.

I popped the vase on the kitchen counter. Fleetingly, I touched one of the red blooms and thought of the tall, willowy blond cop. Fox was such cutie. I sighed. Wrong man, wrong time. It couldn't be helped.

But at least there was the solace of his dad.

Quinn. Now what sort of action did he have in mind? Hmm. I let my imagination take flight!

The Fox boys were late but I forgave them because they'd picked up coffee from a nearby cafe. As we drove to the station, I inhaled the coffee and gave them the little information I had on the body.

Ely and another sergeant were already in the crew room. Ely lifted his eyebrows as the three of us came in together.

'This is becoming a habit,' I heard him say to Burton. 'I wonder what's going on.'

I acted as though I hadn't heard the comment and said, 'Have you a name for our body, Ely?'

'No. I only just got in myself, boss.'

'Get on to it, then. Fox can help you check the missing person reports. I'm going to see Rachel.'

'Sure you don't need me to come along too?' said Ely.

'No. You're more important here.'

'Shame. I could do with seeing that earth goddess.'

'But could she cope seeing you?' said Quinn. He settled down at one of the desks and put his feet up, nursing his injured arm on his flat stomach. 'I'll chill here until I hear from you, Eve.'

'Is your shoulder hurting?' He was looking grim round the edges.

'Nah. Not really.'

'You should be resting.'

'I will when you do.' He gave me the ever-so-slightest of smiles.

Rachel Gath was in green scrubs among endless shiny steel work benches. The red and green tinsel teddy earrings had been replaced with psychedelic pink and blue striped fish with big goggly eyes.

'So, what killed him, Rachel?'

'The guy swallowed a bullet.'

'I didn't think he'd been shot.' I hadn't noticed any blood at the scene.

'He hadn't.'

'But you said – '

'I said that he'd swallowed a bullet. I wasn't channelling some pulp fiction speak, DI Rock. I was stating a fact. The guy swallowed a bullet. Actually, several of them.'

'What?'

'It's my guess he'd been force-fed until he choked. When I cut him up his gullet was full of bullets. Glock slugs to be precise. He died of asphyxiation with bullets lodged in the throat. Guess he just couldn't keep swallowing, poor bloke.'

'How bizarre.'

'Yep.'

'Anything else I should know about?'

'I guess he was of retirement age, in reasonable health and had been shot on another couple of occasions, judging by the scars. Once in the leg and another time in the shoulder. His suit was good quality.'

'Oh. So he could be a respectable businessman with a dark side?'

'Maybe. But that's for you to find out.' She smiled. 'I'll give you my full report once the toxicology results are back.'

Back in the crew room, Ely was setting up an incident board.

'Still no idea who our man is?' I asked.

'Not at this stage. But give me time.'

'Okay. Keep at it. Someone must be missing him. Oh, and by the way, we've got an appointment with an informant at noon.'

3

'You sure you're up to this, boss?' said Ely as we pulled away from the police station later that morning. 'You're looking peaky.'

'I'm fine. I'm just tired. The heat's getting to me.'

'You should take more time off.'

'Because I'm hot and tired? Do me a favour, sergeant. I wish everyone would butt out and stop treating me like a soppy invalid.'

'Yeah, but you've taken a battering. It was a rough couple of weeks, what with the bombs and stuff. No one would blame you.'

'That's all behind me. My arm is as good as new.' I flexed it and winced. Well, almost. I'd left the sling off this morning to give me more mobility, but I was already regretting it. I'd have to be careful not to overdo it. I didn't want any health setbacks.

More for bravado than anything else, I said, 'I'm tough, sergeant.'

'Tell me about it. You're a legend. I would have taken as much sick leave as possible, especially with Christmas in the equation.'

'But then you have a home and a loving wife, Ely. I'm bunking with an anal nun and volatile teenager. That isn't conducive to recuperation, happy Christmases or anything else.'

'Fair comment. With all due respect, boss, your mum is scary.'

'She's in a class of her own,' I said drily. 'Now, let's get this show on the road.'

I was keen to get some good, solid, uncomplicated police work underway after my ten days of sick leave.

'This is the story, Ely,' I said. 'We have a bloke who reckons there have been interesting art thefts from a western suburbs gallery. I'm not sure what the interesting bit means but no doubt all will be revealed.'

'That's strange. No art thefts have been called in as far as I'm aware.'

'I know. I checked. But apparently the art is unusual and very valuable. Which raises the question – why hasn't the gallery reported the theft? Anyway, this guy is keen to talk to us.'

'Is this bloke one of your usual snouts?'

'No. It was a cold call. He rang yesterday, about the same time you were doing the Funky Chicken with one of the secretaries.'

'Gibbon.'

'It looked like a chicken from where I was sitting.'

I read out the Cranberry Court address and Ely clocked the details into the GPS. It must have been a new subdivision north of distant Yanchep because the GPS didn't recognise the address and we had to go on instinct.

Almost an hour later, we arrived at one of the far-flung new outer suburbs, consisting of more sand than houses. The odd finished house stood here and there. A few others were under construction, but otherwise the place was bristling with surveyors' pegs and not a lot else.

'Hard to believe this will be a thriving metropolis in a couple of years,' said Ely as we cruised through the wide, empty streets. 'It's soulless.'

Over the top of my sunnies, I viewed the moonscape. The heat rippled up from the road. The bulldozers had spared only the occasional stumpy eucalypt or banksia, for whatever flimsy reason.

It reminded me of my sad patch of scorched earth in Subiaco, though on a much bigger scale.

'Don't you live in one of these new suburbs?' I said.

'Yeah, but it has more going for it than this. Trees, for starters. Do you reckon that house over there is our destination?'

The house sat proud, like a boil on a buttock. Nothing hindered the view. Not even an apology for a tree.

Ely parked the car out the front of the limestone block house. The front garden was open plan, with an established, neatly cut lawn. Uniform tussocks of lime green and dark maroon native grasses were alternatively planted along the border, with an oversize, over-the-top Gothic fountain in the middle.

'This colour-coordinated designer garden looks out of place in this sandpit,' I said.

'I don't know. They've done a good job. Better than me and we've been in our place almost a year now.'

'You think this is good?'

'Yeah. It's cool. They're setting the standard for the rest of the gardens once they begin to happen.'

We walked up the pale pink paved driveway to the house. Ely looked down at the pavers.

'These look similar to the ones the wife's ordered, but pinker,' said Ely, squinting slightly. 'Yeah, it's the same design. I'm not sure if I like them, now I've seen them *in situ*.'

'Bit late to realise that, buddy.'

'Not really. I could get Teagan to sell them on eBay and then we could choose something less eye-watering. These are really quite zany. Too many edges. It makes me feel like I'm teetering on the edge of a seizure.'

I could see what he meant. It was crazy paving at its most insane.

While the driveway was creating loud zig-zags on the brain, everything else was dead quiet. Not a bird, or cat, or even a cheery chirruping cicada was making its presence felt.

'This place is weird,' I said to Ely. 'Where is everyone? It's like a film set without the actors.'

'Yeah, but it is a public holiday, boss. The tradies are off at the beach.'

Ely rang the doorbell and knocked on the white-panelled front door. 'Nobody's home,' he said. 'What a surprise.'

'Somebody must be in. He made an appointment.' I checked the address. We had the right house. Anyway, there weren't any others to choose from in the street.

While Ely carried on his non-musical percussion of ringing and knocking, I wandered around to see if I could access the rear of the house. An impenetrable high white metal fence surrounded the back garden. There was no way I could see inside.

I completed circuit of the fence and ended up out the front again. I squinted through a window. My face was reflected back at me. The interior blinds had been pulled down, masking whatever was beyond.

When Ely stopped knocking, I thought I heard a slight noise in the garage. We exchanged a glance and heard the scuffle again. I hefted the handle and the big double door swung upwards.

The garage interior was dim. It took a moment for my eyes to adjust to the gloom and then I saw him: a slumped figure tied to a kitchen chair, bang in the middle of an ominous dark stain.

'I think we have us a body, sergeant.'

'I'm not dead yet,' said the body, totally freaking me out.

'I'm sorry,' I said, my heart pounding faster than Bolt's feet. 'My mistake.'

'You took yer time getting here.'

The man's voice was as scratchy as rough-grade sandpaper and he was one of the fattest, ugliest people I'd seen in a long while. He had odd tufts of wiry black hair shooting haphazardly from his flaky skull. More hair sprouted from his ears and nose. That nose was wide, as if it had been randomly flattened with a cement slab, which may have been the case, for all I knew.

'We didn't know it was urgent or we would have used the siren. I'm DI Rock and this is Sergeant Ely. Are you the person I spoke to on the phone yesterday?'

'Yeah. Great to meet you guys.' His tone was full-bore sarcastic. 'But quit shooting the breeze. I'm trussed up like a Christmas turkey and bleedin' everywhere. It's no picnic.'

He was right; it looked nothing like a picnic. 'Sorry,' I said again. I tugged at the cords. 'Who did this to you, Mr–?'

'And are they still here?' added Ely, doing a swift reccy of the garage.

'I already lost one finger for talkin', mate, so I'm saying nuffink.'

'Perhaps we should hack off another one,' said Ely

conversationally as I got out my pocket knife to slice the rope. 'To loosen up his vocal cords. What do you think, boss?'

'Typical police brutality,' said the man.

'Call an ambulance, Ely, and stop giving the bloke a hard time,' I said as the man gave Ely the evil eye from his one good peeper. The other was covered with a black patch, like a Jolly Roger pirate, but without the jolly.

'Yes, boss.'

'Don't bovver on my account,' the man called after Ely. Ely ignored him and went outside to phone.

I sawed through the cords to free the cycloptic troglodyte. He rose unsteadily to his feet and then almost pitched over into the pool of blood.

I grabbed him by the arm. My fingers burrowed deep into his doughy flesh. 'Do you want to sit down, Mr–?'

He shook me off. 'Do me a favour. I been sitting down too long as it is.' He staggered a couple of steps and then slid to the floor, clutching his injured hand to his chest as he turned a nasty sludge grey.

'Steady, buddy,' I said. 'The ambulance will be here any moment.'

I scanned the garage for anything remotely bandage worthy and spotted what I was looking for. A pile of folded laundry sat on a stainless steel counter next to a large freezer. I zipped over, grabbed a tea towel and returned to wrap the green checked cloth around the man's bloodied hand.

'Slow, deep breaths,' I said. 'Nice and easy.'

The bloke just grunted and melted further on to the floor on his fat haunches.

I spied his missing digit lying in its own sticky red goo a few feet away from us. I pulled out a plastic forensic bag from my pocket, gingerly picked up the finger and sealed it in the bag. It needed to be kept cold if there was to be any chance of stitching it back on. I trotted back to the freezer to look for something suitable – ice blocks, frozen peas, whatever – to pack around it for preservation.

'Don't go in there,' said the troglodyte, twitching in his squat position, his one good eye doing cartwheels.

'It's no problem,' I said and lifted the freezer lid. 'A bit of ice will keep your finger nice and fresh for the surgeon.'

'I don't care about my friggin' finger.' He twitched more vigorously, I presumed because of the pain.

'It's worth the chance,' I said. 'You got any frozen veg?' I rummaged about and grabbed a frosted bag.

As the ice crystals fell away, I was eye-balled. Literally.

'Ahh!' I dropped the bag. 'What the–?' I picked it up again. Maybe they were frozen marbles? Nope. Right first time. Eyeballs. A half a dozen or so of them. 'Omigod.' I threw them down and slammed shut the freezer lid.

'Damn,' said Trog.

'Why've you got eyeballs in your freezer?'

He ignored me.

'What are they? Cow? Pig?'

He still didn't answer.

'Goodness, they're not human?' I was damn well joking. No way would they be, but worryingly, the guy did his one-eyed shifty slide away thing and I got concerned.

'Hey, mate, *tell me they are not human!*'

'You shouldn'ta gone in there,' said Trog sanctimoniously. As if it had been *my* fault I'd found the eyeballs.

'And you shouldn't have people's eyeballs in your freezer!' My stomach contents turned liquid and I was in danger of contaminating the crime scene, which I hadn't done in a very long time.

'Medics should be here soon,' said Ely sauntering back into the garage. He took one look at my face and said, 'Bloody hell, boss. What's wrong? You don't look so good. You're not going to faint on me, are you?'

'Hell no. But take a look in that freezer.'

Before he could, the ambos arrived.

I sucked in a steadying breath and read the trog his rights to remain silent, blah-de-blah, and arrested him. 'Do not let this man out of your sight,' I said to Ely, handing him the bagged pinky.

'He's got some tough explaining to do as soon as he's been seen by the medics.'

'What's he done?'

'I'm not sure yet. But there is some seriously disturbing gear in that freezer.'

The ambulance crew wheeled the trog out on a stretcher and I called for back-up. While I waited, I debated whether or not I should search the house. It wasn't sensible to do it solo, and against protocol, but, hey, I reckoned that if anyone had been hiding inside, they would have sneaked off due to all the activity. And I didn't want to hang about with a freezer full of dead eyes. It creeped me out.

I did a rapid search of the house. It was sparse and spotless, which I put down to being new. The hushed, dim rooms failed to give up secrets. There were no finger-loppers to confront, no empty-eye-socketed people in dark corners tip-tapping away with their white sticks. In fact, there was nothing to arouse any sort of suspicion.

Reluctantly I returned to the garage and regarded the freezer. Oh boy. I did not want to have another look inside, but I was compelled to discover if other frozen delights were nestled in the chest. I pulled on a pair of disposable gloves, gritting my teeth against the pain it caused my arm, and tentatively shifted the bag of eyeballs to one side, barely using my fingertips because I really, really didn't want to touch them.

I picked up a pale blue Tupperware box. It sported a label that said it contained chicken noodle soup from some long ago September. I prised off the lid and stared at the contents.

No soup I'd eaten had looked like that. I looked more closely. The frozen bits looked awfully like tongues. Not big ox ones that you could buy from the butcher if you were that sort of home-spun, old fashioned freak who liked to make Mrs Beeton's pressed meats, but smaller tongues. Lamb? Surely not human ones? But there again...

Against my better judgement, I opened another plastic box that had once held fat-free, chocolate chip ice-cream. It was filled with kidneys. Neatly arrayed. Like on a butcher's display tray. There wasn't a chocolate chip in sight.

I slammed down the freezer lid. Someone else could do the frozen stock-take. I wasn't up to it.

I stumbled outside into the harsh afternoon sun to suck in as much air as possible. It didn't help. I emptied my lunch next to the row of tussocks, spoiling the garden's horticultural perfection.

'Sick,' said Burton an hour later when he'd turned up with the forensic team. 'Dead sick.'

I hoped he wasn't referring to my lapse of professionalism in the garden.

'Who would keep eyeballs in their freezer?'

'That's what we're going to find out, sergeant.'

'I don't fancy the job of itemising everything. Who knows what's going to be in that Bluebeard's chest. I pity the poor sucker who gets that gig.'

'Get ready to feel sorry for yourself then, Burton. You're doing it.' I left him to his grisly task and caught a lift back to the station.

Ely looked up from his desk.

'I've a name for our fingerless man: Lionel Duggins. A small time dealer. Been inside a couple of times but nothing major. He still hasn't come round after surgery.'

'We'll go see him tomorrow then, first thing.'

My arm was aching. The pain sapped my energy and enthusiasm for the job. So much for being tough.

'I give up,' I said. 'I'm going home.'

'About time, too. You look like death. Do you want me to drive you?'

'Thanks, but no. You keep on here. See what you can dig up on Duggins. The more we have on him the better. It should give us a bit more leverage during the interview than squeezing his finger stump.'

Exhausted, I rang for a taxi and went straight back to the St Immaculata barracks. I sneaked in the back kitchen door, slunk up to my room, stripped off and slept like the dead until early evening.

I blinked awake, disorientated. The sleep hadn't done me much good. I still felt like hell. I was hot. My head now throbbed along with my injured arm. I'd overdone it. I needed painkillers. Groggy and heavy-eyed, I lay flat on my hard bed, my tummy rumbling out the Ride of the Valkyries. Okay, I needed sustenance, too. And a shower to sluice away the sweat. With an effort, I got up, showered, put on my crumpled blue dress for decency and then raided the medicine cabinet and fridge, in that order. No one seemed to be around so I piled up a plate with cold turkey and minted potatoes – cooked to perfection by my daughter – and returned to my sick cell.

The following morning I felt more robust. The headache had gone and although the arm still pinged when I moved it, it was bearable. I dressed in my regular clothes, did minimal stuff to my hair and face, and made my way downstairs.

From halfway down the staircase, I could hear voices and laughter. I entered the kitchen. Chastity was having breakfast at one of the stainless steel counters. She was smiling broadly with her eyes shining, which was hardly surprising, because she was flanked by my current two most favourite men.

'Morning all,' I said. 'And to what do we owe this pleasure?'

'We anticipated you'd want a ride into work,' said young Fox. 'So we swung by.'

Quinn gave me an assessing look. 'Where did you get to yesterday?' he said. 'We were waiting to give you a lift home.'

'Sorry. I bailed out mid-afternoon.'

'Ely said you weren't feeling too good. How are you faring this morning?' He came over and kissed my cheek, his hand lingering on my shoulder. The unexpected, intimate gesture momentarily robbed me of speech. I glanced at him, suddenly shy and self-conscious.

'I'm okay,' I said a mite huskily. Chastity giggled and I snapped to attention, though I felt like giggling too. So not cool.

'Tea anyone?' I said. I couldn't offer coffee. Sister Immaculata and Chastity regarded it as the Devil's brew and had banned it from the premises.

'Chastity's already asked us. But we're going to pick up a coffee on the way in,' said Fox.

'Sounds like a plan.' And this coffee addict was prepared to skip breakfast for a much-needed, delicious shot of caffeine.

'What about breakfast, Mum? Aren't you having anything?'

'I'll get something on the way.'

'So I have to eat on my own again?' She said with a petulant twang.

'No. On second thoughts, I think I'll have some toast. You two sure you don't want some? It's gluten-free.' I gave Quinn a hard stare. This was his daughter. He could suffer too.

'Well, yeah. That sounds awesome,' he said and glimmered one of his smiles at Chastity. 'Adam and I are starving.'

'We are?' said Adam.

'We are,' said his dad.

So instead of quality takeaway coffee, we had tea and toast, and left a more cheerful daughter washing up the breakfast dishes. I had to give Chastity her due; she was a lot more domesticated than me.

'What's with the starving bit?' said Fox in the car. 'We had a huge fry up this morning.'

'Sometimes, son, one has to take a bullet for the team.'

'And she appreciated it,' I said.

'Happy daughter, happy mother,' said Quinn drily.

'You got it.'

Traffic was busy, though not as bad as in school term time. We made it into the city by ten, just in time for the morning briefing. Sodbury, my opposite number, was back from annual leave and presiding over the meeting. We slipped in and sat down.

Sodbury cut to the chase. 'Wisteria Place has been busted into,' he said and a surprised murmur rippled around the crew room.

Wisteria Place was an underground safe deposit facility in St George's Terrace. It was hidden in the bowels of the former Newspaper House, an impressive 1930s modern classic building that wouldn't have been out of place in an English city. Wisteria

Place touted a fine reputation as a cast iron haven for gold, gems and other costly treasures. It had never been breached in all the time I'd been a cop.

'Hooley dooley,' said Burton. 'I thought the place was built like Fort Knox.'

'That was the impression,' said Sodbury. 'But every bloody safety deposit box was emptied of its contents over Christmas. Cleaned out good and proper. Not a brass razoo left.'

'But what about the alarms?' I asked from my back seat location. 'Didn't they go off?'

'Yes, and what the hell are you doing here, DI Rock? You're meant to be on sick leave, recuperating in bed or something.'

'I'm not sick and I don't own a bed any more. It got blown up, remember. I'm better off here.'

Sodbury blinked his close-set, squinty eyes and waved a pudgy paw in the air. 'Whatever. I don't have the energy to argue.'

He did look tired. At the best of times, Sodbury wasn't the picture of health. In his late fifties, he had sparse sandy hair, a squashy, wide red nose that sported an impressive network of purple spidery veins and a chest wheeze that sounded like an articulated truck's air brakes. Usually his complexion was the colour of rich tomato sauce. Today it resembled grey porridge. Obviously the holiday season hadn't been kind to him. One too many prawns on the barbie, perhaps?

'If the alarms went off, why didn't anyone check?' I said. 'Wisteria Place has the same rating as the Perth Mint. The place would have been high priority. Weren't uniform onto it?'

'Nah, the alarm company contacted the owners who had their security firm personnel do a perimeter search. No police were deployed. Apparently the guards couldn't see anything untoward. All the entrances were locked.'

'Inside job then?' said Burton.

'No point speculating, Burton. We have to find out for sure. Or you do. Go and see what you can dig up.'

'When was it discovered?' Quinn asked.

'Not you too! You're not meant to be here either, Fox. What the hell's wrong with you all?'

'As my bed was blown up too, I thought I'd hang out here, along with DI Rock.'

'You people should get a life.' Sodbury wiped the sweat off his grey face and said, 'The burglary was discovered early this morning when the staff came in after the Christmas break.'

And with that he clutched his chest and slumped to the floor with a nasty gurgle.

After a moment of stunned silence, it was action stations. Burton had just done his first aid refresher course and so yelled a lot of high pitched, panicky instructions which no one listened to. Headless chooks had nothing on it. I didn't rate Sodbury's chances with our half-baked expertise, so I called for an ambulance.

Everyone was emotionally exhausted by the time the ambos arrived and did their stuff. Sodbury was still alive – barely – and was wheeled away. Relieved that the crisis was over, some went outside for a smoke and others hit their poison of choice from their desk drawer and filing cabinet stashes.

Quinn was no exception and downed a hefty whisky. 'That was a close call,' he said. 'I think Burton needs another refresher course, and soon.'

'We all do and no drinking on duty.'

'Technically, we aren't on duty, Red.'

'As good as.'

I noticed Quinn was rubbing his upper arm.

'You in pain, Quinn?'

'I can handle it. Don't fuss.'

So I didn't. I was no Florence Nightingale. But I did graciously hand him a packet of my painkillers, which I reckon counted for something.

Once we were back in kilter, I put on the leadership mantle. 'Go and find out all the details they've got on the Wisteria Place heist,' I said to Burton. 'I need to know what we're looking at.'

He came back after talking with officers who'd been at the scene.

'No wonder the security guards didn't see anything,' he said. 'The gang gained access via an adjacent elevator shaft in the Ramosa building and drilled through the vault wall with a diamond-tipped industrial power drill.'

'Bloody hell,' said Quinn. 'They were taking a gamble. Drilling through thick concrete would have made a huge din. Surely people would have heard something and called it in?'

'Not necessarily,' I said. 'If this took place on Christmas Day, there was mayhem in the city centre.'

'There was?'

'Yep. Blackouts, fire, gas explosions. A veritable circus.'

'What, Santa's Grotto blew up? Or were you in town, sweetheart?'

'Hah, very funny.'

'All I'm saying is that chaos seems to follow you, Red.'

'Only since you've been around. Usually my life is as boring as bat poop.'

'So what are *you* saying? That it's our synergy causing the action?'

'I wouldn't go that far.'

'Don't diss it, babe.' He gave me his oh-so sweet smile that was too reminiscent of his son. Or was that the other way round? Anyway, on cue, lust clutched my gut.

I scowled. These Foxes had no sense of timing.

'So,' said Quinn, his smile deepening as he picked up on my discomfort. 'What was going on in the city on Christmas Day that was so exciting no one heard a high-powered drill cracking concrete?'

'All the emergency services were deployed to evacuate the CBD because of fire. Some electrical cables went up and triggered a gas main explosion. You really didn't know anything about it?'

'Our Christmas had been cancelled, remember?' His expression was wry. 'So we decided to take Adam's boat to Rottnest Island and chill out in one of the bays.'

I felt a pang of envy. I hadn't been to Perth's holiday island in years. While the Fox men had been out in the great blue yonder, enjoying endless sun, sea and sky, I'd spent the day holed up in my poky office, eating party pies and answering calls from dodgy snitches. No prizes who'd had the most fun.

'It was awesome,' said Quinn, rubbing it in. 'There were no bombs, no fires, no hassles.' He gave me that look again.

'I don't court that sort of action,' I said defensively.

'Babe, with you around, it's to be expected.'

'It's not intentional.'

'You attract trouble, Red. It can't be helped.'

Against all the odds, I decided to take that as a compliment.

'So,' I said. 'You reckon that the CBD fire wasn't a coincidence? That it was organised to create a diversion?'

'Yeah. Classic tactics. With all that pandemonium going on, it would have been easy for the gang to get their gear in, drill through the concrete and make as much noise as they needed.'

'You know for a fact it was a gang?'

'It wouldn't have been a solo job, Red. It would take some heavy action to get that hole drilled, let alone cart the stuff away.'

'True. So, suspects?'

'Not off the top of my head. We'll get the boys to trawl through the files.'

Half an hour later, Fox strode into the incident room. He waved a computer print-out in the air to get my attention. 'I might have something, boss. Terry Beard was released a week ago.'

'Well, well. That's a name from the past,' said Quinn.

'Who's Terry Beard? Should I know him?' I said.

'He'd be before your time, Red. He's an old timer. A career thief. Knocked over high street jewellers on a regular basis with a mate. Am I right, Adam, or am I right?'

'Yep, as usual,' said Fox. 'Beard and this other guy would walk into top-end jewellers, whisk out their handguns and take what they could. It was a nice little earner, until Beard got caught.'

'Who was his buddy?'

'He was never arrested and Beard never blabbed.'

'He's been inside several times since then. The last stretch was for an Eastern States heist that went pear-shaped.'

'I thought he'd died a while ago,' said Quinn. 'He must be 70 plus.'

'But would he be our man?' I said. 'This job is far more ambitious than robbing high street shops.'

'Who knows? Send Burton to find him and bring him in.'

'Even if he didn't do this one, a jewellery store robbery on Christmas Eve fits his MO. Ely's got details.'

Before he could follow that up, the chief came in and announced that, because of my body bits in the freezer case, which the office had duly dubbed Operation Popsicle, Quinn would be in charge of the Wisteria Place heist.

'But chief,' I said, annoyed. 'I'm capable of running both investigations. And DI Fox is still injured.'

Quinn didn't say anything, but his highly raised eyebrows gave him away. He wasn't impressed by my outburst. Tough. I wanted the case.

'So are you,' said the chief, thrusting his finger in my direction. 'But I'm not holding that against you. We're short-staffed. Resources are stretched to the max because of the holidays.'

'But...'

'That's why you can have one case each. I don't want either of you overdoing it. That's an order.'

'But, sir?'

'Did you hear me, Rock?'

'Yes, sir. Sorry, sir.'

'Really, I don't know what's going on,' said the chief. 'This is usually our quiet time of year but we seem to be experiencing a crime spike.'

'We've just been talking about that, sir, and decided it's DI Rock's fault,' said Quinn. 'Trouble and Eve go hand in hand.'

'That's not fair,' I protested. 'This batch of crime has no connection with me.'

'What about the body in your skip?' said Ely.

'An unhappy fluke. Do we know his name yet, sergeant?' I said, slapping his impertinence down.

'No, boss.'

'Nice try, Red, but don't change the subject,' said Quinn. 'Trouble stalks you. We'll probably find everything bad that's happened over Christmas is connected to you.'

A ripple of laughter went around the room. I didn't join in. Quinn's prediction might just hold true. I appeared to be going through a disaster phase. Maybe my planets were out of alignment.

'Yes, well, maybe,' said the chief with a rare flash of humour. 'I'm watching you, DI Rock.'

'You don't have to agree with him, sir,' I said indignantly.

'But DI Fox has a point, Rock. Think of all that action before Christmas.'

'Do we have to? That was an aberration.'

He ignored me. 'And, because of that, I have plans for you.'

'What sort of plans?'

'I'll let you know in due course.'

I didn't get a good vibe about that.

'Keep me posted on developments,' he said and returned to his hallowed office on the top floor with its sweeping views of the Swan River.

'Damn,' I said to Quinn after the chief had gone. 'That's one beauty of a case. The biggest we've had, if the haul is to be believed, and I miss out working on it.'

'Relax, Red. We can liaise on both cases,' said Quinn. 'It's not an issue.'

But it was with me. I would have loved to sink my teeth into a good old-fashioned heist rather than a sicko case of possible cannibalism. That was a bad analogy. Don't think of biting and human flesh! Blah.

I retreated to my office to do paperwork. Adam Fox followed me in.

'I'm heading out to Wisteria Place to assess the crime scene. Would you like to come with me?'

'It's not my case.' But that didn't mean I wouldn't mind going with him!

'Yeah, but you'll be having an input anyway. You heard Dad.' He smiled. 'And it would be nice for us to spend a bit of time together. Just the two of us. Even if it is to do with work.'

'I don't know, Adam. I don't think it's a good idea.'

'You don't want to see the damage first hand? Come on, Eve. I know how your mind works. You'd love to view the crime scene, breathe in its smell and get it into your system. Have a ride in my car.'

Yes. I would. All of the above. Especially the car.

'Okay.' I tried not to sound too keen. 'Sounds like a plan.'

'I'm coming too and we'll take my car,' said Quinn, sauntering into my office as if he owned it. He had an interesting expression on his face. I wouldn't say a good one. More assessing. Lethal, even and I wondered how much of the conversation he had heard.

'You don't need to,' said Fox. 'You're looking tired, Dad. You can rest here.'

Quinn's expressive brows lifted just a fraction. 'She's out of bounds, Adam.'

Fox stared levelly at him.

'It's too messy,' said Quinn. 'You know it is.'

Okay, so he'd heard enough. Oh boy.

Fox slapped down the paper on my desk, turned on his heel and stalked out. I was glad that no one else had witnessed the encounter.

'I keep telling him,' said Quinn. 'But he won't listen.'

'So that's why there's tension between you.'

'Yeah. All because of you, sweet cheeks. You shouldn't encourage him.'

'I wasn't. I don't. But now you've annoyed him we'll have to find another ride to Wisteria Place, because I *do* want to see the crime scene, even if the case isn't my baby.' I kept my tone light and disinterested and collected every single sheet of paper on the desk so that I wouldn't have to make eye contact.

Quinn waited a beat. I could feel the heavy weight of his gaze on me. I shuffled the papers and then pretended to read the top sheet.

He sighed. 'I'll go and rustle up a lift,' he said and walked out.

I sighed too and plonked the sheaf of papers in my already full in-tray. It was then I realised the top sheet was upside down. Oops. I hoped Quinn hadn't noticed.

4

Burton was our man. He drove us to the vault, which was busier than a Boxing Day sale. Police, forensics and goodness knows who else were milling about. Some people, who we were told were the owners, were corralled into a corner so as not compromise the scene. They looked absolutely apoplectic, which you would if you'd just been fleeced of your clients' mega wealth along with your own. I left Quinn exercising his vast reserves of charm on them while I went with Burton to view the actual scene of the crime.

The underground vault was huge. There was lots of dust. Lots of empty safety deposit boxes. And a hole.

The hole wasn't that big, but large enough to allow a man to squeeze through. Along with millions of dollars' worth of booty.

'It must have taken them ages,' said Burton. 'There was a lot of gear, let alone making the hole through a metre thick wall of concrete.'

'At a guess, they worked over a couple of nights or more,' I said. 'Which is probably why they chose this window of opportunity, what with the combination of weekend and public holidays.'

'Yeah, I reckon.'

'I don't suppose there were any witnesses?'

'Uniform are doing a sweep of the nearby premises to see, but we're not holding out a lot of hope.'

Quinn joined us and we spent a while soaking up the atmosphere and then left, giving the owners a wide berth.

Back at the station, the place was buzzing as everyone got on with their various lines of inquiry. During a lull in my own particular investigations, I contacted my insurance company. I was fed up not having my own wheels. My arm hurt, but I was coping. I was sure I'd be fine driving. I had to be, because I hated being reliant on others. It curtailed my movements. I was used to my independence, of going to places on a whim, such as Indian restaurants and bottle shops. I was prepared to wait a while for the house pay-out but I needed money to replace my dead car, and I wanted it now.

The insurance clerk didn't share my logic and turned me down flat. I then spent a long, irritating phone call trying to convince him that the company should at least stump up the funds for a hire car while they decided on whether or not, and how much, to pay out. He said he would get back to me, but not until after the New Year.

Frustrated, I marched into the incident room to see what was happening there. No one had put a name to the body in the skip, no progress had been made on the jewellery theft or on the safety deposit box heist. Things were stagnant which made me even more antsy.

I returned to my office and slammed shut the door.

While I'd been away, Quinn had settled himself in my office chair, with his feet propped up on my desk and his eyes closed. He cranked open one eye and frowned when he saw me. 'Why you looking so mad, Red?'

'I need a damn car.' I shoved his feet off my desk and stood over him, waiting for him to vacate my chair. 'Being without wheels is driving me nuts.'

'So buy one.' He stood obediently, towering over me, looking like a warm, cuddly bear with his blond hair muzzed and a faint fuzz of growth on his chin. He'd shed his earlier edgy mood.

'With what? My money was tied up in the house. I've zilch. What's the point in having insurance if they won't shell out when you most need it?'

'Keep your hair on.' He ruffled that same sad, shorn hair. 'There's probably just a glitch in the system.'

'You're too generous. I reckon they're stonewalling me. And thanks for reminding me about my hair.' I slapped away his hand.

'It's cute, in a skin-head pixie kinda way. And you can have my car for the duration.'

'Really?' I stared at him disbelievingly. 'You'd trust me with your car? But you love your car.'

He smiled. 'Babe. I'd trust you with my body, so why not my car?'

I had an instant blood rush. His body, eh? I forgot the car for a good 30 second lust attack.

'Hello! Earth to Red.'

'Sorry. I was thinking of something else.'

'I bet you were,' and he grinned before leaning forward and brushing his lips against mine. 'And now you're thinking of it even more...'

With his one good arm, he pulled me in close so I was hard against his chest. Our gazes meshed, our breath mingled, it was only a millisecond before our lips met in satisfying heat.

There was a long, l-o-n-g moment before we came up for air.

Oh boy.

My anger had evaporated. I felt at peace with mankind. I may have even had a silly grin on my face.

'You're one hell of a woman, Eve.' He kissed me again, more thoroughly this time, so my insides dissolved to mush.

I snuggled closer. 'We need to spend some time together,' I said.

'My boat will be out of dry dock soon.' He gave me a knowing smile.

Wild Thing had been the scene of my undoing 17 years ago. It looked as though it was going to be the scene of my undoing once again.

Bring it on!

'It'll be like going back to our roots,' he said and I wondered if the pun was intentional.

Seventeen years ago I'd met Quinn at a party. There'd been an instant lightning bolt of attraction. The upshot was four days on his boat *Wild Thing* doing, well, wild things. I wouldn't have left except I'd an interview with the police academy. When I'd returned to the quay that evening, Quinn and the boat had sailed away and out of my life. Gone for what I thought was forever.

Until two weeks ago.

Now here we were and I couldn't believe I was going to have a second crack.

'I can't wait,' I said and reached for him again.

'You'll have to, but we can still do this...'

'This is very unprofessional,' I murmured a bit later.

'But good.'

'Yes, but we'll get caught if we're not careful.' I pulled away from him, took a couple of steadying breaths and straightened my rumpled t-shirt. 'I'd better find out how our fingerless guy survived surgery.'

Ely was actually doing that, but I had to think of something to diffuse the heat.

'Ah, yes, the man with the full freezer. Sounds as if you've got a gourmet feast of a case,' he said with a dry chuckle.

'Don't go there. It's horrific.'

'Who is he?'

'Lionel Duggins. He has form but for nothing major. I'll be interviewing him in hospital with Ely.'

On cue, Ely knocked and poked his head around the door.

Goodness, that had been a close call. I didn't glance at Quinn in case I gave the game away but I could feel the stain of heat on my cheeks, so that probably gave it away anyway.

'Sorry to interrupt, boss.' His eyes darted between us and I could feel him absorbing the atmosphere like a true detective. 'But Duggins is well enough to be interviewed. Do you want to go to the hospital now?'

'I reckon. The faster we move on this, the quicker we can get rid of the disgusting case. It's giving me the creeps.'

'Good luck,' said Quinn. 'I'll see you later.' The corner of his mouth twitched with the barest of smiles.

As we drove there, Ely said, 'I wonder where the rest of the bodies are?'

The freezer had been chock full of various body parts. As well as the eyeballs, tongues and kidneys, there were livers and hearts and a couple of ears. There was also a skinned torso, minus arms and legs.

'The boys are going to dig up the garden today,' I said. 'Maybe they'll find the remains of the bodies buried under the lawn.'

'It wasn't lawn, boss.'

'What do you mean?'

'It was fake stuff. Some plastic job. The guys just need to peel it back before getting down and dirty with the shovels.'

'No wonder that grass was blemish-free. Even I could have had a spotless lawn if I'd splashed out on plastic grass by the metre. Why hadn't I thought of that?'

'Never mind. It would have been wasted.'

'How do you work that one out? It would have looked damn good out the front of my place.'

'You still would have blown it up.'

'Gee, thanks, Ely.'

'My pleasure.'

We reached the hospital entrance and Ely said, 'There were six tongues, you know. Which means six bodies.'

'I can do the maths,' I said. 'It's nasty, any which way you look at it.'

'I wonder if we'll be able to identify them all.'

'Goodness knows. Let's hope Duggins can fill us in some details to speed things along.'

That same said Duggins was sitting up in bed like an obese cane toad with a sparse frizzy afro. His hand was heavily bandaged, his eye black-patched. His skin colour was rosier than the previous day, but not by much. It still resembled putty.

'Mr Duggins. Lionel Duggins,' I said.

'Go away. I'm sick.'

'Not too sick to talk to us.'

'I am.'

'No, you're well enough.'

'Who says?'

'The doctor. Now quit fooling,' said Ely. 'Or I'll squeeze your hand until you squeal.'

This earned us a fierce, one-eyed scowl. 'You're wastin' yer time. I dunno nuffink.'

'That's for us to decide, mate.'

Duggins glared back.

'Tell us about your freezer contents,' I said.

'Weren't my freezer.'

'Whose then?'

'Not tellin'. I wanna keep the rest of me fingers. I'm not stupid.'

'You've got protection.'

'Yer mean that kid outside me door? He couldn't fight his way out of a wet paper bag.'

'Actually, Officer Clark is a black belt,' I said, even though I had no idea if Clark knew the first thing about karate, origami or any other Eastern practice, let alone have a high grading in it. But I thought it would make Duggins feel safer and more inclined to cough up information.

'The house is rented under your name, mate,' said Ely. 'Which means the freezer is yours too.'

'No, it don't. The bloody thing came with the house. It's nuffink to do with me.'

'And the contents?'

'I dunno nuffink about that.'

'But you knew what was in there,' I stated. 'You didn't want me anywhere near the freezer in case I saw what was inside.'

Duggins shrugged. 'I dunno what you mean and I dunno nuffink about that freezer, see, or the gear inside.'

'How long have you rented the house?'

'Two months, give or take a week.'

'And you never looked in the freezer in all that time? Do me a favour, Lionel.'

'Nah. Why would I?'

'Don't lie to us, mate,' said Ely and he sat next to Duggins. His hand hovered over the gauze swathes protecting Duggins' pinky stump. The doc hadn't been able to stitch the finger back on. There had been too much damage or something. I hadn't inquired too closely. I didn't need to know the intricate details.

Duggins stared sullenly at Ely. 'Touch me and I'll do you for assault.'

Ely stared back without flinching. 'As if I'd want to hurt you, Lionel.' And we had another tense stand-off.

'Mr Duggins,' I said, fed up with their bull mastiff display. 'Who cut off your finger?'

'Can't remember.'

'Try harder.'

'Me head hurts.'

'Poor dear,' said Ely and shifted his hand meaningfully over the bandage. 'A couple of days ago you contacted us because you had information. Now you don't want to talk. What's the deal here?'

'There's no deal. I changed me mind. It's no crime. I don't wanna talk no more.'

'Duggins,' I said. 'There's a freezer load of body parts in your house so I think you are going to have to do a great deal of talking to explain what the hell's been going on.'

'I told yer, that stuff's nuffink to do with me.'

'Okay then. Let's get back to your finger. Who sliced it off?'

'They didn't slice, they sawed.'

Ouch. I hoped the saw blade had been sharp.

'Who *sawed* your finger off?'

'I dunno. Never seen 'em before.'

'We have a witness.'

'Really?' He didn't believe me, but an old lady living nearby had given one of the officers the information.

'That witness stated your assailant is a regular visitor to your place.'

Duggins glare at me. 'If yer know, why ask me?'

'Because it's better coming from you.'

He thought for a moment. Ely flexed his fingers. Duggins sighed. 'What's the point, anyway?' he said. 'The stuff's Danny Pike's.'

'By "stuff" you mean body parts?' I said.

Duggins gave a half-hearted shrug, his one eye shifty as it did a rapid 360 degree rotation.

'So you *did* know about the freezer contents,' said Ely. 'Naughty Lionel for lying.'

'It's still nuffink to do with me, sarg.'

'Who's Danny Pike?' I asked.

'He's a butcher.'

A butcher, eh? Now, why wasn't I surprised? 'Where can we find him?'

'Subi farmers market. He's gotta stall.' Duggins hesitated, shifting uncomfortably in his narrow hospital bed. 'Selling gourmet stuff. Snaggers and the like.'

A cold shiver rattled my bones. 'You're not saying...'

'I'm not sayin' nuffink, lady.'

A double negative, but I didn't push the point. I really didn't want to know if cannibalism was involved until I really had to. My fertile imagination was already in overdrive, causing my stomach to churn and bile to rise in my throat.

'Was it Pike who hacked off your pinky?' said Ely.

'No.' He did the eye-shift thing again.

'I don't believe you.'

Duggins did his customary shrug.

'Was it anything to do with the information you were going to give us?' I asked.

He squirmed and looked at the ceiling.

'Duggins?'

'No.'

'Are you sure about that?' said Ely.

'Stop hassling. I'm in pain.'

'Enlighten me, Lionel,' I said. 'What was the information?'

'I got nuffink to say. The pain's made me forget.'

Ely put his hand gently around Duggins' bandaged hand and applied a little pressure. Duggins yelped.

'It's true. I can't remember what I was gonna tell you guys.'

'You're a lousy liar, Duggins,' said Ely.

'Let me help you to remember. You told me you had information on an art theft from a Claremont gallery,' I prompted.

Duggins did a one-eyed scowl and Ely squeezed again.

Duggins yipped. 'Oh, that. Now I remember.'

'Good man.'

'But I still don't wanna talk about it.'

'Shame, because you're going to have to. Which gallery? What was taken? And how do you know?'

'The stolen stuff had nuffink to do with the freezer junk.'

Ely and I exchanged a significant glance.

'I'm just saying, for the record,' said Duggins. 'There's no connection.'

'We never said there was,' I said.

'That's all right then.'

'So what was stolen?'

'Dunno.'

'Lionel, you're telling porkies again.'

I wished Ely hadn't used that metaphor, what with the cannibalism bias.

'Somefink special,' said Duggins with a grouchy pout.

'Define "special"?' said Ely.

'It wasn't on show to the public,' said Duggins, clearly uncomfortable. 'Just for select collectors.'

'What was so unique about it?'

'I dunno. I'm no arty fart.'

'Can you describe it?'

'Nah.'

'Try.'

'Gimme me back my phone; I'll show you instead.'

We exchanged glances. The phone was in the evidence room at the station.

'Just tell us.'

'Nah. Too hard.'

I felt he was time-wasting, but he wouldn't budge. Reluctantly we drove back to the station, got the phone released into our custody and returned to the hospital.

Ely handed Duggins the mobile. The troglodyte trolled through his files with an impressive one-handed deftness. He passed the phone to me. I squinted at the picture of gaudy flowers on a yellow background.

'That's it?' I said. 'You wasting our time, Duggins? Because I won't be happy if you are.'

'That's the gear,' said Duggins.

I handed the mobile to Ely. 'I see what you mean,' he said. 'What's so special about that? It looks kindergarten standard. My three-year-old niece could do better than that.'

Duggins snatched back the phone and got up some more pictures. 'Here, look closer,' he said, thrusting the phone towards me. 'Take your time.'

I did. It still didn't look like much. But then, like Duggins, I'm an art philistine. I scrolled down the screen. There were dragons and cartoon characters, the odd heart and loads more flowers. One canvas resembled a patchwork quilt, the individual squares of different hues, sepia through to dark coffee.

A horrible thought popped into my head. But no. I was just being over-imaginative after our previous conversation.

But there again...

'Are these done on parchment?' I said.

'Yeah.' Duggins nodded.

I thought of the haul from Duggins' freezer.

Of the eyeballs and offal.

Of the skinned torso.

Yeuwk.

'Now yer see why they're special,' Duggins in sullen triumphant. 'There's a big market for them works. They fetch huge amounts. Up to half a million smackers.'

While Ely was still figuring it out, I swallowed hard and said, 'Who's the artist?'

'Various tattooists,' said Duggins. 'Unless yer mean who does the final prep and installation?'

Ely croaked as he caught on.

'So who?' I said. 'Pike?'

'Pah. He's nah artist. I told yer. He's a butcher.'

Butchers were pretty handy with knives, which could mean... 'Did Pike prepare the skin for the artist?' I asked.

Duggins hunched down further into the bed, a hunted cast in his eye. He plucked at the hospital bedclothes. 'I'm saying nuffink more.'

'Who are the artists?'

'I want my solicitor.'

'And I need some air.' I left the room and made it to the restroom just in time. At this rate, I was going to turn into an anorexic vegetarian.

5

WE DRANK INSIPID VENDING MACHINE COFFEE THAT CURDLED OUR insides while we waited for Duggins' solicitor. I was on my third cup when he arrived.

'DI Rock?' he inquired.

'Yes?'

'Georgio Papadopolous. Mr Duggins' solicitor.'

I tossed back the coffee dregs, threw the paper cup into the bin and stood to shake hands.

I had to tilt my head to meet his eye. My, the guy was A1 model material. He'd even give young Foxy a run for his money, which was saying something. He was tall, slim and dressed sharper than a paper cut in a tailored black suit, which I guessed was top-of-the-range expensive. His black hair was shorter than mine and had far more style, which wasn't difficult. His eyes were clear pale green and startling and he had a big glossy black Ned Kelly beard that was at odds with his suave suit and slick profession.

'Nice to meet you at long last,' he said, with a distinct American undertone to his voice. 'Your reputation precedes you, DI Rock.'

Ely snorted.

'It does,' said Papadopoulos with a widening smile. 'You'd be surprised.'

'I won't ask what sort of reputation. I don't need to know. And this man with the bronchial complaint is Sergeant Ely.'

'Mate.' The two men shook hands.

'Lionel Duggins is in there,' I nodded to the room. 'We'll wait for you to have a chat and then we need to interview him.'

'Of course.' Papadopoulos disappeared into the room.

A few minutes later, he reappeared. 'My client wants to co-operate,' he said with a pleasant smile. 'Do come in.'

He settled us into chairs like a consummate host and then stood behind us, leaning against the door like a bodyguard. I didn't like having him out of my sightline. I felt I'd been outmanoeuvred, but that might have been my paranoid personality.

Duggins gave him an unhappy glare from his one working eye. 'I don't feel so good,' he said. 'I'm not up to being interviewed. I feel sick. Can't we leave this till another day?'

'Just answer the questions, Lionel,' said Papadopoulos. 'The sooner you start co-operating, the sooner it'll all be over and you can concentrate all your energies on getting better.'

'So Mr Duggins,' I said. 'For the record, who owns the contents of the freezer?'

'I already told yer. Danny Pike. It had nuffink to do with me.'

'But the art did?'

He glared at Papadopoulos and was given the go-ahead. 'A bit.'

'You have pictures on your phone, so you must be involved more than *a bit?*'

'I wasn't. The pix were fer me own records.'

'Which gallery was involved?'

He stared at the lawyer and then said with reluctance, 'Fine Art on the Terrace in Claremont.'

'And what was taken?'

'Some art from an exclusive collection.'

'When?'

He looked at Papadopoulos. 'Christmas Eve.'

There was a knock on the door and a nurse came in. 'Sorry to disturb you,' she said. 'It's time for Mr Duggins' meds.'

'We'll leave you to it,' I said to Duggins. 'We'll be back tomorrow with some more questions.'

Papadopoulos followed us out into the hospital corridor. 'Here's my card,' he said. 'Give me a call when you next want to interview Lionel.'

'Thanks.'

'Good meeting you, Eve.'

I wondered when I'd given him permission to use my name.

The Fine Art on the Terrace gallery owner was camper than a V-dub pop-up van.

Small, round and bespectacled in unflattering powder-blue too-tight skinny jeans, a lemon silk shirt topped with a dandyish bow tie and curly silvery-blond locks, he was your full-blown arty type. The fact that his name was Jeremy Sweet just added to the cliché.

'But I haven't reported any theft,' he twittered when we flashed him our badges and said we were investigating his art theft. 'How did you know about it?'

'A tip-off.'

'That's strange. But I don't want to press charges.'

'So the art has been returned?'

'Well, no, Detective Inspector.'

'So it was stolen?'

'Taken, not stolen.'

'Semantics, Jeremy. Who *took* it?'

'I'd rather not say, if you don't mind.'

'Actually, I do mind.'

'Oh dear.'

'What's the problem?'

'If I tell you, he might hurt me, Detective Inspector.'

I thought of Duggins' butchered pinky. 'Danny Pike,' I said matter-of-factly.

Jeremy blanched like a Christmas almond. He tugged at his yellow silk shirt collar, dislodging the symmetrical perfection of his natty pink tie.

'He stole the pictures?'

He nodded, his Adam's apple bobbing. 'He said they belonged to a friend. He's scary, Detective Inspector. He said he'd turn me into sausage meat. I believed him.'

'Do you have a photo record of the artwork?'

'Oh, but of course. That's standard procedure.'

'And?'

'I'm sorry?' He shuffled from one pink and cream winkle-pickered foot to the other.

'The photographs.' I reined in my impatience. 'May I see them?'

'Well, if you really must.' He went over to his laptop and found the file. The artwork didn't improve with a second viewing. I concentrated on the two letters on the bottom right-hand corner of one of the pictures: LD.

'Do you know Lionel Duggins?' I said. Jeremy's cheeks bloomed a blotchy, uncomplimentary maroon.

'Yes.' He sounded curt.

'So he's the artist?' I hazarded.

'Oh I really don't know about that,' said Jeremy. 'I doubt if he is any sort of creative being. But he organised the delivery.'

Okay, so Sweet didn't like Duggins. Understandable, neither did I.

'You do realise what the artwork actually is?' I said.

'Yes, of course. It's representative of our contemporary culture.'

'That's one way of describing it. But do you know what the medium is?'

'Ink on parchment,' he said promptly.

'Actually, Jeremy, I think it's ink on dead people's skin.'

'No!' I felt he wasn't as horrified as he should have been.

'Yes.'

'But that means...'

'Yes, Jeremy. People have died for the sake of naff art.'

'Not naff, Detective Inspector.'

I rolled my eyes at him. 'Naff *and* sick. The question is, was the skin inked before or after death?'

We went straight back to the hospital, contacting Georgio Papadopoulos to tell him we were on our way. He was there when we arrived.

'I appreciate your promptness,' I said to him. 'We don't often get such co-operation from defence lawyers.'

'A little co-operation goes a long way. I believe in building relationships.' And he winked – yes, winked – as he left us to go and prepare Duggins for the interview.

'Smarmy git,' said Ely under his breath. 'Reckon he's trying to soft soap you.'

'It'll take more than that to get me on side with the lawyer species,' I said.

Papadopoulos came back and invited us into Duggins' room. Duggins was slouched low on his pillows. He wasn't thrilled to see us again so soon.

'You're the artist,' I said to Duggins.

He snorted. 'Do I look like an artist? I'm no butcher, neither, before yer go makin' any more accusations.'

'Come on, Lionel, what was your part in all this? Your initials are on the canvases.'

'Not mine.'

'LD. Or is that just a coincidence? Hmm? I don't think so.'

'Yer can't pin it on me just cos I share the same initials with someone. That's crazy.'

'Give me something to go on, then. Like the artist's name?'

'Look, I rented out me garage to Pike. It was easy money. I also delivered artwork when asked. That's it.'

'I want the artist's name.'

'I've nuffink else to say.'

He pressed his lips in a purposeful line. We left him in a self-imposed mute state on his hospital bed.

On the way out, we passed a diminutive figure in a big straw hat talking to Officer Clark.

'Grapes,' she said to him, holding up a brown paper bag. 'For poor Mr Duggins. Is it all right if I just pop in to say hello? I won't stay long.'

Papadopoulos caught up with us in the hospital foyer. 'Thanks for going easy on Duggins. He's in a lot of pain. Let me know as soon as you need to see him again.'

'We will.'

'How about a drink sometime?'

It was on the tip of my tongue to say *probably not* when I had a rethink. It might be politic to keep him on side.

'That would be nice. Thank you.'

'I'll give you a call.'

'Really?' said Ely as we got in the car. '*Really?* You'd go for a drink with that dude?'

'It can't do any harm,' I said.

'I wonder what's in it for him?'

'You never know, Ely, but he might just fancy me.'

Ely turned to look at me. Before he could stop himself, his eyes flicked to my red-fuzz disaster and then back to me. There was a heap of *you-gotta-be-kidding-me* in his expression.

'Or not,' I added.

'No disrespect, boss, but you don't look his type.'

'Just tell me how it is, sergeant.'

'Well, personally, I think he'd go for a more sophisticated type of woman. Classier. Younger.'

Ouch.

'You didn't have to go into specifics.'

'Oh, I'm sorry, boss. I thought you wanted my opinion.'

'Right.'

'My mistake.'

Back at the office, things were already winding down for the day. Someone was taking orders for food and so what could I do but order a Rogan Josh? Over the curries, tacos and sushi cartons, we discussed what progress everyone had made. Basically, we hadn't. We made sketchy plans for the next day and then officers began to peel off to their respective homes.

'Okay, boss. It's getting late. Do you want a lift home?' said Ely. 'Unless you've made other plans?' He gave a nod in the direction of Quinn, who was chatting to one of the other sergeants on the other side of the office.

'No, no other plans.' If Ely thought Quinn and I were an item we'd been too obvious. I adopted a cool, indifferent tone. 'A lift would be good. Thanks, Ely.'

Cyclone Clarry was gathering momentum in the Timor Sea. Its impact on the city was oppressive humidity and wild, abstract cloud formations. We drove towards St Immaculata's with Ely's favourite rap music drumming through our skulls. At times like this I really, really missed my own car and the glory of silence. As we neared the school, I asked Ely to pull into a picnic area on the Swan River foreshore near the university. 'I can walk from here,' I said.

'Is that a good move, boss?'

'The exercise will do me good.'

'But what about Hugo Maine?'

Darn, I'd forgotten about him.

'I doubt Maine's worked out where I live yet and there's no certainty he's going to bother with me anyway. I should be fine. The school is just around the corner.'

'But, boss...'

'And I want to smoke. The school's a smoke-free zone.'

'I'll wait while you inhale your poison and then I'll take you home.'

He wouldn't budge on the idea. He pointed out in no uncertain terms how dangerous Maine could be and so we sat side-by-side on a park bench, overlooking Matilda Bay, watching the play of lights on the dark water with the odd ghostly apparition of a pelican bobbing by, while I enjoyed a cigar. It had been a while since I'd had one. Sister Immaculata and Chastity didn't approve of smoking, but cigars, red wine and hot curries were my chosen vices.

And Quinn.

And Fox.

Ah, vices. Well, today I had enjoyed curry, Quinn and now a cigar. I could round it off with a red once I was back in the St Immaculata barracks. Nice thought. Four out of five was pretty good going in my estimation, and especially with my abysmal track record.

A slight wind ruffled the water but didn't do much to relieve the hot air. I didn't mind. It was pleasant just being there. I didn't often get the opportunity to sit and do nothing. Perhaps that was one of the reasons I enjoyed a smoke so much: the peace and meditative few minutes of just being, without doing.

Neither of us spoke. We let the slumberous warm evening wash around us until Ely's phone beeped and broke the spell.

'It's the wife,' he said. 'I'd best get back.'

'Thanks for babysitting me.'

'No worries, boss.'

My self-imposed bodyguard took me back to St Immaculata's and dropped me round the back of the premises.

I sneaked inside the school building. It had just gone ten. The place was cloaked in darkness. Chastity was probably watching a film in her room or had gone out with friends, and my mum was chanting Hail Marys, sacrificing virgins or doing whatever nuns did at night.

I quietly made my way through the silent kitchen with its rows of stainless steel counters, through the connecting corridor towards the entrance hall to access the main stairs to my room. Then I heard muted voices.

I stopped and listened, more to determine how close the people were rather than to hear what was being said. I didn't want to be rumbled and get dragged into any conversations. I was tired and over the human race for the day. My narrow, chaste bed beckoned.

It didn't take long for me to realise that the intense, whispered discussion was going on between Sister Immaculata and someone else. I stayed stock-still in the doorway, hoping they hadn't seen me. One of them moved into my line of vision. I could easily make out the penguin silhouette of my mother because she was dressed in her usual severe nun's habit. She stalked into the dimly lit vestibule, gesticulating madly at a figure shrouded in shadow.

My curiosity was piqued. I strained to hear the heated conversation, but I was too far away to decipher the actual words, just the sibilant angry tone. The school's old creaky floorboards were not conducive to stealth, so there was no way I could risk getting any closer by creeping across the polished floor.

I'd made a good call because the argument abruptly came to a head.

Sister Immaculata hissed venom at the person who'd briefly stepped into the half-light. It was a man in dark blue overalls; that was all I could tell. He had a dark beanie pulled over his hair. He said something low and furious to her and then left the building. The Iron Nun closed the heavy jarrah door with a decisive clunk, drawing fast the bolts, like some medieval gaoler in a *Blackadder* episode.

I hugged the hall's black shadows and held my breath. Sister Immaculata stomped into her office and slammed the door. You didn't need to be a rocket scientist to know she was one hell of a ticked-off nun.

Expelling my breath, I slipped out of my sandals and swiftly went upstairs to my room.

So, what was all that about? Who had mum been arguing with, and about what? She was usually so restrained and cool – actually more icy than cool. Where had this fierce heat come from? But hey, it was none of my business. The school was mum's domain. I didn't get involved if I could help it.

I made it to my room without further incident. I stripped off, slung a towel sarong-style around me and padded off to the communal bathroom. It was good to wash away the filth and sweat of the day.

Back in my room, I enjoyed my fourth vice of the day and sank a couple of wines before dozing off.

Two in the morning and the moon was brighter than a Mensa student. But that wasn't what had woken me. The silver moonlight had fooled the resident kookaburra and his mates into thinking it was time for their merry dawn chorus. I couldn't hack the hilarious noise or the light, so I got out of bed to close the window and draw the curtains.

As I swung the window shut I caught a slight movement in the deep pool of shadows near the gymnasium. Immediately, my professional instincts leapt to high alert. I strained to see more but there was nothing. Maybe I'd been seen? I carried on closing the window and stepped back into the room, out of sight.

I waited a few moments and then peeped out. The courtyard was empty. I must have imagined the movement in my sleepy state. To make sure, I decided to find a better view of the gym for another look.

For modesty's sake, I pulled on my t-shirt and underpants and hoofed it along the corridor to one of the other vacant student rooms. Peeking out of the window, I spotted what I presumed to be a man. He was wearing dark overalls and hat, like the guy in the foyer a few hours before, and pushing a large wheelie bin. He disappeared into the gym and then came back into the moonlight before disappearing again, this time around the corner of the building. He was back in seconds with another wheelie bin. He repeated the process twice more.

Well, that was odd. It wasn't refuse collection day, and anyway, the bins were usually collected from around the back early in the morning. The school caretaker was off during the holidays, so it wasn't him, and no tradie would be doing work at this time of night. It was hard enough to get them to front up in daylight.

I didn't hang around to watch any more but scarpered back to my room. I thought about donning my jeans, but decided the new stiff denim would be too difficult to get on quickly with my one fit hand. Forgoing socks for speed, I pulled on my sneakers, tucking the laces into the shoes. I tried to put my holster on but failed because of my gammy arm. I could carry my Glock but I needed my phone for its light and with only one able hand, I had to make a choice. Gun or phone? I needed to see and not necessarily shoot, so the phone won out.

I jogged along the corridors, down the stairs to the kitchen and unlocked the back door. I figured that by going out the back way I wouldn't be seen.

Quietly, I made my way past the bank of rubbish bins, taking time to glimpse in each one. Some were empty, one had recyclables and the other usual domestic waste which didn't smell too good. At the end of the line of bins, I turned into an alley that took me to the front courtyard – and tripped over the solid body of Horace. I went down hard on one knee and swore as ripely as the gunk festering in the bins.

'Thanks, Horace,' I hissed at him as I writhed in pain, trying to be as quiet in my suffering.

I shone the phone's pencil light bang in his face. His eyes glowed back at me like two huge glass marbles. He blinked once and then nonchalantly wandered off into the night, unfazed by my antics.

Once I'd got a handle on my pain, I limped along in his wake until I reached the end of the alley. I switched off the light. It was redundant here because the moon was doing an excellent job this side of the building. The lawns and flowerbeds were gilded silver, transforming the pedestrian garden into a bewitching fairyland.

But I wasn't here to appreciate botanical beauty. I was on a mission. I scuttled down the pathway towards the gym, hugging close to the brick wall, keeping well into the velvet shadows. As I approached the gymnasium, I stopped and listened. There was the whine of mosquitoes and nothing else. Even the kookaburras were mute. I moved forward, slowly this time, my muscles tense.

The gym door was shut. I twisted the doorknob and pushed. The door didn't give. Okay then, so whoever had been here just now had a key. I followed the path to where the person had been getting the bins. A dark, boxy van was in the parking lot. I snapped a picture of the registration number with my phone and then peeked in the van's back window. As I raised up on my toes to look inside, I heard the crunch of loose bitumen under someone's foot.

Before I could respond, something soft and sweet and smothering was shoved firmly in my face. I fought against it, but whoever held the cloth was stronger than me and kept the offending stuff hard over my nose and mouth for what seemed like an eternity.

Blackness won out.

6

Whoa!

I came to with a start as cold water hit me full in the face. I jerked upright and I wished I hadn't. My skull hurt like hell. I slumped back onto the lawn, jittery from my rude awakening. The smell of wet grass and dirt filled my nostrils. I became aware of a fast, rhythmic tick-tick-tick and then a thrum. Water hit me full-on again, the fat drops as hard as rice grains stinging my skin. It took me a groggy moment to realise the school watering system was doing its early morning routine and I was lying directly in the path of one of the heavy duty sprinklers.

The moon had gone but it hadn't yet been replaced by the sun. It was the deep darkness of pre-dawn and I couldn't see a thing. I patted the grass around me, trying to find my phone. Tick-tick-tick, thrum, and I received another drenching. Dammit, I'd drown at this rate.

Feeling wonky and uncoordinated, I scrambled to my feet and staggered forward, right into the path of another rush of water that sent me sideways into a flowerbed. The sickly scent of rose-scented geranium bloomed around me. I was badly disorientated and had no idea what part of the garden I was in. As I grappled to get up, my t-shirt snagged on a rose thorn. I tried to untangle myself and got stabbed in the hand and tore the wet fabric of my newly purchased top.

After a few more tumbles, false starts and bore-water dousings, I managed to find the school's front steps and get out of the path of the relentless sprinklers. I sat on one of the concrete tiers. The surface was rough and cold on my buttocks. I slouched forward, leaning my head against my one good forearm. Goodness, I felt hungover. What the hell had been on that cloth? Who had done it? And why?

I stayed there for a few minutes, gathering my reserves. My knee throbbed, my hand hurt, my head was cracking and I was soaked to the skin. Really, I needed to get back inside the school and ring the station. But I didn't fancy finding my way in the dark. I had enough injuries as it was. I presumed that whoever had knocked me out had long gone. There was no rush. I'd sit tight and wait for dawn.

I hunkered down, shivering and fed up with the world. But I wasn't on my own for long. Horace meandered along and sat beside me. Not close enough to offer warmth, but near enough to be companionable. We waited together until black night inexorably melted into pearl grey dawn.

Once I could see my way clear, I limped, cold, stiff and sore, back inside. I snapped on the bedroom light to collect some dry clothes and caught my reflection in the full length mirror. Oooh, not good. My hair was worse than Ronald McDonald's and my ripped wet t-shirt was see-through. Absolutely nothing was left to the imagination. Phew, I was glad no one had seen me.

Except for my attacker!

Which wasn't an uplifting thought and so I shoved it away.

I grabbed my clothes, hastened to the bathroom and tried to lose my embarrassment under the biting hot water. The shower was blissful. I let the hot water massage my chilled flesh until I began to feel more human and less drowned rat. Even the pounding in my head lessened slightly.

I rubbed the steam off the mirror once I was dry and took another peek at my reflection. I was a sucker for punishment because there was no way to escape the stark truth: I was a walking – make that limping – disaster. My body was littered with insect bites and tri-coloured bruises, some of which had faded to a green-brown, others were new and blue, obviously collected during the night, and my black eye was deep purple with a halo of sick ochre. At least the cuts from a week ago weren't as prominent.

I padded back to my room in my dry t-shirt and crawled into my bed to catch up on some shut-eye.

Understandably, sleep eluded me. I began making a mental list of all the things I needed to do, which included organising a replacement phone if I was unable to find the other one, finding out what had been going on in the night, and buying some concealer to make myself look more presentable to the world.

Or at least to the Fox men: I had my standards.

By six, I was in the kitchen, eating a banana for breakfast and drinking tea laced with painkillers. I read a three-day old newspaper, checked to see if my zodiac sign prediction had been correct and by seven, I headed to the gym. No, I hadn't made a premature New Year's resolution to get trim, taut and terrific. I wanted to see if there were any signs of the night before's activity and search for my phone.

I swung by to collect the gym key from the master board in the Iron Nun's office but the door was locked. I trotted around to the gym anyway and tried the door. That, as expected, was locked too. I quickly checked around the area. Nothing seemed amiss. Of course, the van had long gone from the parking lot. I checked the lawn and flowerbeds for the phone and, unsurprisingly, came up empty handed.

I made my way back to the kitchen. It had fired up since I'd left it. Now it was a right little party scene with Chastity whisking up eggs in a stainless steel bowl and chatting to the gorgeous Foxes.

Adam turned as I came in and held up one of the three takeaway coffees sitting on the table. 'For you.'

He obviously didn't want a repeat of yesterday's tame tea.

'You *are* staying for breakfast though, aren't you?' Chastity asked him.

'If there's enough,' said Adam, shooting a glancing at his dad. He was learning, bless him.

'There's plenty,' said Chastity.

'We'll stay then. Thanks.'

Quinn looked me up and down as I sipped the cappuccino.

'Bad night, Red?' he said. 'Or a good one? You look hungover.' He reached over and tousled my wild Orphan Annie hair but there was a serious edge to his voice. 'Nothing to do with Ely?'

I gave a perplexed frown. 'What do you mean?'

'Did you two stop off for a drink or three on the way home?'

He sounded jealous, which was ridiculous. I attempted to smooth my curls back down.

'No. Of course not. But there was an incident last night.'

'Oh here we go,' said Chastity. 'You're doing police speak. You can talk to us normally, you know, Mum. We're not your minions.'

'Actually, I am,' said Fox. 'What sort of incident, boss?'

I filled them in on my night-time experience. 'We need to get the key to the gym as soon as Mum gets up and see what was going on in there,' I said. 'I couldn't tell from the window. I was too far away.'

'Did you memorise the van's reggo?' asked Quinn.

'No. I didn't think I needed to. I just snapped the pic and tried to look in the back. After that, nothing.'

Sister Immaculata joined us in the kitchen ten minutes later while we were tucking into fluffy scrambled eggs on toast. I repeated my night's adventure for her benefit and asked for the gym key.

She wasn't impressed. 'For goodness sake, Eve, you were probably imagining it. You're causing a fuss about nothing.'

'I saw someone, I checked out the van and I know without doubt that I was drugged and left on the lawn for a good drenching. How the heck could I have imagined that? I was soaked to the skin!' Partly because I'd had very few clothes on, but I wasn't going to share that with the Fox boys. They didn't need that wet t-shirt image lodged in their psyche. 'And my phone was stolen.'

'Are you sure you weren't drunk and just misplaced the phone?'

'Mum!'

'Well, you do have a reputation, Eve.'

'I was dead sober.'

'Well, then there's another alternative: you were sleeping-walking.'

'Cool,' said Chastity.

'Don't be ridiculous,' I snapped. 'I don't sleep-walk.'

'You used to as a child.'

I gave her a hard stare. 'That's the first I've heard of it.'

'It's never been relevant before,' she said airily. 'You were dreaming.'

'Some dream. I got impaled by a rose.' I held out my gouged hand.

She pursed her lips. 'You should put some antiseptic on that or it may get nasty.'

'I have. Humour me, Mum. Let me have the key so we can check things out. If nothing's amiss then that's the end of the story.'

Except it wouldn't be, but she didn't need to know that.

With a huff, she handed over the key, still maintaining that I was mistaken. She didn't come with us to the gym, but Chastity gambolled along, bending young Fox's ear, while Quinn loped along by my side.

'How are you feeling, Red?' he said.

'Bruised and stiff. But then I was feeling like that before. I'm now more so, due to lying on the wet grass for I don't know how long. And I've a cracker of a headache, which is probably because of the knock-out drugs. I'm grateful the guy didn't punch me out. Or kidnap me.'

'Or kill you.'

'Now *that* would have been excessive.'

'You should have called it in rather than investigating on your own.'

'I wasn't sure anything bad was going on. I didn't want to cry wolf.'

Or Fox.

Which was true. But I was also worried. The man had looked like the one the Iron Nun had been arguing with in the foyer. Was Sister Immaculata up to something? She'd been too adamant I'd dreamed up the whole episode. I was loath to say anything to Quinn and Adam at this stage. I wanted more to go on before I implicated my own flesh and blood.

What really worried me was that the intruder had a drug on hand to use in an emergency. Who carted that sort of stuff around? Not an ordinary thief, that's for sure.

Ah, but saying that, my darling mother had history when it came to drugs...

As did my daughter. Both of them had thought their use of drugs had been justified. Perhaps the same applied to this intruder?

And what was the story behind those wheelie bins? What was being transported in them? I very much doubted it was refuse.

We got to the gym and unlocked it. We were met with echoes of silence. Nothing in the airy hall was out of place. The others wanted to search the car lot and surrounds, even though I'd already done so. I humoured them but, as before, there was nothing of interest. Fox followed the path around the back of the gym.

'Hey, come here,' he called.

We followed his voice. There, at the rear of the building, by the common boundary with our neighbour, the barren sandy patch was strewn with rubbish. Three bins worth. A fourth bin had been tipped into a culvert.

'Case closed,' said Quinn matter-of-factly. 'Someone was illegally dumping trash.'

I wasn't convinced. Something didn't smell right and it wasn't just the festering prawn tails in the fourth bin.

'It doesn't explain my drugging,' I said.

There was a loaded silence from the others.

'I wasn't drunk,' I protested. 'I hadn't touched a drop.'

'Hey, we didn't say anything,' said Quinn.

'But the inference was there.'

'If you hadn't been drinking wine then Gran might have been right and you were sleep-walking,' offered Chastity.

I decided not to push it. I knew what I'd seen, what I'd experienced. I didn't need the endorsement of these three stooges. I would keep an eye out for other unusual activities at the school but I wouldn't bother keeping the Fox boys in the loop.

We trekked back to the kitchen, this time Fox and Chastity in front of us. Brother and sister. *The half didn't count.* Chastity touched Fox's arm and we could hear her girl-woman giggle. Quinn tilted his head to look at me. He raised one expressive eyebrow.

'Okay!' I said. 'I'll talk to her.'

'Good.'

'But not yet.'

'Eve!'

'I've things to sort out.'

'Like?'

'I've got my own dad issues to work out before I dump dad stuff on Chastity.'

'Don't leave it too long. It would be hard on her if she makes a fool of herself over Adam.'

We watched the young couple, Chastity trying to keep abreast as Fox lengthened his stride, trying to maintain his distance without being too obvious.

'I know. That wouldn't be good.'

'Understatement. It would be grossly unfair.' Quinn glanced at me. 'Have you spent much time with your dad yet?'

'No. But I need to rectify that. It's on my to-do list.'

Back in the kitchen, we told the Iron Nun about the rubbish. She was unimpressed and said she'd organise with the gardener to tidy it up and find out which neighbours were missing bins.

She also told me to lay off the booze.

It took all my self control not to yell at them all.

7

ELY AND BURTON WERE IN A HUDDLE, HAVING A DEEP AND MEANINGFUL as the three of us marched into the incident room. Ely straightened. I could tell from his expression that he had news and that it wasn't good.

'Hey, boss,' he said.

I held up my hand. 'Stop right there.'

Obediently he did, cocking his head to one side, waiting with coiled patience.

'I'm not going to like this, am I?'

'No.'

'Hit me with it then. But gently.'

'I can't. There's no easy way to break this. Duggins is dead.'

'What!' I hadn't been expecting that little snippet. But damn, I still had a shed-load of questions to ask him. 'He was all right yesterday. What happened?'

'Heart failure is suspected but we'll have to wait for the post mortem.'

'That leaves us thin on info. We'll have to check out this Danny Pike and hopefully unearth some facts. Is it the farmers market today?'

'Tomorrow.'

'Of course it is. We don't want to have things too easy. What else do we have to go on?'

'Not a lot.'

'What about Duggins' house? Anything interesting on the garden excavation?'

'They're still working their way through the back garden. Nothing so far except black sand.'

'That's disappointing. I was certain a load of corpse bits were buried there.'

'Me too.'

'Okay, we've a freezer full of human remains. Surely there is something we can do to move this case forward?'

'We could go back to Sweet?'

'Because?'

'Find out more about the stolen canvases. For all Duggins' protestations, the two things are probably linked.'

'Yeah, I suppose. Just give me a few minutes and then we'll go.'

I ducked down to pathology and found Rachel Gath hunched over a bench taking tissue samples from what looked like a tongue. I didn't want to know if it was one from Duggins' freezer.

'Hey, Rach.'

'Hey, yourself. You here about the bin body? I emailed you the report first thing.'

'No, I wasn't. But while I'm here, can you give me a quick run-down?'

'He'd been in the skip for approximately 12 hours. He been killed elsewhere and dumped. There were no drugs in his system. Or alcohol.'

'Ta.' I hovered.

She blinked at me over her mask. 'What?'

'Is there any chance you can do a blood test?'

'When?'

'Now.'

'Which body?'

'Mine.'

She looked at me for an elongated moment, her large, doe-like eyes quizzically assessing. She came to a decision, put down her scalpel and straightened. 'Want to give me a little more to go on, DI Rock?' she said, sounding formal.

'It's a need-to-know-basis, but I want to know if there are any traces of a knock-out drug.'

'Why don't you go to the doc?'

'I haven't time – and I don't particularly want to.'

'Hmm. I won't get into trouble for this?'

'No. I'll take the rap if there's any fall-out.'

She still wasn't convinced. 'I'm not in the habit of taking samples from the living.'

'Come on. It's no big deal.'

'I don't believe you.'

'Okay. It might be, but I want to be sure of my facts before I commit to any action.'

'You might regret this,' she said, preparing a syringe and vial. 'Because there's a reason I only work on dead people.'

'Which is?'

'I'm not very good at taking samples from the living.'

She was right but I gritted my teeth and tried to think of anything else but my butchered vein as Rachel extracted my precious life blood.

'There,' she said triumphantly. 'Done!' She patched me up and then patted my cheek. 'You'd best put your head between your knees before you keel over.'

I hadn't felt great before. Now I felt worse. I must have looked terrible because she said, 'You okay, Eve? I didn't think I'd done that bad a job.'

'I've a cracking headache.' It was too early to swallow more painkillers to combat it.

'If you took drugs that might be a side effect.'

'I didn't take anything. It was forced on me.'

'Oh. I see.' She gave me another curious glance but didn't push for further information. She said she'd get back to me when she had the tox results and, feeling fragile, I shuffled off to find Ely.

He gave me a strange look. 'You sick or something?' he said.

'No. I've just been talking to Rachel. She was cutting up a tongue.' I wasn't going to let on about my night-time adventure. At this stage, the less who knew about it the better.

'Chopped tongue? That explains it then. I don't think I'll have deli meat in my sandwiches for a while.'

'Me neither.' *Make that forever.*

Fine Art on the Terrace was open for business. We entered the hushed interior. The gallery was based in an old Federation-style house with high, pressed-tin ceilings and big square rooms. The walls were painted startling white and the jarrah floors were glass-like in their high gloss finish. It was a bigger version of my cottage and how I'd envisioned it being, once the renovations had been completed. I squashed the bitter thought. That was a sad, dead dream.

We didn't see Jeremy Sweet to begin with, but we heard his twitter. On further investigation we found him in a room where he was busily showing a smart couple some large and bright abstract canvases. He didn't see us and so we ducked into another of the rooms to wait until he was free. The room – Ely's choice – was full of nudes. Sometimes it was hard to work out what the subject's gender was, but then you could say that about some of the actual people we met on our job.

We heard the couple leave and popped out of our side room. Sweet jumped with a rodent squeak when he saw us. Today he was dressed in tight red trousers, white silk shirt and red spotted bow tie. I can't say it was a big improvement on yesterday's blue and lemon pastels.

'How long have you been here?' he demanded, his eyes darting in all directions. He tugged at his tie. His tongue flicked back and forth to moisten his thin lips which looked as though they may have been tinted with red gloss to match his trousers. They didn't.

'Not long. We need to ask some more questions.' I said.

'Why?'

'Lionel Duggins died yesterday.'

'And?'

'You don't seem surprised, Mr Sweet.'

'Why should I be? I wasn't emotionally attached to him. I don't feel surprise or anything else, Detective Inspector.'

'You didn't like him much.'

'I didn't like him at all. Not that I want to speak ill of the dead.'

'But you did. Why didn't you like him?'

'He was rude and odious.'

'And that's the only reason?' I pushed.

'Isn't that enough?'

I left it for now, though I wondered if there was more to it. 'Those pictures that were stolen?' I said. 'Can we see the others from the same collection?'

'What collection?'

'Come on, Jeremy, we know there were other pictures. Lionel told us about the exclusive exhibition. We want to see it.'

Sweet's eyes ping-ponged in all directions. 'Why?'

'Stop answering us with another question,' snapped Ely. 'It's very irritating. We want to see the collection, and now!'

'But it's private.'

'And this is a murder investigation,' I said. 'Nothing is private. Show us the collection, Jeremy.'

Sweet swelled, his face turned red with indignation. 'All right. If you must.' He went to the gallery front door and locked it, switching around the open-close sign with a snap. 'This way.' And he toddled like a Poirot impersonator down a corridor towards the back of the gallery. He unlocked the final door and switched on the light.

The walls were covered in small, dark-framed pictures. We walked around in silence with Sweet trotting at our heels, huffing and puffing like a little red steam engine. 'I really don't see this is relevant,' he said. 'This art is not connected to the stolen pieces.'

'How so?'

'That art was sub-standard. I should never have agreed to exhibit it.'

'Sub-standard in what way?' I asked, peering closely at one of the pictures. I was still having difficulty getting my head around the fact that these were tattoos. On skin. From dead people.

'They'd been done by amateurs. These are professional.'

'You can tell the difference?'

'Yes.'

'How? These look pretty similar to the ones in the photos.'

'The smell for starters. And the execution of the art. Oh, and the canvas quality.'

I was still hung up on the first difference. 'Smell?'

'Yes, the canvases hadn't been properly cured. They were decomposing.'

I stared at him in horrified wonder. Was he serious? Well, judging by his earnest expression, yes he was.

I gulped. 'How did you source them?'

Sweet hesitated.

'Come on, Sweet. Spit it out. Unless you want to come down to the station to answer our questions?' said Ely.

'No, no,' said Sweet. He took a breath. 'They were offered to me. Through a mutual acquaintance. It's the first time I've exhibited this sort of work. I very much doubt I'll do it again.'

'Why? Duggins told us that these buggers fetch big figures,' said Ely, waving his hand dismissively at the canvases.

Sweet poked his glasses back up his nose with his middle finger and didn't say anything.

'Well? Do they?' pushed Ely.

'What would that low-life know?'

'I don't know. But do they?'

'It's a niche market.'

'How many have you sold?'

He waited a beat. You could feel his mental tussle on whether or not to tell us.

'Sweet?'

He sighed. 'See how many red dots on the labels?' He pointed to the white card under one of the artworks. The card listed the exhibit number, title and price. 'That'll tell you how many I've sold.'

We swiftly scanned the room. There weren't any red dots.

'So you do a rip-roaring trade, then,' said Ely, heavy on the irony.

'There's not a great deal of interest in tattoos in the western suburbs. Clients prefer abstracts and landscapes.'

'Discerning,' I said.

He shrugged. 'Everyone's tastes are different. Have you finished? I'd like to reopen the gallery.'

'For the moment,' I said. 'Let's go, sergeant.'

We left Sweet sweating in his red and white finery and swung by a lunch bar. We gave a wide berth to the smoked meats and hams and bought ourselves some cheese and onion rolls oozing cholesterol and deliciousness. We headed back to the office where it was a bustling hub of activity.

I gave a sweep of the incident room. Quinn was nowhere to be seen. No doubt he was making huge inroads with the Wisteria Place case while I was coming up against fresh air on mine. I cosseted myself in my office and demolished my roll. The comfort food did just that and I didn't feel so bad. I licked my fingers, wiped them on my jeans and stared at my in-box. It was spilling over with reports and files. Sighing, I prepared myself to shift the backlog.

After I don't know how long, there was a tap at the door and young Fox cruised in looking fresh and wholesome and loose-limbed sexy. I wanted him there and then on the desk, on the floor, against the wall; I wasn't choosy.

He held two mugs of coffee. He set them down on the desk and gave me this deep-eyed, smouldering look he did so well.

'How are you going, Eve?'

Was it my imagination or was there a whole heap of subtext in his question? While my brain was trying to figure that out, my body was liquefying and beginning to burn.

'Fine,' I said and tried not to respond to his dimples. He was so damn cute you just wanted to pick him up, take him home and *do* things.

But I wouldn't.

Because I was in lust with his dad.

But it was tricky all the same. I knew I could swing either way: I was a sucker for Foxes.

'No after-effects from your early morning soaking?' he said.

I wasn't sure if he was alluding to my supposedly drunken state or just the reticulation drenching. 'No, I'm all good. Just tired.' My head was still sore but I didn't want to let on how sooky I felt. 'Nothing a good night's sleep won't fix.'

'This might help.'

'What, the coffee?'

'No, this.' He moved behind me and began massaging my shoulders, his thumbs strongly, rhythmically stroking my tense muscles while his fingers kneaded the soft tissue. Pleasure and pain. An exquisite combination.

I gave an involuntary groan. I did so love his massages.

'Too much?'

'Yes. No. It's sore, that's all.'

'Don't overdo it.'

'I shan't, Adam.' I was touched at his concern and, in spite of my good intentions to keep my distance from the young Fox, I relaxed under his seductive touch.

'For the record,' he said, close to my ear. 'I don't think you were drunk.'

'Thanks. I'm glad someone believes in my sobriety.' I twisted around to smile at him. Hah. His expression gave him away.

'Oh, right, you were just being kind! I'm disappointed.' I wriggled away from the delicious magic of his hands and the proximity of his mouth.

'You've been under a lot of pressure these last few weeks,' he said, straightening and recovering his ground, employing tact, or so he thought.

I wasn't so easily duped.

'Anyone would have a few drinks given the circumstances. You wouldn't be the first.'

'I hadn't been drinking, Fox.' I didn't tell him I'd had a blood test and could prove it.

'Hey, I'm sorry. Maybe you dreamed it all.'

'I wasn't drunk, I didn't dream it, I know something was going on and it wasn't the dumping of Christmas trash.'

'Forget I said anything.'

'Forgotten.'

But it wasn't. I stood and gathered some paperwork together for something to do and to show him our discussion was over, as I had done with his dad.

'Look, I'm here if you need me to take you home or anything,' he said. The *anything* was loaded with possibilities.

'Thanks.' I tried not to shiver at the *anything* even though I was annoyed he thought the worst of me. 'I'll keep that in mind. But there's work to do.'

'Well the offer's there, Eve.'

'Thanks.'

He hesitated.

'What?' I said.

He looked as though he was going to say something profound but then Quinn walked in which put paid to anything Fox was going to impart.

'Keys,' said Quinn. 'For you.' He dropped them in front of me. 'It's in the carpark. Burton will show you where. Which means,' and he cast a swift, meaningful glance at his son. 'That you won't be needing lifts home any time soon. Or anywhere else come to that.' And he walked back out.

I looked down at the keys and then up at Fox.

Our eyes locked.

'He's lending you his *car*?' He made it sound as if his dad had lost his marbles.

'Yes. What of it? Wouldn't you lend me yours if I asked?'

'No.'

'Harsh.'

'But sensible. Man, he must have it bad.'

'Because he's lending me his car? Oh, come on, Adam. It's just a car.'

'Serious? That's his baby.'

'Obviously he doesn't mind sharing.'

'But he does. I only get to drive his car when it suits him.' He paused. 'So it must be to his advantage to lend it to you. What does that tell you?'

'That he's a control freak?'

'No offence, but I doubt if anyone could control you, Eve.'

He followed his dad out of the door before I could reply.

I wasted no time in searching out Burton to show me where Quinn's car was parked.

'It's a heap of junk,' he said.

'It's vintage,' I countered.

'Same difference.'

I patted the car's bonnet before sitting in the driver's seat. The leather was cracked and worn, the dash covered in dust, but I felt more empowered than I had in days. 'If anyone wants me, tell them I'm busy.' I said and headed for freedom. It felt so damn good I wanted to shout and scream at the top of my voice. How uncool.

In fact it was soooo good, I didn't return to the station but cruised over to the safety deposit box facility to have a quiet wander around without an entourage. Clark was on guard duty with another officer who I recognised from my tiger-snakes-in-the-toilet incident.

'Boys,' I said. 'What's happening?'

'Nothing. Not even a snake infestation,' said Clark, who had a reputation for his questionable wit.

'Very funny Officer Clark,' I said. 'Were you on duty when Duggins died?'

'Affirmative, DI Rock.'

'Talk me through his last few hours.'

'You were there for most of them.'

'Sorry?'

'He died just after you left. Didn't you know?'

'No. But he wasn't at death's door, just grumpy. How can he have suddenly upped his toes and died?'

'You came and went with Sergeant Ely. The lawyer dude went back into the room for a minute and then left. Duggins died maybe fifteen minutes after that.'

'So soon?' I'd presumed he'd died in the night.

'Yeah. It was a surprise all round. Especially for Duggins, I bet.'

I ignored his flippancy. 'What about the woman in the hat? Wasn't she going to visit Duggins?'

'Yeah. The old duck popped in with some grapes. She left not long after you. Maybe five minutes later.'

'Did you get her name?'

'No.'

'Because?'

'She was old and didn't look like someone who'd be a threat to Mr Duggins or anyone else, come to that.'

'That wasn't your call to make. You should have taken her name, Officer Clark.'

'Sorry, DI Rock.'

'Did she go in before or after the lawyer?'

Clark frowned in concentration. 'Can't be sure. Maybe after.'

'You should know for sure, Clark. It's your job.'

He said resignedly, 'Sorry, DI Rock.'

'What else has been happening here?'

'Forensics have been collating evidence. I don't think they've found anything of note.'

I still wasn't keen to go back to the station, so I took myself off to Cranberry Court. A couple of officers were replacing Duggins' lawn, rolling the fake grass back over the dirty sand.

'Anything?' I asked hopefully.

'No. But we'll be starting on the front garden in the morning,' said one of the officers.

I left them to it and went back to St Immaculata's.

Perhaps I'd overdone it, seduced by my new freedom, because my headache was now steadily progressing into a migraine with blurred vision, jagged lines and star-bursts. I needed to lie down before I threw up.

'You all right, Mum?' Chastity asked as she passed me on the stairs.

'Migraine,' I said. 'Gotta crash.'

I slept for 12 hours straight. In the morning I still felt brain-bruised and nauseous. Reluctantly I called in sick and spent the morning in bed with a wet cloth over my eyes to block out the torturous light.

Thankfully, the migraine lessened to a dull ache as the morning wore on. I grew twitchy. Fed up with being cooped up in my hot, tiny room, I decided to give Henry Talbot a call and have a shot at the father-daughter thing.

After witnessing his body language on Christmas Day, it was obvious Henry wasn't comfortable socialising at St Immaculata's. I didn't blame him. I wasn't either. So I rang him and floated the idea that we could meet up for coffee at a place of his choosing.

'On your own?' asked Henry.

'That's the plan. Mum and Chastity are busy. Is that a problem? Would you prefer we all met up together.'

'No, I'm not in a great rush to see your ma again so soon. But what about colleagues? Will any cop boyfriends be in tow?'

'Not today. They're working and I've taken a sickie.'

'Well, then, I accept your invitation, Eve. Coffee and cake would be delightful.'

'Do you have a favourite haunt?'

Henry mentioned The Dog's Breakfast. I'd never heard of it but he gave me directions to the Fremantle cafe and we agreed to meet in an hour.

The dingy dockside cafe was an interesting choice. It was alive with seagulls. Loud heavy metal music pumped from within. The racket was going to make it difficult to hold a normal conversation and I wondered if that had been his intention. The place shimmered in the suffocating heat against a backdrop of cargo ships and cranes.

Because I couldn't see Henry inside, and I didn't want my migraine reignited by the hellish music, I opted for an alfresco table for two that had a sticky plastic grey surface and a dog-eared menu with food stains. The vicious-eyed gulls strutted about between the tables, and sometimes on top of them, gorging on discarded chips and burger buns. I ordered a wussy ginger and lemon tea in deference to my delicate head and sipped my way through it until it was cold. Henry turned up wearing a blue and yellow Hawaiian flowery shirt and wide shorts that did nothing for his spindly white legs. He had on big eighties dark glasses and a flowerpot-man sunhat. I now realised where my fashion sense came from.

He looked around, checking I was indeed flying solo.

'Still no boyfriend with you?' he said, confirming my suspicion.

'No.'

He gave a slight smile and I wondered why. Didn't he like my choice of men? And what was it to him anyway? He hadn't been in my life, like, forever.

We sat opposite each other and I actually blessed the overspill of music. Conversation was a stuttering nightmare as we tried to find common ground.

'Okay,' I said, deciding to be proactive and force a dialogue between us. 'Why did you want to make contact with me after all these years?'

'Didn't I say?'

'Not in so many words.'

'I thought it about time. I'm not getting any younger. You're my only child.'

'I see.' Though I didn't.

'I would have been around before now but your mother wasn't keen.'

'But she's fine with it now?' She was hiding it well if she was.

'She's coming around. Slowly.' He dipped his head and winked over the top of his sunglasses. 'She needs careful handling but then you'd know all about that, living with her.'

I made an executive decision. 'Why don't you come and have dinner at St Immaculata's tonight?'

'Oh, I don't know about that, Eve. Your mother may not like it. Christmas wasn't a big success.'

'It never is. Don't take it personally,' I said. 'And this will be a more informal affair.'

I cajoled him, thinking that it would be better for the four of us to get to know each other over a meal. We made a time and I went off to buy some food.

Back at St Immaculata's, I told them about the dinner date. The Iron Nun was less than thrilled.

'Why bother?' she said. 'It's not going to change anything.'

'It doesn't have to,' I said. 'We can simply enjoy a family dinner.'

'I think it's a fabulous idea,' said Chastity and she helped me cobble together a vast lasagne and salad.

Halfway through our culinary bonding time, while I was grating a mountain of cheese, my mobile beeped.

'Don't answer it,' said Chastity.

'Hah, that's like saying don't breathe,' I said and picked up the phone. 'DI Rock.'

'Boss, thought you'd like an update on the Duggins' excavation.' It was Burton. 'They found bones under that big ugly fountain.'

'Bingo.'

'Just about gave the team hernias trying to move that bloody edifice.'

'Were there enough remains to identify anyone?'

'The gorgeous Rach reckons they belong to a dog.'

'Oh. Right. A waste of time then.'

'Never say that. There's a chance they'll find something under the poncy pink driveway. It's going to be dug up in the morning.'

'You'd better tell Ely. He might score some extra pavers for his new home.'

Burton laughed. 'I'll pass that on.'

'Thanks for the update. I'll catch you tomorrow.'

I returned to my domestic duties and got stuck back into the cheddar grating. Frustration gnawed at me. I hated it when progress was slow. But at least I was doing something positive for my family.

Henry turned up early. I was in the shower and Chastity on her phone. Sister Immaculata had to step up and entertain him. When I entered the room ten minutes later, you could feel the crackle of frost. It wasn't an auspicious start.

The evening went downhill from there. Sister Immaculata didn't thaw but adopted her grumpy bullfrog mantle, glaring at Henry through most of the dinner. Charity was snitchy because

I'd told her to turn off her phone while we were eating. Henry was jumpier than one of Horace's sixty million fleas, which I suppose was not surprising as the women in his life were acting like Macbeth's three witches, with the Iron Nun as principal hag.

'This is nice,' I said chewing on a forkful of lasagne. Chastity had been heavy-handed with the garlic. It was strong enough to make the eyes water and keep away a swarm of vampires.

'Yes, very,' said Henry valiantly.

In reality, the atmosphere was as painful as an ingrown toenail. Whatever topic of conversation I introduced generated monosyllable answers. I tried to engage Henry in discussion about his art career and life in general. The answers were briefer than a G-string and I decided that my father was socially autistic, along with my mother. Goodness, I didn't stand a chance. No wonder my social life was an on-going train wreck.

Eventually Henry asked a couple of questions of his own, mainly about my work and what I was currently investigating. I told him I wasn't allowed to discuss my professional life, which killed that particular line of conversation.

Dinner abruptly ended once the last plate scrape ceased. No one wanted dessert or a cuppa. Henry said he had to go and none of us tried to stop him.

My attempt at happy families had been a failure. Again.

I escorted Henry to his car and we didn't arrange a time to meet again.

He drove off and I stood in the dark, watching the tail lights of his car disappear down the street.

As I turned to go back inside, I caught a flash of something out of the corner of my eye. I stared hard into the darkness but everything was still. I presumed it was Horace.

Or at least, I hoped it was.

Back in the kitchen, the Iron Nun and Chastity were sitting side-by-side with their hands cupped around mugs of tea. So much for not wanting a cuppa.

'That was a blast,' I said conversationally. 'Walking over hot coals would have been more enjoyable.'

'It wasn't that bad,' said my daughter. 'He just needs time to get used to us.'

'No he doesn't,' said my mother. 'He needs to go away and not come back. He's trouble.'

'That's rather harsh,' I said.

'But true.'

8

THE NEXT DAY, CHASTITY AND MY MOTHER WERE ALREADY IN THE kitchen eating their breakfast by the time I came down. We said desultory good mornings and then I fixed myself a bowl of muesli and chopped banana. I perched on a high stool at the stainless steel counter just as Chastity got a phone call. Whoever was on the other end brought a rosy flush to her cheeks. She left the room in a flurry, abandoning her eggs.

I wondered who had caused the breathless excitement and doubted she would tell me.

'Last night wasn't a huge success, was it?' I said to the Iron Nun.

'It was a waste of time,' she said.

'Next time might be easier.'

'There won't be a next time.' She cleared her throat as if she was getting ready to announce prize winners at the school's open day. 'You need to move out, Eve,' she said.

I choked on my muesli and sprayed the table with soggy oats. I hadn't been expecting that opening gambit. 'Really?'

'Yes. I wouldn't have said it otherwise.'

'You've changed your tune. A fortnight ago you said I could live here.' I mopped up the mess with a tissue.

'It was never an open ended invitation.'

'Gee, thanks. That makes me feel warm and fuzzy.'

'I offered you a temporary stopgap to help you out. You should be grateful.'

'I was. I am.'

'But we have a full contingent of girls booked in for the first term.'

'There's still five weeks of holiday to go.'

'But the rooms need to be prepared. They take time.'

'I can move into the attic.'

'There's too much clutter up there.'

'The basement, then.'

'No. I need you out of the school.'

'But, Mum, I've nowhere to go!'

'I would like you out by Friday.'

Which gave me all of six days.

At the station, I bewailed my rapidly approaching homeless state.

'I'm looking for a house-mate,' said Rachel Gath as she hovered in the entrance of the crew room clutching a sheet of paper. 'You can share with me, Eve.'

'Don't do it, Rach,' said Ely. 'You'll end up destitute or dead.'

'Yeah, look at me,' said Quinn. 'I'd gladly have her stay on my boat, except I don't have one anymore. She blew it up. That's why I'm bunking with Adam.'

'I did not blow up your boat!' I protested.

'As good as, Red.'

'Now, Rachel, do you know the reason why our boss here is homeless?' said Ely.

'No.'

'I thought not. Well, you know that place where you had to deal with the body in the skip?'

'Yes.'

'That scorched piece of dirt used to be DI Rock's home.'

'Oh come on. That was a bomb site.'

'I rest my case.'

'Really? That was Eve's home?'

'Yep.'

'You're not having a lend?'

'Nope. And like DI Fox's boat, the house exploded. As did her car.'

Rachel gave me a wide-eyed look. 'No offence, Eve, but I think I'll take a rain-check on the house-mate idea,' she said. 'Sorry, pet, but

I value my little home. I've worked hard to save the down payment.'

'It's not a problem,' I said. 'I'd probably do the same in your shoes. I'll just go and live in a cardboard box under the Narrows Bridge. Don't worry about me.'

'Would you like me to play the violin for you, boss?' said Ely.

'Shut up, Ely. Anything about the bones under Duggins' fountain, Rachel?'

'Most of them belonged to a dog. Possibly a Rottweiler.'

'And?'

'The other one was a marrow bone from a cow. Judging by the teeth marks, it had been the dog's dinner.'

'That's disappointing. So we just keep on digging.'

'May I have a private word with you?' Rachel said when everyone had dispersed to their various tasks.

She followed me into my office, closed the door and laid the A4 piece of paper down on the desk in front of me.

'There were traces of chloroform in that blood sample I took,' she said.

'I thought as much.'

'Are you going to tell me more?'

I decided it might be better if at least one other person knew what had happened. I gave her a brief summary of the night's events. 'I presume yesterday's migraine was triggered by it?'

'Yes. More than likely.'

'Any idea how long I would have been out for the count?'

'Judging by the amount in the blood, you probably would have been unconscious for 10-15 minutes, give or take.'

'Is that all?'

'They would have had to keep administering it if they wanted to keep you knocked out.'

'So they only wanted me out of the way for a few minutes. Long enough to drive off, I suppose.'

'Any idea who it was?'

'No. Maybe.' The image of Hugo Maine rose before me. But why would he pick on me? Why not Quinn, who had spearheaded the drug bust? I'd just been a small cog in the wheel – except for taking down the actual Santa-clothed drug dealer. Unless, of course, Maine was trying to get to Quinn through me.

'Are you going to tell the others?' said Rachel.

'Not yet.'

'You should.'

'I'll think about it.'

'Eve, you might be in danger.'

'Tell me about it.'

'Is that why your house and car exploded?'

'It could be the same person...'

She looked at me with her Bambi eyes and blinked. 'Aren't you scared?'

'No.' I lied, but being frightened didn't achieve anything but acute paralysis so I ignored it

Rachel left only to be replaced by Quinn.

'What's Rachel got to say for herself?' said Quinn. He was holding a bulky package wrapped in brown paper under his good arm.

'Girl stuff,' I said. 'What's new on the Wisteria Place case?'

'Not a lot.' Quinn chucked the package in front of me on my desk. 'This is for you.'

'Why?'

'It's a present. You would have got it earlier if you hadn't cancelled Christmas.'

'What is it?'

'Open it and see.'

I just stared at it.

'Be brave.'

I cut the twine and peeled back the paper to reveal cracked brown leather. Blood rushed to my head. Really? Truly? I lifted it out of its nest of white tissue and shook it into shape. Oh my. It was! A genuine flying ace bomber jacket complete with insignia.

'It's to replace the one you lost in the explosion.'

'Oh *Quinn*.'

'I thought it'd be useful.'

I hugged it to me. 'Thank you.'

'You're welcome.'

'It must have cost you a fortune.'

'Half a one. Put it on.'

I gingerly threaded my dodgy arm into the sleeve. Quinn shrugged the jacket around my shoulders with his good arm, helping me get my other arm into the sleeve. One handed, he dragged the lapels together and looked deep into my eyes. 'It fits. Cinderella will go a-crime hunting.'

I could feel the colour climbing up my neck and infusing my cheeks. This was the office. We shouldn't be doing this!

I ducked away and did a twirl.

'What do you think?' I managed to say after clearing my husky throat.

'It's a bit big on you,' he said. 'But it'll give you room to grow.'

'Hah. I think it's perfect.'

'Most women would prefer a pretty frock.'

'One day you'll realise I'm not most women.'

'I already do.'

I spun around again and said, 'I saw Henry yesterday.'

'How did it go?'

'Not a great success. I think I'm too old to take on new things.'

'Things as in relationships?'

'Yeah.'

'Oh babe.'

'But you can be the exception, if you want.' Hell, but I sounded pathetically needy. Where was my grit?

He grinned. 'I'll hold you to that.'

'Can't you just hold me?' I wanted his arms strong around me, damn the office. I'd taken such a battering these past few weeks. I just wanted to feel safe, to be held hard and fast.

By Quinn.

Or by Fox!

'What? Here? Now?' And he looked at me assessingly and then

out at the busy crew room before returning to cock an eyebrow at me. 'Really, Red? You up for it?' He took a step towards me.

'Okay, maybe not.'

'Coward.' He smiled. 'But later...'

'Yeah. Later.' But I would probably have lost the urge by then.

9

WE GOT A CALL. THE MORNING'S EXCAVATION OF LIONEL DUGGINS' driveway had been aborted. Someone had beaten them to it. The paved forecourt had disappeared and a socking great big hole had been left in its wake.

'Which logically means there was something to be found there,' I said to Ely as we drove to the site.

'A body or two?'

'More than likely.'

Two police officers were milling around outside the house.

'Wasn't someone on duty here during the night?' I asked them.

'Well, yes. Technically,' said Officer Clark. 'But they were called to attend a brawl at the Tallington Tavern at midnight. It was going down and all nearby units were requested to assist.'

'A set up?' said Ely.

'It would hardly have been a coincidence,' I said. 'Whoever dug up this would've had to have the machinery all ready to go. There would've been only had a small window of opportunity to clear the decks.'

'We asked around but there aren't any witnesses,' said Clark.

'What time did the officers get back here?'

'About 4am and it was all done and dusted by then.'

There wasn't much we could do. We left the crew looking for any shred of evidence to lead them in the right direction but I didn't hold out a lot of hope. We returned to the station, picking up lunch on the way.

Because we still didn't have a name for the skip bin corpse, I decided to make that my priority, to deflect my frustration on Operation

Popsicle. So, with a mug of instant coffee and my lunchtime egg mayo and salad roll by my side, I scrolled down the missing persons file, beginning with the most recently reported ones.

None of the misper faces matched the well-fed florid countenance of the dead man. I got sidetracked looking at the profiles of a few young men, as you do. I hovered over one in particular. He was an Irishman with a raft of tattoos. I sat there, staring at his wild, colourful skin.

'Enjoying the eye candy, boss,' said Ely. He perched on the desk by my side and viewed the screen. 'Aren't we pretty enough for you? I reckon we're far cuter than him.'

I only half listened and didn't reply.

'Boss?'

I held up my hand for silence. I focussed on the misper's left arm. I had seen something similar only a few days ago. The design must be a generic one. I checked the date he was clocked missing. He'd been reported missing six months ago by the warden of the city central backpacker hostel by the railway station. I wondered *what if* and my imagination ran riot. But it seemed too far-fetched. I took a bite of my crusty roll and carried on scrolling down the file.

'May I talk now?' asked Ely, who was still patiently waiting, swinging his leg backwards and forwards.

'Go ahead.'

'The farmers market is on today,' he said. 'Do you want to interview Danny Pike?'

I chewed and swallowed. 'Yeah. I suppose.'

'You don't sound too enthusiastic.'

'Don't mind me. I'm just playing with ideas in my head and coming up with weird scenarios.'

'Want to share them?'

'Not at this stage. Come on, let's get this visit over and done with.'

I whisked up my jacket and then thought twice. Humidity and leather didn't go. Reluctantly, I hung it back over my chair. Never mind. I'd have plenty of opportunity to wear it once the weather broke.

Danny Pike wasn't difficult to locate. He had a tidy queue of western suburb yummy mummies waiting to buy his expensive gourmet sausages, complete with "Gran's Secret Ingredients". I shuddered to think what those ingredients were and wished I hadn't consumed that egg bap. Thank goodness I hadn't relaxed my ban on meat and gone for a sausage roll.

'Want some snaggers, missus?' he shouted over to me. 'Special deal for you, darlin'.'

'I don't think so, Mr Pike.' I did the badge flashing routine.

Pike, a burly grizzled individual, didn't blink an eye.

'Wot can I do for yer, DI Rock?'

'You can come down the station, Mr Pike.'

'Why?'

'To help with our inquiries.'

'About?'

'A few things, but Lionel Duggins for starters.'

'That piece of scum.'

'Save it for the tape.' We hauled him off down the station, leaving his young underling in charge.

'So,' I said half an hour later. 'You know Lionel.'

'I rent his garage for my butcher's van and keep some of my surplus stock there. I live in the neighbouring suburb so it's nice and convenient.'

'So the freezer is yours?'

'Which freezer?'

'In the double garage.'

'Yeah. That's mine.'

'And can you tell me what you keep in it?'

He gave me a curious look. 'Sausages. A few bits of choice offal. What else would I keep in it?'

I gritted my teeth. 'Human eyeballs, kidneys, tongues...' The egg mayo shifted in my stomach.

He laughed. 'Get real, lady.'

'I hope they aren't your Granny's secret ingredients?'

'You're one sick woman. Sage and onion with a little stout. Now

I'm gonna have to kill you.' He laughed again, this time at his own sick humour, before he realised I wasn't joining in. 'Joke,' he said.

'Not funny,' I said.

'I don't hold with cannibalism,' said Pike. 'That's for the oddballs.'

'Then explain why there were human remains in the freezer.'

'I can't. I didn't put them there. I don't go around cutting up dead bodies. I'm a butcher of animals, not people.'

'And you expect us to believe you.'

'Yeah, I do. I've done nothing wrong. Duggins must have put the stuff in there. Ask him. He works for an undertaker. Maybe he's renting out space to those guys too. But if he's using my freezer for other gear, I'll have to have a very strong word. That would be a health hazard. I don't want to jeopardise my food handling licence.'

'So you maintain you knew nothing of the body parts?'

'Only the animal ones.'

'Did you cut off Duggins' finger?'

He swore. 'Why would I? And if he said I did, he's a lying bastard.'

'Duggins is dead, Mr Pike.'

He opened and closed his mouth a couple of times. 'Well, I'll be damned. When did he cark it?'

'A couple of days ago.'

'Poor bugger.'

I changed tack. 'So why did you steal the artwork from Fine Art on the Terrace?'

'Oh, that.' He shrugged as if it was no big deal. 'I took it, I didn't steal it. The stuff belonged to someone I know. That fool at the gallery wouldn't release it. I was simply doing a friendly favour.'

'You're telling me the artist wanted them back?'

'Yeah. She had a buyer for them. Wanted to cut out the middle man and make more money.'

'She?'

'Yeah. Poor old duck. Life's tough on a pension. Any extra bunce makes her life a little more comfortable.'

'So, this woman, does she have a name?'

'Lucy Drew. She's house-sitting for a friend of mine. She's the sweetest old girl.'

LD: The initial in the corner of the canvases.

'Where can we find this Lucy Drew?'

'Hey! Don't you go intimidating her, DI Rock,' said Pike. 'She's a vulnerable old lady.'

'We don't do intimidating, Pike. I just want to verify what you've told us.'

'You be gentle with her.'

'Always. Now where does she live?'

Pike grudgingly gave us her address.

We grilled him for a while longer without luck. There was nothing to hold him on and so we released him.

'You know, boss,' said Ely. 'That Lucy Drew. I'd forgotten about her, but I think she's the same woman who tipped us off about Duggins' assailant being a regular visitor. I'll check it out.'

'The plot thickens,' I said. "Get onto it quick and then we'll go for a visit.'

'Lucy Drew?' I said when the elderly house-sitter finally cranked opened the front door a few centimetres. She nodded and I introduced Ely and myself.

'May we come in?'

'Oh I don't think so, dear. This isn't my house, you see.' She peered up at us from behind huge magnified glasses that gave her a look of a myopic praying mantis.

'Makes no difference. We need to speak to you.'

She hovered and I pushed open the door, easily thwarting her. Ely and I walked into the house. A terrible smell whacked us in the face. It caught nastily at the back of our throats, making us gag.

'Pwor,' said Ely. 'What's that stench?'

'Formaldehyde, if I'm not mistaken. And decaying flesh,' I said, remembering our conversation with Jeremy Sweet.

'Really?' said Ely.

'It can be a little strong,' said Miss Drew. She was diminutive. Her face was as white and creased as crumpled silk. Her sparse hair was cut in a style similar to mine so you could see the baby-pink skin of her scalp. She wore a baggy plum-coloured tracksuit and joggers, all of which had seen better days.

We followed her tiny figure through to the open plan living area, where the smell was worse. The place was littered with "canvases" at various stages of development. Lucy Drew hadn't perfected the art of preservation. Not nearly. Some looked decidedly sinister, others plain ill.

There was a fish tank over by the bay window. Some things were floating in it and they weren't fish. I stepped closer and wished I hadn't.

'Omigod!'

'What?' said Ely but I ignored him and ran outside to suck in large lungfuls of fresh air. When I had myself back in hand, I returned to the house.

'What the hell *are* you playing at?' I asked her. 'You've got eyeballs in there!'

'I'm not playing, DI Rock. This is serious art.'

'You call this art?' I waved my hand in a wild gesture.

'Bloody hell,' said Ely and it was his turn to leave the room.

'Yes. I call that piece *Eyes to Sea*. It's my bold attempt at something cutting edge,' she said with pride. 'I'm attempting to be relevant in the art world. Damien Hirst got away with putting dead stuff in formaldehyde, why shouldn't I?'

I could appreciate her logic even if I didn't think she had what it took to be one of the world's wealthiest artists.

'It's illegal to use human remains like this.'

'I don't see why.'

'Where did you get the–' I grappled to find the right words and failed. '–bits from?'

'My dear friend Lionel got the body parts from the funeral parlour. He only took them from bodies that were going to be cremated. It was a tidy arrangement.'

She gave me a reassuring smile. 'Relax, dear. Nobody was killed in the quest for art, if that's what you're suggesting. The people were already dead. Lionel brought back pieces he thought I could use in my installations. I took what I needed and whatever I didn't use he took back to work. You could say we were recycling.'

'What were you going to do with the kidneys and tongues?' Ely asked. His face was bland but I could sense his disgust.

'Oh they weren't mine. I'm vegetarian.'

Ely choked again.

'So only,' and I couldn't believe I was having this discussion, 'the eyeballs in the freezer were yours?'

'Well, yes and no. I didn't want those particularly. They were the wrong colour. Lionel was going to take them back to work.'

'And the other stuff in the freezer? Who did that belong to? Danny Pike?'

'Oh, you know dear Danny?'

'Yes.'

'Lovely man. Decent.'

'So they were his?'

'I guess so, dear. But I wouldn't swear on the Bible.'

I changed tack. 'Did you know that Lionel Duggins is dead?' I asked her.

'Yes. Poor man.'

'And we're having a post mortem done to see what killed him.'

'Very sensible.'

I had a thought. 'Did you visit Lionel at hospital on Thursday?'

'Well, yes, dear. I took him some grapes. Red ones. Seedless. I think they were called Sweet Celebration or Crimson something. Do you know the type?'

'No.'

'You should try them. They're very tasty and quite crunchy.'

'Concentrate Miss Drew. This is important. You may have been the last person to have seen him alive.'

'How interesting.' She blinked at me with polite interest.

'How did you know he was in hospital?'

'Word gets around.'

'So you can't remember?'

'No, dear. Not off the top of my head. I get a little muddled nowadays. It might be my age. Or the latest tablets the doctor gave me.'

'Would you have any idea who would want to cut off Lionel's finger and why?'

Her large glasses glinted so it was hard to read her expression.

'Do you, Miss Drew?' I pushed. 'Because you had been watching his place. You gave a witness statement.'

She drew herself up, straightening her birdlike shoulders and folding her hands in her lap. Her lips pursed and she shed her sweet persona. 'No. I don't. But he deserved it. He tried to sell my canvases without my permission. He wasn't a trustworthy man.'

She gestured to the assorted canvases propped up against various surfaces. 'My body art pieces. He stole them and took them to this place in Claremont.'

Her reedy voice hardened. 'He wouldn't tell me which gallery he'd used.' Her eyes glinted behind the scarlet-rimmed spectacles. 'He'd done a deal with that dreadful Jeremy Sweet. I wouldn't deign to put my work in his parochial little gallery. Anyway, with the help of a dear friend, I *persuaded* him to tell me where he had taken them.'

'By cutting off his finger.'

'Don't be ridiculous. We simply frightened him. My friend then retrieved the artwork for me. I intend to sell them to collectors on e-Baby. There's big money to be made on-line, you know. Cured body art is all the rage.'

'I think you mean eBay,' said Ely.

'Whatever, young man.'

I ignored them as my imagination was running riot, thanks to the frozen skinned torso.

'Are these real tattoos?' I asked, not really wanting to know.

'What do you mean, dear?'

'Were these taken from human bodies?' I didn't like to add "dead or alive".

'Oh no, dear.' She wasn't shocked. 'I don't have those sorts of connections. This is the poor man's body art canvas. I used pigskin and inked in my own designs.'

'Where did you get the pig skin from?'

'Dear Danny.'

'How come Duggins was involved?' I said.

'He was my partner.'

Ely made a strangled sound of shock.

'Business partner,' Miss Drew said sternly. 'I'm not that sort of woman, sergeant.'

'Sorry, my mistake, Miss Drew,' said Ely.

'We shared the profits on any art sales.'

'Did you make a lot?'

'No.'

I didn't know if I believed her or not, but it was a novel way to eke out the pension.

'Aren't we going to arrest her?' said Ely as we got back into the squad car.

'Not yet. We'll send someone to pick up the canvases and find out if she's telling the truth about them being pigskin.'

'What about the fish tank.'

'That's definitely got to go. It's a stinking health hazard.'

'Some vulnerable old lady! She's a fruit loop.'

'She not your run-of-the-mill geriatric.' I conceded.

'If my granny tattooed animal skins we'd have her locked up in a psych ward before you could say pickled brains.'

'That Damien Hirst has a lot to answer for. Fancy wanting to emulate him.'

Ely fiddled with his phone and then whistled through his teeth. 'You should see this, boss. It's the old bird's Facebook page. Take a look.'

He handed me the phone. The page was simply called Lucy Drew's Skin Art and there were poor quality images that were similar, if not the same, as those on Jeremy Sweet's computer and Lionel Duggins' phone.

And, worse, there was a dodgy photo of the fish tank.

I wrinkled my nose. I could still smell the formaldehyde in my nostrils and taste it at the back of the throat. Whether it had lingered or was in my imagination, I don't know, but it was pretty foul.

10

WE RETURNED TO THE STATION TO ORGANISE A WARRANT TO SEARCH Lucy Drew's premises and seize her so-called artwork. On our way back to her house, I told Ely to swing by the backpacker hostel.

'Why?' he asked.

'I want to speak to the warden about a missing backpacker.'

'Is this anything to do with the misper eye candy?'

'Yes.'

He raised his brows in enquiry but I didn't elaborate. My theory was still taking shape in the dark recesses of my mind. I wasn't ready to share in case he thought I was signing up for the funny farm.

The Barrack Street hostel was housed in a three-storey crumbling relic of the gold rush days. It had sour cream, pock-marked masonry that had been colourfully tagged by graffiti artists to head height. Remnants of black cast iron lace clung to the eaves and balconies. I reckoned it wouldn't be long before developers got their greedy, grasping hands on it and transformed it into a corporation edifice or an upmarket hotel for the well-heeled traveller.

The place was quiet for a Saturday afternoon, as to be expected, with only a handful of dishevelled multinationals lounging around, staring moronically at their little screens. Why weren't they out there, experiencing the sun and surf, the great Aussie outdoors, rather than composting in the dingy common-room?

We rang the tarnished bell that sat on a jarrah reception counter that must have been highly polished back in its day. Now it was scuffed, scratched and dull, like the rest of the building. No one jumped to attention. We dinged the bell again. A grubby blonde, pierced like a tailor's pin-cushion, took pity on us, but only after we flashed our badges. She told us the warden wouldn't be in until after six and then returned to her texting.

Ely and I drove on to Lucy Drew's and got there the same time as uniform. We flashed the warrant and the officers wasted no time bagging up the artwork, giving the old bat a wide berth.

'This is an outrage,' said Miss Drew, wild and angry behind her magnified spectacles. Her whole demeanour bristled hostility.

'But necessary, Miss Drew.'

'Why? I can't see that my art is of any interest to you philistines.'

'You've broken the law, Miss Drew. You could be facing charges of necrophilia.'

'That's ridiculous.' Her fury gathered. 'I shall get a lawyer.'

'That's your prerogative.'

She harrumphed and then said, 'What will you do with my art?'

'Check it out. You may get some of it back in due course, but not the tank of eyeballs. Anything containing human remains will be destroyed in the appropriate fashion.'

We took her to the station and charged her while she loudly proclaimed her innocence and annoyance in equal measures. Ely told her to shut up and save it for the interview as he shut her in a cell. He was over the granny histrionics.

Mid-afternoon, we got the call to say Lucy Drew's lawyer had arrived and that she was ready to be interviewed.

'Brilliant,' said Ely when we discovered the defence lawyer was Georgio Papadopoulos, complete with glossy beard, wide toothy smile and pinstripe business suit. 'Mr Georgio Gorgeous,' he added under his breath.

'Careful, Ely,' I said and then greeted the tall American. 'Mr Papadopoulos.'

'DI Rock. Lovely to see you.'

'I didn't expect us to meet again so soon.'

'No, but a bonus. For me at any rate.'

I refrained from answering.

'Are we still up for that drink?'

'Of course.'

'I'll call you.'

'I'll look forward to it.' I could feel seismic disapproval radiating from Ely. He really didn't like the guy, which was fine. He didn't have to, because he wasn't the one being asked out for a drink.

The interview went as expected, with the old biddy maintaining, shrilly and adamantly, that she'd done nothing wrong.

'I'm an artist,' she said. 'I've been one for years. I hit my straps when I took up china painting in my fifties.'

Papadopoulos flicked me an expressive look and half winked. I tried not to smile in response.

'All artists are expected to push the boundaries,' she said. 'That's what we do.'

'Using human body parts is beyond the pale,' I said.

'My client accepts that now and is sorry. She had no idea she was breaking the law,' said Papadopoulos, although Miss Drew was far from contrite. Her whole demeanour hummed irritation. 'And she says she won't do it again.'

I raised my brows at Miss Drew. 'Really, Miss Drew?' I said.

'Of course I won't. What do you take me for? A fool? I don't want to spend my final years behind bars. I've got things to do.'

'How long had you been experimenting with human remains?' I asked her.

'A few weeks. Lionel suggested it as he was able to source material.'

'Did he supply anyone else?'

Her bony shoulders pistoned up and down. 'Not to my knowledge. He never mentioned anyone else.'

We didn't get much more from Miss Drew and terminated the interview. She was released on bail and I presumed Gorgeous Georgio took her home.

I returned to the hostel on my own just after six. The place was now a teeming pit of dreadlocks, garlic and sweat. I felt old, all the exposed flesh, tanned and firm, and the buzz of adrenalin and expectation. Oh, to be young again.

The guy at the desk, whom I presumed was the warden, was checking in a couple with minimum English. He looked as he'd just ridden out of the surf on his board, with sand-matted bleached hair, faded t-shirt and low-slung shorts. He'd be an ideal pin up for the stereotypical surfie.

I waited while he patiently tried to make himself understood and watched the flotsam and jetsam of nationalities wash around me. I thought I recognised one of the hostellers and tried to work out where I'd seen him in the last few days. While I mentally worked my way through the various places, I cast my eye over the communal noticeboard. It was a montage of casual jobs, live music gigs and car adverts. I swung back to get another look at the young backpacker but the kid had disappeared. With that, the warden finished with the Korean backpackers.

'Can I help you?' he said.

I discreetly showed him my badge, introduced myself and said, 'Are you the warden?'

'Yeah.' He glanced at the badge. There was a slight shift in his posture; he stood slightly taller, pulling back his shoulders, puffing out his chest, adopting a quasi-aggressive silverback gorilla stance. I guessed he'd been in trouble with the police in his not-so-far-off youth and now he was on his guard.

'Your name?'

There was a five-second delay. 'Mitch Sumner,' he said with reluctance.

'See, now that wasn't too difficult, was it, Mr Sumner?'

He shook his head but didn't look convinced.

'Was it you who reported a backpacker missing about six months ago, Mr Sumner?'

He gave me a wary glance and defensively crossed his arms over his chest. 'I guess.'

'Do you still have his things?'

He hesitated.

'Mr Sumner?'

'Yeah. Come this way.' He took me to a back room. 'See those rucksacks? Those belong to several guys who have failed to claim them; who disappeared for whatever reason.'

'Why didn't you report them missing?'

'I did.'

'Oh. When?'

'Months ago.' He re-crossed his arms. 'So who are you interested in?'

I glanced at my notebook. 'Charlie O'Toole. Do you remember him?'

'Yeah. He stayed here on and off. Is he in trouble?'

I didn't answer him.

'Is he dead?'

'I don't know.'

'So why have you come about Charlie and not the others?'

'Because of his tattoos.'

He frowned. 'Were they special?'

'I don't know. But I recognised the design from somewhere else and thought there may be a connection.'

'I don't know if it's relevant, but the other blokes had tattoos too,' said Sumner.

My blood ran cold.

'What sort of tattoos?'

He scratched his shaggy head of damp hair, showering sand on to the floor. 'Usual stuff I guess. Dragons, demons, women, flowers. Can't say anything really stood out.'

'Let me clarify. Did these men have lots of tattoos?'

'Yeah, I guess. Full blown sleeves. Torsos completely covered.'

'On each of the guys?'

'Yeah, I reckon, though definitely Charlie. But it was a while ago now. I can't be dead certain of the others.'

'Can you give me their names?'

'I've got them on the computer.'

'Can you email them to me?'

'Sure thing. I'll do it now.'

We went back to the registration desk.

'How come you remember Charlie's so well?'

'We did a bit of surfing together and he had a couple of tats done while he was here.'

'Oh? Do you know who did them?'

'Not off hand.'

'You okay with me taking the missing backpackers' belongings?' I said while he copied and pasted the names into an email and flicked it to my in-box. 'I'll give you a receipt for them.'

'Not a problem. They're just cluttering up the storeroom. Might as well clutter yours instead.'

He helped me load them into Quinn's car. I took them to the station to be itemised.

Unfortunately, the backpacks didn't hold anything of interest, just crumpled clothes that smelled of mushrooms and minimal toiletries. The following day I would get Burton on the job to find out who these men were and if they were still listed as missing.

I headed home much later than expected. I hummed a catchy little song to myself because Quinn's vintage Holden didn't have the luxury of anything that could generate music. It didn't have the luxury of air conditioning, either, and so my lovely leather jacket lay on the passenger seat next to me.

I was getting into my stride and hitting the chorus when a dark car screamed at me out of nowhere.

I wrenched the steering wheel right and then left; pain shot up my injured arm. I narrowly missing a parked car on one side and a street tree on the other as the other car's tyres squealed like a strangled cat and spun off in the opposite direction. I slammed on the brakes and took a few deep breaths while the Holden rocked to a halt in the middle of the road. My heart was racing. My arm was on fire. Dammit, it had all happened so quickly, I hadn't had time to take in any details of the other vehicle.

Next minute, I saw a car – the same car? – bearing down towards me. I wrestled the Holden's column gear stick and took off as fast as I could, fishtailing up the street as the headlights gained on me. I whisked into a side street, then another, and pulled into someone's driveway, killing the lights.

A minute later the dark car roared past.

Bloody hoons! This sort of behaviour was not on, especially in a quiet residential area. I'd let the traffic boys know and get them to keep an eye out in the district.

Once my pulse was less frantic, I restarted the car and puttered home. I cruised into the parking lot. As I locked the car door I heard a chink of something metal. Still zinging from the hoon incident, I spun around, fully alert, and stared into the blackness. I strained to hear more: frogs, the traffic rumble, a distant siren.

There was a distinctive scrape.

'Is anybody there?' I said into the night.

What a damn fool question. If there had been, they wouldn't answer, now would they? Because they were hiding in the shadows for a good reason – like, not to be seen.

I thought of the other night, of the man shifting bins, me getting drugged...

I decided, for sanity's sake, that it was probably Horace. But still, I didn't want to hang around to find out. I legged it straight for the house, fumbled open the lock on the kitchen door and slammed it behind me. I didn't want to admit I was rattled.

My imagination was blooming and thinking the worst – like the noise could have been made by Hugo Maine or one of his thug off-siders. I blamed Ely. His comments the other night must have got to me. Bombs and snakes were still nasty, vivid memories. So was my recent drugging.

I made sure the door was firmly bolted behind me, not just locked with the Yale key. I was taking no chances. I leaned against the door, clutching my jacket to my heaving chest, and allowed my breathing to slow to a less erratic rhythm. My gaze fell on a moving mountain of orange. Horace was curled up on the one easy chair in the kitchen corner. He'd raised his head and one unblinking marble stared at me. A whisker twitched.

Okay then, the noise hadn't been made by the cat. Oh boy.

But be sensible; it could have been a neighbour's moggy. Horace wasn't the only cat around here, just the one with attitude.

Or it could have been a rat. Though it would have had to have been a hell monster rat to make so much noise.

I berated myself for being so frightened. There must have been a logical, pedestrian reason for the noise. I was being fanciful. Maine would have got to me by now if he was interested in revenge. And the man with the bins? Well, I wasn't so sure about him and his motives, but it was none of my business if he wanted to dump his Christmas refuse on the school grounds. The Iron Nun was more than capable of dealing with that issue.

With that determined thought, I went up to the student quarters to shower and sleep.

Unfortunately, sleep didn't want to come. My tummy rumbled. I'd missed tea and I considered trekking down to the kitchen for a snack. The more I thought about it, the hungrier I got, but I was too much of a coward. I didn't like the idea that someone might be lurking outside. Instead, I took painkillers to deaden the fierce ache in my shoulder and hoped my liver would cope.

Sleep, the bugger, eluded me. I lay in the dark, my eyes wide, wide open, my body restless. As the tablets worked and the pain lessened, my mind began to spin. What had I actually heard out in the school yard? Had there been anyone there? If so, who would it have been? And should I investigate?

I wasn't keen to, which irritated me. I was being wimpy. For heaven's sake, I was a police officer, employed to maintain law and order and to keep the public safe. If someone was out there and up to no good, I should deal with them and not hide away like a sissy.

I lay there a little longer until I couldn't bear it any more. I pulled on my jeans, got my gun and tiptoed back downstairs. Because my t-shirt was white and I didn't want to be seen, I unhooked Mum's cloak from behind the kitchen door. She wore this over her habit in winter and the heavy black material satisfactorily shrouded me from head to toe. My eyes were accustomed to the dark so I didn't need a light. I unlocked the door and slid into the frangipani-scented night with my heart beating faster than a rock 'n' roll drummer on speed.

I hugged the shadows as I headed for the car park. Everything was silent in the immediate vicinity, although the muted sounds of the city played out like a familiar musical score. I stealthily moved closer to the old Holden, and stopped.

Uh-oh, I hadn't been expecting that: there was a van parked right next to it. It looked remarkably like the one from the other night.

I stood stock still, listening, making sure it was safe to move closer so I could read the registration plate. The night was hot and airless, the cloak was heavy and far too snug for a summer's night. Added to that, I was dead scared. Perspiration beaded my upper lip, trickled down my temples, between my breasts, down my spine. Even the backs of my knees were weeping heat and stress-induced sweat.

But all seemed quiet.

I took a small step forward and waited. I became aware that there was another smell mixing with the flower-perfumed night.

Cheap tobacco.

Someone was smoking nearby.

What should I do?

Suddenly, the thought of being out here, alone, to rumble an intruder, wasn't such a grand idea. What if they rumbled me?

The gun felt insubstantial in my slippery grip. I changed hands and wiped my uninjured one on the habit's rough material, and then resumed my hold of the Glock.

I took a step backwards. Retreat seemed the most sensible thing to do.

'Hey,' said a man.

Eek! He'd seen me!

I have an adage that's held me in good stead. *When the going gets tough – run.* I clutched the gun tight while preparing to sprint for my life.

'Is that you, Immac?' he said.

Immac? Did he mean Sister Immaculata? If he did, he made Mum sound like some sort of hair removing ointment.

But what to do? Stay? Run? Shoot?

I opted for a non-descript *Mmm* in reply.

'Come and give us a cuddle, Immy,' he said.

Freaky! Who would want to cuddle the Iron Nun?

'No.' I tried to mimic Mum's taciturn no-nonsense tone, hoping my voice wouldn't sound cracked and pathetic.

'Come on, you saucy cow.' He gave a dirty chuckle. 'I know you like to play hard to get, but I know better. The good old days aren't that far behind us, lovely. How about a kiss and a cuddle while there's just the two of us, eh?'

A glowing cigarette butt was tossed on to the bitumen and a figure emerged from the deep shadows of the plumbago hedge. He stamped the butt into the ground with his boot. He was tall and bulky, but it was too dark for me to see his features.

'I've got time if you have,' he said suggestively. 'How about it, darlin?'

'No,' I said mimicking Mum again. 'I'm busy.' And I shot off back to the school.

'You don't know what you're missing,' he said and I heard him laughing. 'Except you do.' Luckily, he didn't follow.

Back in my room, sweating like a pig, I flung away the cloak and flopped down on my narrow bed, panting.

What should I do? Obviously, the bloke knew Sister Immaculata. But what was he doing lurking about the school grounds and wanting a bit of "how's your father" with my mum – *who was a scary nun?*

And was it the same van as the other night? What the hell was going on?

I was confused, which wasn't an unusual state of affairs.

I decided to sleep on it and maybe, just maybe, tackle Mum in the morning.

11

THE KOOKABURRA CHORUS WAS AT IT TOO EARLY FOR ANY NORMAL person – and I included myself in that category.

'Okay, guys,' I yelled out the window. 'Give me a break.'

They didn't but flew off to a higher vantage point and launched into even more outlandish hysterical laughter. If my arm had been up for it, I would have thrown a boot at them. Instead, I had to be content with slamming shut the window.

I went back to bed to grab some more shut-eye, but sleep wasn't co-operating. My arm hurt too much, the hunger pangs hadn't gone away, and it was already too flipping hot to do anything but sit in icy air con, which, as my room lacked such sophistication, meant I had to get up, get dressed and go into work.

On my way out of the door, I restored the cloak to the door hook, shovelled a couple of spoonfuls of cold lasagne into my mouth, swallowed more painkillers, and then went off to meet the day.

The Holden was parked in glorious isolation. I had a quick scout around and found three cigarette butts on the ground nearby. I bagged them up, just in case, and popped them in the glove compartment. Then, keeping a weather eye open for a coffee van along the Crawley foreshore to complete my hasty breakfast, I headed towards the city centre.

Five minutes later I received a hit, of the vehicular rather than caffeinated variety.

As the car spun out of control, my immediate thought was of Quinn.

He shouldn't have lent me his car.

His precious Holden had lasted less than three days in my custody before some nutter side-swiped me on Riverside Drive and drove me into the path of an oncoming "P" plater. Only the quick thinking of the young guy saved us both from annihilation.

It didn't save our cars though.

'Quinn,' I said some minutes later, clenching my phone so hard my knuckles turned white with the pressure.

'Sweetheart.'

He sounded warm and sleep-burred, as though he'd just woken up. Which was a possibility, as it had only just gone six.

'Did I wake you?'

'Nah. Just lying here on the deck, listening to the slap of water on the hull, looking up at the endless blue. It's going to be a scorcher of a day, babe. A real beauty.'

'Mmm.'

'Wanna catch up for breakfast?'

As I'd already deposited mine at the side of the road and was now feeling decided shaky, sweaty and nausea-clammy, I declined.

His sharp investigative mind must have picked up the subtleties that I wasn't very enthusiastic.

'What's up?' he said.

I wasn't sure quite how to phrase my answer.

'Spit it out, Red. Don't be shy, honey.'

I took a deep breath. 'I'm sorry.'

I'm glad he couldn't see what I could see. His car would make his heart bleed. The accident was being mopped up by police. Two tow truck teams were dealing with the crumpled wrecks. The medics were still patching up the "P" plater who'd been on his way to work.

I sensed Quinn's stillness at the other end of the phone.

'For what?' he said and now he didn't sound sleep-burred at all.

'Your car.'

I could feel him pulsate down the line. 'What about my car?'

'I've had an accident.'

'I should have known it. Dammit, Red.' I heard a thump, as

though he'd smacked the deck with his fist. 'I thought you'd take more care. You know how much that car means to me.'

'Hey, it wasn't my fault.'

'I didn't say it was.'

'But you inferred it.'

'Yes. I suppose. I'm sorry, but trouble dogs your every move. What are the odds? My car!'

'I couldn't help it.'

It was his turn to take a deep breath. 'Are you hurt?'

'No. Not really. But thanks for asking.' Did I sound narky his concern was more for the car? Maybe.

'What do you mean, not really?' His voice was sharp and I wasn't sure if it was due to annoyance or concern. Perhaps a bit of both.

'A bang to the head but there's no concussion. A bruised shoulder, sore neck, hurt foot.' I'd floored the brake so hard it was surprising I hadn't punched a hole through the metal and hit tarmac. 'But your car wasn't so lucky. It's being towed away.' I watched one of the tow trucks manoeuvre into the early morning traffic flow and head off to the garage with the mangled Holden in its unhappy state.

'What happened?'

'This car came out of nowhere. I didn't stand a chance.' I reiterated that it wasn't my fault, but I don't know if he believed me.

'I'll find Adam and we'll come and get you.'

'No need. I'm hitching a ride to the hospital in the ambo with the other victim.'

'I'll meet you there.' He rang off before I could argue.

Both the kid and I were released following a thorough check-up.

Fox turned up while I was sitting on the wall outside the hospital, kicking my heels against the stonework, feeling sorry for myself. My arm was back in a sling and I'd been given another shed-load of painkillers.

'You look awful,' he said as he sat next to me and slung an arm around my good shoulder.

'Thank you. That's just what I wanted to hear.'

'Best get you home.' He hugged me to his side and I let him; it felt good and necessary for my well-being. But then I thought of Quinn. I didn't want him catching me snuggled up to his son. I shifted a little away, though not a lot, from the embrace, trying to put a bit of safe space between us.

'Where's your dad?'

'Back at the boat.'

'Oh. I thought he was coming too. He did say.' Was he that mad at me for killing his car?

'He'll be pushed to find his own way in. I was already at work when I heard about your bingle. One of the traffic boys tipped me off.'

That made me feel a mite better. Quinn hadn't abandoned me.

'Why were you in so early?'

'I was dealing with the Eastern States guys, following up leads on the Wisteria Place heist.'

'Anything?'

'Not at this stage. It's slow progress.' He kissed the top of my cropped curls. 'Let's get moving before I get a ticket. I'm parked in a loading bay.'

'Where to?' he asked as we sat in the Spitfire.

'The station.'

'Not home?'

'Definitely not home and I'd better tell your dad where I am in case he comes looking.'

Fox sighed meaningfully as I texted Quinn, but I ignored him.

'Were you in his Holden when the accident happened?'

'Yep.'

'Oh dear. What sort of shape is it in?'

'An interesting one. Like a mangled banana.'

'Ouch. Dad's not going to like that.'

'He didn't.'

Back at the nick, I escaped to the ladies to tidy myself up. I stared at my reflection in the mirror. My vain heart sank. It would be kind to say I looked elfin-like, but in reality I was more an anorexic orang-utan on chemo. There wasn't much I could do about it. I threw water on my face and patted it dry with a paper towel and sluiced out my mouth to get rid of the sour taste of vomited lasagne.

I attempted to improve my hair by alternatively fluffing it up with my fingertips and smoothing it flat, but nothing worked. It needed more length but that would take time and patience, both of which I lacked.

What more could I do to enhance my looks? Well, I could raise a little colour. I pinched my cheeks in an attempt to infuse a red tinge but it didn't help much. I now resembled a plague victim with a terminal, hectic fever.

In the crew room, people were beginning to traipse in. I gave an airy general wave and escaped into my office. Fox was already in there. He had a mug of tea and a couple of plain biscuits waiting for me.

'This should make you feel better.'

'Ta.' I nibbled at a digestive and cautiously sipped the over-sweet tea. I didn't want a repeat chunder performance, especially not in front of Nurse Fox.

'Are you sure you're okay to be here?' he said. 'You're looking peaky.'

'Don't fuss. I've got work to do and so do you.'

I shut my eyes briefly once he'd gone. Too little sleep, too much pain and too much aggro with cars, plus the worry of strangers wandering around St Immaculata's. I should rethink my life. For now, I tried to put all that to one side and get on with my investigations. I had a dead man to identify and Operation Popsicle to crack.

I steadily drank my tea as I went back through more missing person files and highlighted those I thought relevant to my case, including the five reported by Mitch Sumner. Feeling more robust, I took myself off to the evidence room and had another gander at the festering backpacks.

Quinn found me there half an hour later, slowly sorting every single item with my one good hand, including screwed up pieces of paper. He lounged against the door jamb and gave me an assessing once-over.

'I saw my car,' he said instead of hello. 'You had a lucky escape.' He then walked over and bear-hugged me, ignoring the embarrassed young officer tagging gear at the other side of the room.

'I'm really sorry, Quinn.' I said into his chest. He smelled of warm man and sea. A winning combination. 'Do you think it's salvageable?'

'As in parts or in its entirety?'

'Either.'

'Who knows? But at least you're safe. That's the main thing.' He kissed me on the top of the head, just as his son had done a couple of hours before and then released me. 'What are you looking for?'

'Anything and everything that might throw some light on why these men disappeared. These backpacks are from the city hostel and belonged to young men who have disappeared over the last six months.'

'How is this related to your investigations?'

'I'm not sure yet. I'm feeling my way.' I smoothed out a piece of cheap, lined notepaper with my forefinger and thumb. There was a partial telephone number written on it in blue ballpoint. I put it to one side and continued my systematic search.

Quinn picked it up, read it and put it back down again. He picked up another twist of paper and absently straightened it out while he said, 'That body in your skip was Terry Beard.'

I glanced up and frowned. 'What, the jewel thief who'd just got out of jail? So he wasn't involved in the Wisteria Place theft, then.'

'Doesn't look like it.'

'Bang goes that theory. I wonder why he was dumped in my skip.'

'Fluke.'

'Perhaps. Hopefully. I wonder if he did the high street robbery.'

'He did. He's captured on CCTV as large as life.'

'So he was mugged, murdered and thrown into the bin.'

'Looks like it.'

'And whoever did it also took his gun.'

'A Smith and Wesson, yep.'

'Oh. Not a Glock? Okay, so that means he wasn't suffocated by his own bullets.'

'No.'

'Any of your pet informants know anything? Any gear being fenced? A gun being sold on?'

'Nothing's been offered out there yet, but it's early days. It's still the holiday period. Even the crooks take time off to enjoy their ill-gotten gains.'

He placed the tiny scrap of paper next to the other one. 'Same type of paper, ink and writing,' he said. 'And with the first three digits of that number.' He pointed to the other piece.

'Hmm. I'm pretty sure these came from the hostel noticeboard. There was a small advert with phone numbers written underneath in strips so that you could tear off the info if you wanted to contact the person. I think I'll go back and visit, see what the ad was for and get myself a number.'

'How? You don't have a car. You killed it, remember?'

'How could I forget? Anyway, Ely should be available.'

He wasn't, but young Fox promptly came to my rescue.

'I'll take you,' he said with his sinful, cherubic smile which gave me the feeling there was a double meaning going on. 'Unless you have a problem with that, Dad?' There was a challenge in his question and the smile wasn't as cherubic.

Quinn shrugged. 'As long as you behave yourselves, I don't have a problem.'

'I'm here too,' I said. 'And I'm more than capable of conducting myself appropriately.'

Both men gave me the same expression of disbelief. Nice to know they thought so highly of me.

Midday at the hostel and barely anyone was around, including the warden, who was no doubt riding the breakers at Cottesloe. I went straight over to the noticeboard. There was a space in the jumble of posters and pamphlets where the advert had been.

Fox came up behind.

'What are we looking for again?'

'An advert. It's been taken down since yesterday, which I don't think is a coincidence.'

'There doesn't appear to be anyone around to ask about it.'

'I'll come back this evening and speak to the warden.'

'Fancy a drink before we go back to the station?' said Fox.

I did. And him. But I said no.

'Coward.'

'Yep.'

He snorted a laugh. 'One drink won't hurt, Eve.'

'I didn't say it would.'

'Then let's do it.'

In a moment of weakness I agreed, because I was sure he was still talking about the drink. If he wasn't, well, I could handle myself.

'Serious? Where shall we go?' He mentioned Jinxed, a nifty new Matilda Bay restaurant where, if you hit it right, you could spot the dolphins at play in the bay. It was a special place. One more suited to a date than a casual afternoon drink. I didn't want him thinking he was in with a chance.

'I was thinking of a flat white in the mall.'

'Live dangerously.'

'I do. Often. But at this moment I want to play it safe. I've already had enough excitement today. A straightforward coffee would be nice.'

'You deserve more.'

We compromised with a no-nonsense coffee at Jinxed. A young waiter showed us to a secluded table where Fox and I enjoyed a pleasant half hour interlude. Actually, it was more than pleasant, if I was honest. It lifted my mood and restored my equilibrium.

'Only one thing would make this absolutely perfect,' said Fox in his dreamy way. He was gazing out at the still, clear water. Only a trio of playful porpoise and a mob of black swans, occasionally dipping their long, slender necks into the brink, interrupted the endless blue.

'What would that be?' I immediately regretted asking as he turned towards me and I caught his expression.

'A kiss.'

The air seared heat.

He reached for my uninjured hand and tangled his fingers with mine.

'But I'm patient.'

Hah. I wasn't, especially if he looked at and touched me like that.

'Behave, baby Fox,' I said, ruing my huskiness. 'Life is difficult enough.'

'Eve,' he said, a wealth of longing in that one word which I don't think I was imagining.

'You said one drink wouldn't hurt me.'

'I would never hurt you.'

'Not intentionally but you might anyway.'

'I'm prepared to take that gamble.'

'But I don't know if I am.'

'Just close your eyes.'

I did.

There was a deep stillness moments before our lips touched.

It was a chaste kiss; gentle, tender, and yet heat consumed me.

This was wrong *but right.*

Good *but bad.*

Inevitable.

And I'd pay for it...

'See?' he said when he broke the kiss. 'That wasn't too difficult, now was it?'

I swallowed with difficulty.

'We'd best get back before we're missed,' I said.

He smiled and briefly touched my mouth with his finger.

'Until next time,' he said.

Oh boy.

12

As soon as we walked through the door, Quinn sprung Fox from my side.

'I need a driver,' he said, his voice grim. His argument was valid: his arm was worse than mine. But he wasn't fooling me. The real reason was to keep Fox clear of my orbit.

Which was a good thing, if disappointing, because I liked having the blond Adonis buying me coffee, teasing, flirting... *and kissing me!*

But really, for sanity's sake, I needed to stick with Ely until my arm was out of a sling and I had wheels. I didn't mind partnering with the young sergeant. He was easy enough to work with. He also got the coffee and second guessed me, like Fox. But we'd both be freaked out if he tried any lip syncing.

Burton poked his head round my door and said he'd been reading through the statements by my neighbours and that one of them had seen someone dressed as a Santa near the skip in the very early morning.

'Did he have the right date?' I asked. 'Because there was that Santa wandering around the suburb prior to Christmas.' I didn't remind him that it had been my dad stalking me, dressed up as a department store Santa.

'The guy was unsure. He'd been half asleep. Otherwise no one saw a thing.'

'Do we know where Beard was staying when he came out of jail?'

'No. It was as if he vanished.'

'But he didn't. Do we have any known associates?'

'I'll get a list.'

'Have you got any info on the mispers from the backpacker hostel?'

'They're all still missing bar one who has shacked up with a local girl and hasn't bothered to collect his radioactive gear from the hostel or tell his family.'

'Let's pay him a visit to see if he can give us anything on the other lads.'

We spent a fruitless afternoon talking to the young man. He was wide-eyed, loved up and tattoo-free. He didn't know the four missing backpackers as he'd only stayed at the hostel for one night before linking up with the girl. It was a wide shot, but I asked him if he read any of the adverts on the hostel board. The boy, bless him, hadn't even realised there had been a noticeboard. He was useless as a witness.

Next we visited Mitch Sumner at the hostel and bombed out again. He had no particular recall of the advert and neither did any of the travellers that happened to be in the common room.

'I'm sorry, DI Rock,' he said. 'I don't pay too much attention to the things that get stuck up on the board. I just do what I have to do to keep this place functioning. It's not my passion, you know, being a warden. I'm just doing it for somewhere to live so I can surf all day.'

I could see where he was coming from. Sensible man. Perhaps I should do a rethink of my life and take a less stressful job?

'If you remember anything, please contact me,' I said. 'However insignificant you think it is, it still may help us.'

'You got it. Happy New Year.'

'You too.' I'd forgotten it was New Year's Eve. 'You out on the town tonight, Burton?' I asked as we walked back to the car.

'Yeah. Off to a party. You?'

'Who knows? I'll see how I feel.' My arm was sore and I felt all-over bruised, tired and fed up, so I guessed it would be another night in, sweating buckets in my small cell of a room.

Burton dropped me home on his way back to the station. St Immaculata's was deserted except for Horace. Where was everyone? Horace heaved himself off his cushion on the comfy chair and weaved his way fatly between my legs. I scratched the top of his boofy orange head and got a miaow with attitude.

'You hungry, Horace?' My voice sounded too loud in the quiet kitchen. I gave him some milk and cat biscuits. Then I opened a bottle of Merlot for myself and poured a glassful of the rosy red.

'Cheers, Horace,' I said. 'Here's to us, mate.'

Oh boy. I'd finally hit single cat lady status, sharing significant moments with a feline companion. Bring on the New Year! I stroked him again. He raised his head with a baleful scowl and scuffed me with his open paw, drawing blood, the ungrateful wretch.

I rinsed my hand under the tap and scowled back. As I took my first sip of wine I regarded the side door that led to the bowels of the school. It was ajar.

Temptation loomed.

No one was around. Now was an opportune chance to scout out the basement.

Sister Immaculata wanted me off the premises but I needed somewhere to sleep. I could understand her wanting me out of the student room but why not let me have the basement? Growing up at the school, I knew the basement was cool and dry and away from the hullabaloo of school life. I'd often hidden out there, or the attic, when young. I could buy myself a swag and make my nest there. I would be well out of the way. I wouldn't be a bother to anyone.

Setting my wine glass down, I left the bright, shiny kitchen with its industrial stainless steel counters, and went down the stairs into the dim corridor, passing storerooms of tinned food and other paraphernalia. At the end of the corridor was a big room that had recently housed a month-long sleepover of several former pupils. The beds and chairs were still in place, as were the computers. I was curious that things hadn't been returned to the main school.

In fact, the place still felt inhabited, which was crazy. Maybe Chastity spent time down here. I should ask her.

I wandered through and couldn't shake the feeling that the

place felt more than just lived in. You know that feeling? That something busy had been going on in a room moments before you've walked into it? We experience it during police raids. You burst into a suspect's house and everything looks quiet and normal. But there's a "throb" in the atmosphere. Then, bingo, you find people hiding in cupboards, under beds, up in attics, in sheds with drugs, guns, you name it.

This place had that sort of delayed frenetic energy about it.

I scanned the room. A green wheelie bin stood near one of the tables. Three others were lined up along the back wall.

I went to the nearest one, took hold of the lid – and then the Iron Nun called my name.

'What are you doing down here?' she said sharply.

'Nothing.' I guiltily dropped the lid, ruing I'd hadn't had a chance to peek inside.

It was typical I'd been caught in the act of snooping. My mother had a radar for bad behaviour. That was why her school was so successful. She had the knack of nipping insubordination in the bud.

'I was checking it out to see if there's room for me to bunk down here.'

'There isn't.'

'Really?' I waved my uninjured arm in an arc. 'Looks like it to me.'

'I'm keeping it like this for the Year 12s, as an alternative common room.'

'But I need somewhere to sleep until I get my accommodation sorted.'

'I've already told you, Eve, you are not staying here.'

'Why do you have the bins down here?'

She blinked at the change in subject and said, 'Convenience. I can throw out the rubbish in readiness for the new term.'

'Would you like me to give you a hand?'

'No.' She must have realised how blunt that was. She added a trite *thank you.*

'I don't mind, Mum. I'd like to be useful.'

'You wouldn't know what was rubbish and what wasn't. I can manage.'

She ushered me back upstairs and then closed – and locked – the door behind me.

Why didn't Sister Immaculata want me in the basement? I smelled a proverbial rat and decided to investigate as soon as I got the opportunity.

'Would you like me to order some takeaway for tea? My treat?' I said as I watched her purposefully slip the key into her capacious nun's habit pocket so there would be no way of retrieving that key without knocking her out cold.

'I've other plans tonight.'

'What about Chastity?'

'She's at a sleepover.'

'Looks like it's just Horace and me then.'

'You should go out too.'

'I would, if there was anywhere to go.' I smiled brightly. 'But don't mind me. You have a good night. Happy New Year, Mum.'

I had a reviving cool shower and came back down to the now empty kitchen. Sister Immaculata had gone and Horace had deserted me. Even he could rustle up a night on the tiles with his furry friends. I fixed a cheese and pickle sandwich, collected my wine and retired to my cell.

I lay on the narrow bed with the noisy fan trained on my shower-damp skin. I let my mind meander over Operation Popsicle, tattoo art, the Wisteria Place heist, and wondered what was going on in the basement before falling into a deep, black sleep devoid of dreams.

I awoke sometime later. The water pipes were singing. Someone was showering in the students' bathroom. Chastity must have decided not to stay over. I glanced at the time. Ten. Okay then, it must have been a lame party. The night was still young but I was disinclined to connect with it. Or with anything or anyone really. I rolled over and went back to sleep, only half aware of footsteps and whispers.

With an effort, I surfaced again a bit later. My injured arm was stiff, my mouth was drier than sandpaper. I took a swig from my water bottle. The water was warm and stale. I switched off the fan, casually glancing down into the school courtyard as I did so. My eyes must have been playing up. I had the impression shadows were dancing to and fro. Either I'd drunk too much wine – which I hadn't, as my second glass was sitting on the study table, still half-mast – or there were several people milling about in the courtyard. I wasn't game to find out who they were, not after the last time. If it was Maine and his men, they could rot out there. I wasn't offering myself up for more of his shenanigans any time soon. If it was Sister Immaculata reverting to her bad habits and having a rave up with friends, she was welcome.

I slumped back on my bed and slept like the proverbial.

The morning dawned and I felt fouler than a coop of chickens. I staggered to the bathroom and threw up. I splashed cold water on my face but didn't feel much better. Back in my room, I looked at the wine bottle. It was empty. I didn't remember drinking it. Goodness, was I losing it? But I didn't think so.

In fact, I felt the same as I had when I'd been drugged a few nights ago.

As a precaution, I took my water bottle to the bathroom and managed, in a decidedly hit and miss fashion, to collect some urine. I'd get Rachel to check it for drugs.

I sat on the bed, my head hanging down, aching like nobody's business, trying to muster the will to get dressed. I really needed to clean up my act or my lifestyle would kill me.

I checked the time on my phone and noticed I had some missed calls yesterday. Quinn, Fox, Fox, Quinn, Quinn and Papadopoulos. Hmm. I read the messages. Nice. Basically I could have been out on the razz the night before, with the choice of one of three men, instead of comatose on my virginal bed without even the cat for company.

Well, such was my life.

I debated what I should do with the spanking first day of the New Year and opted for a taxi into work. It was a skeleton staff and I didn't need to be in, but instinct told me it was the safest place to be. I left my pee bottle, with a note discreetly wrapped around it and secured with an elastic band, for Rachel and then fired up my computer and started googling body art.

Mid-morning, Quinn rang me.

'Where were you last night? Why weren't you answering your phone?'

'I was at home, asleep.' *Or drugged.*

'Shame. You missed out on a great night.'

'I wasn't in a party mood.'

'Where are you now?'

'Work.'

'I thought we were all having a day off to recharge the batteries?'

'Mine got a hammering last night. I decided I was better off here.'

'You should lay off the booze, honey.'

'Yeah, well, one day I'll learn.' There was no point trying to explain. Quinn already thought I had a drink problem. I'd wait until I had the tox report from Rachel to back me up on what had really happened.

'You don't want to come out on the boat, then?'

I looked at the computer screen and the sites for cannibalism. Sun and surf sound much more fun than researching sickos.

'I'll be out the front and waiting,' I said.

'We'll be with you in ten.'

'Good party?' I asked Chastity that evening when she floated in the door, euphoric. I was feeling better too; more relaxed and energised by a day on the ocean with my two fab Foxes.

'Crazy,' she said.

'When did you get back?'

She cocked her head to one side. 'Now. Duh.'

'But I thought you came back last night?'

'No. Didn't Gran tell you I was staying over?'

'Oh yes. I forgot.' But I hadn't.

While Chastity chattered about her party and friends, I wondered who'd been showering in the communal bathroom. Chastity had been out and Sister Immaculata had her own *en suite*, so who else had been in the school building apart from me? Hmm.

'By the way, Mum. Look what I found,' she said.

I stared at the ring sitting in her small pink palm. With my vast, non-existent experience of jewellery, I couldn't tell if the ring was worth a lot or was a mere trinket. But with the jewellery shop robbery and the safety deposit box heist, I reckoned the odds were that it hadn't come from a Christmas cracker.

'Where did you find it?'

'Outside.'

'Outside is a big place.'

'It was on the path by the gym. Do you think it's valuable?'

'Maybe.'

'I wonder who dropped it.'

I wondered indeed and thought about those shadowy forms I'd seen the night before.

'I'll take it into work and get it looked at.'

'Aw, can't I keep it?'

'Not at this stage.'

'I wonder if they dropped anything else.'

I was thinking the exact same thing.

'I'm going to have a look,' she said.

'I'm coming with you.'

By the light of our phones we scanned the area, but we didn't find anything else.

'I think you should stay with a friend for a few days.' Like, the rest of the school holidays.

'Because?'

'It's a precaution. A few strange things have been going on.'

'So when I wanted to go away I wasn't allowed to, but now, just as something interesting might happen, you want to get rid of me.'

'It might be dangerous.'

'It probably will be if you're involved.'

'You've been listening too much to Quinn and Adam.'

'They say you're a catalyst for trouble.'

'Only because I've had some unfortunate experiences lately.'

'Well I think you're overreacting. This is just a bit of bling.'

Bling that looked like a platinum and diamond ring worth a bomb.

'Humour me all the same. And Chastity. Don't mention it to Gran.'

'Too late and funny, she said not to mention it to you too. Go figure.'

Now I was even more fired up to get down the basement. My imagination was running riot. I needed to stop it in its tracks before I became totally paranoid. But I had to wait for the right time...

On the first regular working day of the year, I wasted no time in ringing the insurance company to seek justice.

The insurance clerk didn't share my passion and attempted to stonewall me with officialdom.

'But you said you would have things sorted by the New Year,' I said, narked.

'I've been in the office for five minutes. Give me a break.'

'You've had a break. Ten days to be exact. I was counting, waiting for you to be back so you could help me in my time of need. I need a car. I need accommodation. I need clothes. But the car is priority.'

'I'm not sure you qualify, Ms Rock.'

'What?' My blood pressure sky-rocketed faster than a space shuttle.

'It says in my report that the bombings weren't an accident. They were done with malicious intent.'

'Look, buster, I've paid my insurance for years. I expect to be recompensed. I need the money. I don't have a house, a car, or any belongings.'

He didn't say anything.

'Are you listening to me?' I said. 'I'm a police officer. I need wheels to do my job properly.'

'You should sue the bloke who did this to you.'

'It was a woman and she's dead.'

'So sue her estate.'

I could feel anger twisting my gut, my head throbbed with tension. I didn't think it would do me any favours suing my former friend and neighbour's estate. I certainly didn't think I'd get anywhere pursing Maine, whose men had done the actual explosive dirty work for her. In fact it would be more detrimental to me, knowing Maine.

'Or get the police department to reimburse you,' he added.

'But you're my insurance company. What's the point in having insurance if you don't pay up when needed? You can contact the Police Department if you want to weasel out of paying but as far as I'm concerned, you should foot the bill for a rental car at least until it can be worked out who is liable.'

'I'll sort something out and ring you back.'

He rang back two hours later and we had another intense wrangling match. Eventually I triumphed; the insurance company agreed to foot the bill for a hire car.

I collected it from the depot just after lunch. The car was big, white, automatic and shiny new. I hadn't driven a new car, ever. I decided it could get addictive, what with the clean smell, the pristine dash and seats, the absence of daily detritus, and the fact it actually worked without any funny noises.

Ely had been ringing around the various funeral parlours to find out where Lionel Duggins had worked and, in my new chariot, we rode over to Hammer & Sons Funeral Home. We would have gone sooner, except the place had been closed for Christmas, as if people didn't shuffle off mortal coils during the festive season.

Hammer & Sons was on the outskirts of a Wanneroo industrial development. Immaculate green lawns, which I recognised as fake now that I'd got my eye in, led up to the low slung, whitewashed building.

We parked on the forecourt and as we walked across to the main entrance, Ely looked down in distaste. 'I'm really going off these pavers,' he said. 'Teagan is gonna have to change her mind. First a cannibal's house and now a funeral home. I ask you.'

The foyer was simple and tasteful, with muted colours and big vases of what I presumed were fake flowers. Comfy couches and soothing piped music completed the picture.

We rang the bell for assistance and a slim young woman in a navy suit came out from the back to greet us. We showed our badges and asked to see the owner. She escorted us through to the back blocks of the building and discreetly left.

As soon as I met Barry Hammer, I decided the funeral parlour was aptly named. He was a Boris Karloff clone. He had clipped iron grey hair, bushy black eyebrows that were thicker than pork sausages and a corpulent body encased too snugly in well-washed green overalls that bore stains caused by things I didn't want to know about.

'What's the old bugger done now?' he said when we asked him to confirm he knew Lionel.

'I'm sorry to inform you that the old bugger is dead,' I said.

'That would explain why he didn't turn up to work then.'

'You don't seem surprised.'

'I deal with death all the time. It's what people do: they die. It doesn't faze me. And it keeps my wife in silks.'

There was a titter from a back office.

I officially introduced Ely and myself and asked him his full name.

'Barry Hammer.'

'How long had Lionel worked for you?'

'What's that got to do with anything?'

'Please just answer the question.'

'How long, Maggie?' he called towards the office.

'Six months, maybe seven.' Another Boris clone emerged from the office. Her eyebrows weren't quite so bushy, but she wore similarly stained overalls.

'What was his role here?'

'Doing whatever we asked. Preparing bodies, helping out with the services, cleaning up.'

'Was he a good worker?'

'Fair.'

'No problems with him?'

'No. Look what's this all about?'

'Did Lionel ever take body parts home with him?'

The Karloffs laughed in unison. Then they stopped and looked at us in embarrassment when we didn't join in.

'You *are* joking,' said Hammer.

'No,' said Ely.

'Well of course he didn't,' said Hammer. 'Why would he?'

'We understand he was acquiring certain...er...parts for art installations.'

They laughed uproariously again, then abruptly stopped.

'Sorry,' said Mrs Hammer. 'What you're saying is wacky.'

'He didn't,' said Hammer. 'We would have known. We're very particular here.'

'And yet we know he brought certain items back if they weren't used.'

'Blimey. Who would have thought?'

'Me,' said his wife. 'You must admit, he was a bit creepy, Barry.' Which was ripe coming from a Karloff.

'But you didn't miss anything?'

'Like?'

'Eyeballs?'

Hammer snorted. 'No. We've had no complaints either. We have a good reputation.'

'Does anyone else work here?' I asked.

'We've got an apprentice and then casual blokes who get called in to do the pall-bearing.'

'Good to know it's not a dying trade,' said Ely.

'Nice try but I've heard them all, mate,' said Hammer.

'The apprentice's name?' I said.

'Merv Turner. He's not here today. He's got another week off.'

'I'll need his contact details,' I said.

The Hammers obligingly gave them to us and then showed us

around the funeral parlour. It was all very basic. The mortuary wasn't dissimilar to Rachel's domain. Right at the back of the property, where the weedy grass, such as it was, definitely wasn't fake, was a corrugated iron warehouse. Inside were loads of stacked coffins. Some looked quite grand, possibly mahogany with gilt handles, others were decorated in footie colours or flowers. One was on a trestle half-painted with motorbikes.

'What's with the coffin artwork?' I said.

'They appeal to the younger generation. It's a sad fact of life that we get quite a few young blokes. Accidents, suicides, being silly buggers. Merv designs their coffins. It's a nice personal touch.'

We left the Hammers in their hushed house of the dead and got back for the tail end of the afternoon.

Rachel was waiting for me, swivelling back and forth in my grey office chair, eating a muesli bar, her eyes closed as if savouring the flavour.

'Rachel,' I said and she snapped open her long-lashed doe eyes. 'Sorry to wake you.'

'As if. I'm enjoying a little me time,' she said. 'It's been a hectic start to my tenure here.'

'Tell me about it. You have anything for me?'

'I came by to thank you for the yellow peril present,' she said. 'A lovely surprise after my New Year's break.'

'Ah, sorry, Rach. But please tell me it was laced with sedatives rather than alcohol.'

'You must have slept like an elephant, pet. There were hefty traces of gamma hydroxybutyrate.'

Right.

I knew all about that drug since last month's missing girls' case, Operation Paradise. It had been the drug of choice of the St Immaculata vigilante group. They had used it to sedate their victims. Which now begged the question, was some still kicking around at the school? And was Chastity using it on me so she could have an unfettered social life? If so, that girl really needed to be taken in hand. Then I remembered that she had been out that night. So the last man standing was the nun...

Rachel took another hefty bite of the bar and said around the oaty mouthful, 'This is the second time you've been sedated in a week. What's going on, luvvie?'

'I'm not sure.'

'Have you told Quinn?'

'Why would I tell him?'

'I'm not blind, pet.'

'Have you told Quinn what?' and there he was, lounging in my doorway, looking remarkably dishevelled and sexy, though somewhat tired, with his shaggy mane of hair loose from his band so he looked more rock star Bee Gee than a smooth dude cop.

'You look as though you've been in a fight,' I said.

'I have. A verbal one with the damn Wisteria Place owners. They've been hounding me, wanting to know why we haven't caught anyone yet and retrieved their property. But the trail went dead cold at the end of that makeshift tunnel. There's been nothing. Not a peep. And stop changing the subject, Red. Tell me what?'

'That she's been drugged, twice, in a week,' said Rachel sweetly.

'Really?' said Quinn, surprised. 'So it wasn't booze knocking you out?'

'No! I told you it wasn't, but would you listen? No. And what happened to patient confidentiality, Dr Gath?' I said. "Hmm?'

'You're not my patient, pet. You're alive. Eve had chloroform shoved in her face on Thursday and gamma hydroxybutyrate laced in her drink last night.'

'Crikey. Isn't that the same drug your daughter used?'

Your daughter too, I wanted to say, but in deference to Rachel I didn't.

'It's no wonder you look like death with all those toxins in your system. Mind, the bruises don't help.'

'Thank you, Rachel.'

'You're welcome, pet.' She fingered one of her long yellow and black spotted giraffe earrings, looking thoughtful. 'Where did the second drugging take place? Were you on a New Year's Eve date?'

'No such luck. I was at home, kicking my heels.'

'You would have been out if you'd bothered answering your phone,' said Quinn with a grumble.

'In my defence, I was already knocked out. I didn't see your message until this morning.'

'But why are you a target?' said Rachel. 'Or is it your daughter mucking about? I don't want to pry, but does she need professional help?'

'Chastity wasn't there. She was at a party.'

'So who *was* there?'

'My mum.'

'Would she drug you?' asked Rachel doubtfully.

I thought of the Iron Nun. 'Maybe. Possibly. I don't know.'

'That covers all bases, pet. And it sounds as if your mum might need the counselling instead of your daughter.'

'That could be a plan.' Though Sister Immaculata would spit chips if it was suggested.

'Talk us through the evening, Red,' said Quinn. So I did.

'So Sister Immaculata could have spiked your wine,' said Quinn.

'Who's Sister Immaculata?' said Rachel.

'My mum.'

'*Your mum's a nun?*'

'It's complicated.'

'Sounds it.'

'I'll explain over a bottle of Cab Sav one day.'

'I'll hold you to that.'

'Why do you think you were drugged?' said Quinn.

I gave him a level stare and wrestled with my conscience. I didn't know if I was ready to throw my family to the wolves and I didn't particularly want to air my dirty linen in front of Rachel. I tried to keep my private life under wraps at work. Which was hard, given the past few weeks.

'I might wait a little longer before I say anything. I want to gather some more facts.'

'*Red...*' he cajoled. I ignored the appeal.

'In the meantime, you might want to check this out.' I handed him the ring. 'Chastity found it.'

He regarded it for a moment then raised his eyes to mine. 'Where?'

'Need-to-know basis, DI Fox.'

'Red!' Now it wasn't an appeal, but more of an objection.

'You wouldn't believe me anyway.'

'Try me.'

'Another time. Do you think the ring is part of the heist haul? Or even the shopping mall jewellery robbery?'

'I'll get someone to check.'

'Chastity wants it back if it's not claimed.'

'Of course she does,' he said. 'Typical woman.'

We shared a smile.

Rachel cleared her throat loudly. 'Don't get all dewy on me, guys. I haven't finished showing off how clever I am. I've got some results on Operation Popsicle.'

'Good,' I said, though I inwardly thought that it was about time.

'I scored a tissue match on a pair of eyes, ears, a liver, tongue, two kidneys and a heart with the skinned torso. On top of that, we know who he is. High five, guys. Aren't you impressed?'

'Yes, but who is it?'

'Robert Button. A Brit. He is one the missing backpackers.'

'Good result, Rach.' And I did high five her.

'That's not all. I've matched up the various eyes and kidneys with liver and tongues. I've got one more name; Charles O'Toole. We still have unidentified bodies, but we've been liaising with the police overseas and it's only a matter of time for the DNA results to come back from your AWOL backpackers. It's been slow because of the holidays, but I'm sure we'll get some matches.'

'What about Lucy Drew's canvases? Pigskin or human?' I asked.

'Pig, pet.'

'Thank goodness for that. I was having nightmares about that skinned torso.' My imagination had been running away with me. 'I can't believe anyone would want to buy bits of tattooed skin.'

'Especially if it was badly cured. These ones are already disintegrating.'

'Perhaps those canvases at Sweet's gallery have also been done on animal skin.'

'I should do a test on them.'

'Yeah. People can't really be that sick, can they?' But what did I know? Human frailty never failed to surprise me, often in nasty ways.

'And now,' said Rachel, standing up and stretching her arms above her head which emphasised her substantial assets. 'It's time for me to go home and cook dinner.'

'What's on the menu tonight?' I asked conversationally.

'Lamb's fry.'

I pulled a disgusted face. How could she cook and eat that after slicing up people's livers?

'Relax, Eve. I'm joking. I'm on a vegetarian health kick at the moment. See you both tomorrow,' and she patted my cheek and left.

13

Quinn shut the door behind Rachel. He leaned against it as if I was about to escape, which was suddenly an excellent idea. He cradled his injured arm with his good one and regarded me sombrely. I could feel the coiled energy in his stillness: he meant business and wasn't going to be fobbed off.

'Okay, Red why do you think St Immaculata drugged you?' he said.

'Because she was there and had the opportunity.'

'But *why*?'

I shrugged. 'Who knows what drives that woman.'

'You're keeping something back.'

'Not really. I've no hard evidence. It's just a feeling.'

'Come on. Tell me more.'

'But I might be wrong.'

'I'm not going until you spill."

I sighed. It wasn't worth the fight. I perched myself on the corner of my desk and mirrored him by holding my own sore arm.

'Where to start?'

He waited patiently.

'I think I was drugged so I wouldn't witness activity at the school.'

'Like?'

'I think someone is secretly living in the school basement.'

'Okay.' I don't think that was quite what he expected to hear. If anything, it was an anticlimax. 'So what's the deal?'

'I'm not allowed to go down there.'

He snorted a half laugh. 'Eve, darling, that doesn't mean there's a crime being perpetrated. Your mum just doesn't like you living at the school, period.'

'I know but I feel as though things are going on, especially after dark. I saw shadows last night. I've heard voices and footsteps.'

'You could have been hallucinating due to the drugs.'

'Maybe, but I don't think so and it doesn't explain the first time I was knocked out, when you thought I'd had too much wine and Mum said I'd been sleepwalking.'

'Go on.'

'My guess is that someone is illicitly storing stolen goods at the school. Chastity found that ring on the path by the gym, near to where the van was parked. I think gear is being stashed in the basement. But it all sounds so flaky. Why would Mum be involved unless she's a fence, which I very much doubt?'

Actually, I didn't doubt it that much. My mother was a law unto herself.

'Okay,' said Quinn. 'Let's say you're right and stolen gear is being hidden at the school; but no way would your mum be part of the jewel theft or Wisteria Place robbery. That's way off beam.'

I wasn't surprised at his attitude. He hadn't been around for years and had no real grasp of my circumstances where Mum and the school were concerned.

'I accept that it may not be connected to those two cases, but I *know* something is going down at the school, that Mum is involved, and I intend to find out what.'

'Jeez.' He shook his head.

'I'm going home.'

'Is that wise, given what you've told me?'

'I'll be fine.'

He didn't move away from the door.

'I worry about you,' he said, his voice softening.

'Don't. I can handle myself.'

'I know but it doesn't make me feel any better. If you find anything to back your theory, promise me you won't do anything stupid.'

'I'll be careful.'

'Call if you need me.' He levered himself from the door and reached for me, cradling my cheek with his hand. 'And don't get yourself hurt, Red. You've enough battle scars to contend with.'

'I don't intend to.'

'Good girl.' He kissed me a while and then I left with a spring in my step.

Well, so much for good intentions.

As I drove home, I was rear-ended at the Thomas Street traffic lights and shunted into cross traffic so I got side whacked as well and ended up facing the on-coming traffic: Hairy.

My lovely new car hire had lasted barely eight hours and I had a horrible suspicion it had been pranged by the same car that had destroyed Quinn's. But, to be honest, I couldn't be sure. I'd only caught a glimpse of a tinted windscreen in my rearview mirror as I'd grappled for damage control at the intersection. Lots of cars had tinted windows. Maybe I was just paranoid.

I went through the same procedure of tow trucks and hospital. While I waited for treatment in A&E, I rang Quinn.

'Missing me already, babe?' he said.

I wasn't in the mood for flirting. 'No. I need a lift. Can you organise someone to come and get me.'

He immediately shed the teasing tone. 'Okay, what's happened to your car?'

'It's sick, like panel beater sick, and I'm at the hospital.'

You could feel his brain cells chattering away as my words sunk in. 'Dammit, Eve, are you hurt?'

'Not particularly. Just the usual; a sore neck and shoulders. I'm waiting to be seen by a doctor. Are you still at work?'

'I'm on the boat. I'll get a taxi and come for you.'

'That's crazy. Stay put. I'll get a taxi home once I get the all clear. I just want to go to bed – alone,' I added so there was no misunderstanding. 'I'll see you tomorrow.'

It took an age to see the duty doctor. As predicted, there was no major damage and I was given yet another script for painkillers. I was turning into an analgesic junkie.

There were no taxies outside the hospital entrance so I took out my phone to call one. Before I could hit a button, the phone beeped; it was Georgio Papadopoulos.

'Hey, lovely lady, do you fancy a drink?' His smooth American accent was urbane and too damn testosterone cocksure for my current state of mind.

'No thanks.'

'Oh. Well, maybe some other time then.' My lack of enthusiasm deflated his bonhomie.

'It's nothing personal.' I had no idea why I was apologising for turning him down except that he sounded like a kicked puppy. 'I'm stranded at the city hospital. I was just about to ring for a taxi home when you called.'

'Is that all?' He was back to being the upbeat Yank. 'I'll come and get you. I'll be about ten minutes.'

He was there in five. I was impressed.

His long frame eased out of a black sporty number that I instantly coveted.

'Eve, looking good,' he said with a wide smile.

'So speaks a defence lawyer. Come on, Mr Papadopoulos, you can do better than that. There's no jury that needs to be instructed. You can speak the truth without prejudice. I look like a death punk. Admit it.'

His smile widened, if that was possible, and he said, 'Okay, I will admit that you look as if you've been beat up by one of my more challenging clients. But that is completely off the record. What happened?'

'I was in a car accident.'

'Bad?'

'Not in the scheme of things but I have added a few more bruises to my collection.'

'I like a girl with blue-black eyes,' he said with one of his winks as he opened the car's passenger door.

'The lime green touch is good,' I added. 'As is the purple.'

'Very seventies,' he said. 'I approve of retro.'

He slid into the driver's seat and turned towards me, his eyes flicking over my face. 'Are you up for a drink? You could then tell me the stories behind your delightful colour scheme.' He lightly touched my purple-tinged temple, taking me by surprise at his bold intimacy.

I should have been warned and said no and been done with it. But I didn't. I don't know why. In my defence, I did hedge and said a pathetic, '*Well...*'

'No pressure, Eve, but everyone needs a little time-out once in a while and a double brandy would do you good.'

'I *was* going to have an early night.'

'You still can. I shan't keep you up. I'm a responsible adult, you know.' But his smile said otherwise.

'I'm not dressed for anywhere fancy.' It was a last ditch attempt at me being sensible.

'Trust me. I know a nice little place.'

So we went to Jinxed, the hipster hangout on the foreshore, and I got to see the dolphins. *Again.*

'Who was the hunk who brought you home last night?' Chastity asked as she whisked some eggs for an omelette.

'Someone I know through work.' I filled the kettle and switched it on for tea. I didn't want to elaborate on my evening with Georgio Papadopoulos. I was still trying to process it myself.

'Was it a date?'

'No.' I didn't think so, but it wouldn't have taken much to tip the balance. He'd given more than one hint he was up for it. But Chastity didn't need to know that. 'He gave me a lift home.'

'But it was late.'

'We had dinner first. It was no big deal.' Except for the undertones. There had been more to it than just dinner. I just had to figure what.

We'd sat at a small sheltered table on the wide wooden decking that jutted out into the Swan River. In fact, it was the same table I'd shared with Adam a couple of days ago.

I'd felt a little awkward being with the lawyer; that it had been the wrong decision to have a drink with him. As we scanned the menu, I'd blurted out the first thing that came into my head – and it hadn't been the best of opening lines: 'Your beard's impressive, Mr Papadopoulos.'

'Thank you, DI Rock. But I do take it off at bedtime.'

'I bet your wife is happy about that.'

'Oh, it's not a scratchy beard, Eve.' He leaned towards me and his voice dropped to a conspiratorial level. 'It's soft; caressing even. I'd let you cop a feel but it might be misconstrued.'

'Feeling up a colleague's beard would be extremely unprofessional.'

'Unless we were friends and then it wouldn't matter.' He smiled. 'For the record, there is no wife.' And he held my gaze, as if making a significant point.

Uh-oh, how had it suddenly come to this? And what should I say in response?

But then I didn't have to because a young waiter came to our table. He was not much older than Chastity, maybe 18 or 19, with an unruly salad haircut and a rash of tattoos over his arms and neck; probably other places that were covered by his uniform. He looked awfully like the kid who had served me before.

'Good evening, Mr Papadopoulos. Nice to see you again,' he said and briefly acknowledged me with a nod.

'You too, Jimmy. New tattoo?' Papadopoulos gestured to the lad's forearm. There was a black line tattoo of a raven's skull with an arrow through its eye. The skin around the ink was red and raised.

'Yeah. Karl did it yesterday. Cool, eh?'

'Yeah, man. You've a fine collection coming along.'

'I'm building up to a sleeve.'

'Good for you.'

'Yeah. It's cool I can get them for free. Thanks for the tip-off. I wouldn't be able to afford a sleeve otherwise.'

'My pleasure.'

'Are you ready to order, sir?'

Georgio ordered two brandies and then said to me, 'We might as well eat too,' and he ordered seafood pasta for the both of us, ignoring my protests.

'We have to eat, Eve. You'll feel better with food inside of you.' He then asked about my battered face and I told him of my various exploits, including the bombings.

'You must be an exciting woman to be around.'

'Or dangerous?'

'Any partner?'

'I'm sure you've done your homework, Mr Papadopoulos.'

'Back to being formal? Relax. And yes, I admit I have done some digging. You're an intriguing woman.'

'Or are you simply profiling me, arming yourself for when we face each other in court?'

'There is that side to it, too.'

'I appreciate your honesty.'

The food came, we ate and chatted and the time slipped by.

'We should do this again,' Georgio said as he'd left me at the school entrance just before midnight.

'That would be nice.' I blamed my answer on the mixture of brandy, painkillers and seductive company. I was a sucker for alpha males.

'I don't know how you do it, Mum,' Chastity now said. 'You don't seem to go out of your way to attract men but you get them lining up all the same. Just look at Quinn and Adam.'

'Ah.' Now was the optimum moment. But I was reluctant.

'What's with them hanging around all the time? I mean look at you? You look like you've done a few rounds in the boxing ring. You never wear anything feminine. You never do anything with your hair. You smoke, you drink. What's the attraction?'

Ouch.

'As for me,' she said. 'I try to make myself look good, but does Adam notice? No, he watches you instead. I can't work it out. I would have thought Quinn and especially Adam would be more discerning.'

Ouch again.

'Look, Mum, I get that you're a nice person but what am I missing? What's your secret charm?'

I took a deep, steadying breath. 'I have something to tell you, Chastity Rose.'

'When you use my full name, I know I'm in trouble.'

'You're not. I am. Or was.' I took a deep breath. It was now or never. 'Quinn is your dad.'

The whisking abruptly stopped. 'What?'

'He's your dad.'

She stared at me with wide stunned eyes.

I shrugged helplessly. 'I don't know what else to say.'

The whisking resumed at breakneck speed. Raw egg speckled with dried oregano splattered the counter top. She stopped again. Red slashed her cheeks. 'That means – *Omigod*, Adam and I are related! Half brother and sister! That's terrible. Why didn't you tell me before? *Mum!*'

She slammed down the bowl and clutched the bench top, the whisk still clenched in her fist, the egg mix dripping. Her head down, she heaved in big gulps of air.

'Does Adam know?'

'Yes.'

She raised her head and pointed the dripping egg whisk at me. 'That is so unfair.' She gulped a couple more lungfuls and then said with loathing, 'You have ruined my life!' With that, she stormed from the kitchen.

I sat there, statue-like, and realised I'd been holding on hard to the bench top, too. I eased my punishing grip. What should I do? Go after her? I didn't think either of us was ready for that.

The kettle finished boiling but I'd lost the urge for a cup of tea.

Should I call Quinn and tell him I'd done the deed?

I didn't have the urge to do that either.

Sister Immaculata swanned into the kitchen. She looked at the eggy mess, then at me. 'Where's Chastity?'

'I presume in her room.'

'What's happened?'

In for a penny...

'I told her Quinn was her dad.'

'Is he?'

'Yes.' *Why would I have said it otherwise?*

'Does he know?'

'Yes.'

'I see. Have you found an alternative place to live?'

'What?' Where did that come from? 'No, not yet. I'm working on it.'

'Make it your priority.'

Oh, did I feel the love!

I cleaned up the kitchen and then went in search of Chastity. I knocked on her door and she told me in no uncertain terms to go away, so I did. Thank goodness for work!

Ely acted as my taxi driver. 'Where's the hire car?' he said as I got in the car.

'At the garage.' I didn't extrapolate.

'Bummer,' he said.

'You have no idea.'

At the office, the chief gave us a pep talk. He said that the Wisteria Place owners wanted results.

'Don't we all,' said Quinn.

'Has any of the haul surfaced?'

'One piece.' Quinn glanced in my direction. 'A ring. It was found lying in a car park. We're making inquiries.'

'I suppose it's a start. What's the progress on Operation Popsicle?' said the chief.

'Most of the body parts in the freezer have been identified,' I said. 'We're working on who actually put them there. We're trying to find out what happened to the young men between leaving the hostel and ending up, piecemeal, in the freezer.'

'They were all men?'

'We believe so, sir.'

'Any leads?'

'We're trawling through cannibalism and body art internet sites and any local connections, such as tattoo parlours. I want to re-interview the gallery owner to see where he sources his art from. There may be a link.'

'What about this Terry Beard? Any idea of motive for his murder?'

'No, chief. We're trying to trace his movements since he left jail.'

'Well, keep me up to date. This is not a good start to the new year.'

Quinn followed me into my office and shut the door. He reached for me, wrapping his good arm around my shoulders and pulling me close. 'You okay?'

'Yeah.'

'Not too sore?'

'It's manageable.'

'You should take more care of yourself.'

'Yeah, well, I do try but there are other nutters out there who are determined to get me.'

He released me and tousled my lack of hair. 'You're more than a match for them,' he said. 'Now, that ring of Chastity's. It *was* from the Wisteria Place vault.'

'I see.'

'You might, but I don't. What was it doing at St Immaculata's?'

I gave him a level stare. 'Like I said before, perhaps the gear is being stored at the school?'

He sighed deep. 'Yes, it looks as if your theory has legs.'

Ah, a breakthrough.

'And Mum is in the mix.'

'You still think your mum is involved?'

'Yes, in one way or another. This morning she told me to move out. I reckon she's worried. She doesn't want me at the school, nosing around. She's implicated somehow, Quinn.'

'I'm finding it hard to accept. This is the biggest heist in the state's history and she's just a nun who teaches girls from wealthy families.'

'She is also a former hooker who lived on the seedier side of the tracks. Anything is possible.'

'She's got history, I'll give you that. But come on, she's your mum.'

'You mustn't underestimate her.'

'I would never underestimate any of the women in your family,' he said with feeling.

'Sensible.'

'Which means, Red, I'd be happier if you vacated the school, for your own safety. I dislike the idea of you being a sitting duck.'

'I don't believe I'm in life-threatening danger and, anyway, it's best I stay. I can keep an eye on Chastity and work out what's going on in the basement.'

'I guess it's your call, but I don't like it. Not a bit.'

'Don't worry. I'll be fine,' I said robustly, but not really believing it. The school wasn't my sanctuary by any stretch of the imagination. It hadn't been for years, if ever.

I took a deep breath. 'Talking of Chasity, I told her about you this morning.'

'You did?' He was surprised, and pleased.

I nodded.

'About time.' He lightly touched my cheek, just as Georgio had done the night before. I shut down on the similarities. 'How did she take it?' he said.

My throat tightened with sudden unexpected emotion. 'Let's just say she's not a happy bunny.'

'Should I talk to her?'

'Maybe. But it was Adam she was most angry about because now he's out of bounds.'

'Messy.'

'Yep.'

Quinn gave me another one armed hug and kissed the top of my head. 'But it doesn't have to be. Let's catch up tonight and talk about it over dinner. I know a nice little place that's recently opened on the foreshore.'

I squeezed my eyes shut. Surely not?

'I'll see how I feel by the end of the day.'

Ely knocked and poked his head around the door. 'Sorry to interrupt,' he said as Quinn released me. 'But you need to know – Duggins was injected with insulin and he wasn't diabetic. We're looking at murder.'

14

'WHO WERE THE LAST PEOPLE TO SEE DUGGINS ALIVE?' I ASKED ELY and Burton.

'The lawyer git Georgio Papadopoulos and that crazy old bird Lucy Drew who throws eyeballs into fish tanks,' Ely said promptly.

'And nurses?'

'Possibly.'

'Burton, find out who was on duty that day. Include the orderlies on your list.'

'You got it, boss.'

'And what would be their motives?'

'Drew was angry he'd tried to flog her dodgy art and Papadopoulos found him the client from hell.'

'Thank you, Ely. Very informed choices, I don't think.'

'My money's on Gorgeous Georgio,' said Ely. 'What about you, boss?'

'I'm keeping an open mind.' I wished I hadn't agreed to last night. Things could get dicey now Papadopoulos was a suspect.

But I only had myself to blame.

The trouble was, I was too susceptible to the opposite sex. I needed action. I blamed it on the testosterone-packing men who occupied my orbit, tossing out enticing pheromones, causing me gyp.

I'd be all right once – or if – I got myself laid. Peace and harmony would be restored, except that I suspected I had an addictive personality and I'd only want – and demand – more if it was ever forthcoming.

Quinn kept promising...

As did Fox.

And Gorgeous Georgio? *No! Don't even go there.* He was right out. I had enough on my plate with the Fox men. And he was a suspect, dammit.

I dragged my mind back to work.

My immediate priority was to get wheels.

My not-so-friendly insurance clerk wasn't happy when I called him, but then neither was I. Whiplash was giving me grief and I was missing my freedom. I figured it was essential I had my own vehicle because then I wouldn't get hijacked for drinks that turned into dinner and place myself in compromising situations.

The insurance clerk very, *very* reluctantly agreed that I would get another car and it would be ready after lunch. In the meantime, I messaged Chastity and, surprise, surprise, got no response. Then Ely and I visited Jeremy Sweet.

'This is harassment,' Sweet said when we sauntered into the gallery. 'I'll lodge a complaint.'

'Go ahead, Mr Sweet, but we're only doing our job.'

'What do you want this time?'

'Where do you source the tattoo art?'

His eyes pinged in all directions.

'Why do you want to know?'

'Oh no. Here we go again,' said Ely. 'I've warned you before, Sweet, stop answering a question with a question. So let's start again: where do you get your sick bloody tattoo art from, eh?'

'I have a local supplier.'

'Who?'

'The Extreme Body Art Association.'

'Address and contact details?'

Sweet huffed. 'Come this way.'

We went into his office, he found the info on his laptop, wrote it on a hot-pink post-it and gave it to Ely. 'There. Now stop hounding me.'

It was two o'clock and time to get my new hire car. Ely took me to the garage and swallowed a laugh when he saw the car, which wasn't surprising. The car was a much smaller model than my first car. In fact, it was more of a jam jar on wheels.

'Start pedalling,' said Ely. 'You should make it home by bedtime.'

Okay, the car was small, but at least I had transport. I followed Ely to the premises of The Extreme Body Art Association and parked next to him.

The Extreme Body Art Association office was tucked away in the same commercial zone as Hammer & Sons Funeral Home, squashed between a paving warehouse and sad-looking storage hangers. The squat brick building was covered with spray-painted images that were, in my opinion, more sordid than visually pleasant. Weld mesh was riveted over its small windows. The place looked deadbeat and dirty. Except for the spanking new forecourt.

'Look at this,' said Ely in disgust. He scuffed the ground with his shoe and scowled. 'More bloody pink paving. What are the odds?'

'It's because they're on your radar that you keep seeing them. If you were getting blue ones you'd see those everywhere instead. Chill out.'

'Maybe.' He wasn't convinced.

'When are you getting yours laid?'

'Tomorrow. I wish I'd cancelled them. They don't hold great connotations for me, but Teagan refused.'

The office door was open and a vacuum cleaner was roaring somewhere close at hand. Ely shouted *hello* a couple of times.

The vacuum cleaner went quiet and a mountain of a man, decorated rather like the building, emerged from the back blocks, his jaw moving rhythmically like a cow chewing cud. He didn't look particularly friendly.

'Yeah?' he said around his gum. He had a shaved head and bulging muscles. He sported more art than the Tate and Louvre combined. Every inch of visible skin was covered in tattoos. It was hard to determine his age. Anything between twenty-five and sixty. Perhaps even seventy.

'Police.' I gave our names and ranks as I flashed my warrant card.

'I ain't done nuthin wrong.'

'I didn't say you had,' I said mildly.

'Whaddya want then?'

'We want to know what goes on here.'

'Why? Has someone complained? Tell me who and I'll sort it.'

'Relax, mate. There haven't been any complaints,' said Ely. 'You don't have to sort anything. We're just following up on some information and want to eliminate you from our inquiries.'

'I don't like the sound of that.'

'If you've done nothing wrong then you don't have to worry.'

'This is a kosher business,' said the man defensively.

'And you are?' I asked.

'The manager, Karl X.'

'What does the X stand for?'

He gave me a bovine-wide stare as if I was the dense one. 'X is for the X in extreme.'

'Oh I see. So, Mr X, what's your real name, eh?'

He cracked a knuckle and I noticed that he wore chunky silver rings with skulls and snakes on every finger.

'Karl?' prompted Ely.

'Karl Sweet.'

'Oh. Now that's a coincidence and a half. You anything to do with Jeremy Sweet of Fine Art on the Terrace?' I said.

'Not really.'

'Which means?'

'He's my cousin.'

'Oh, and there I was thinking you were his twin,' said Ely.

The bloke gave him a dead-eyed stare.

I intervened. 'So the whole family is into art, then?'

'Did that ponce send you here?' He bristled.

'Yes. He said you provided the artwork for one of his private exhibitions.'

'Yeah, so? That's no crime.'

'We haven't said it is, at this stage,' I said. 'But we want to know more about the art.'

'There's not a lot to know. Basically, it's framed tats. What you see is what you get.'

'And who does the framing?'

'Me.'

'And the tattoos?'

'Me and a couple of others.'

'So is this a tattoo parlour too?' Wasn't Karl the name of the tattooist the hipster waiter mentioned last night? The guy who'd inked his sinister bird skull? That would be creepy.

'Yeah. I do inking here. It pays the rent.'

'And the curing?'

'Yeah.'

I felt I was missing a connection somewhere.

'Okay, you do tattoos, but surely the tattoos you cure and frame are sourced from elsewhere?'

He gave me a shifty look.

'Karl?'

'It's done through the association.'

'The Extreme Body Art Association?'

'Well, yeah.'

'But that's you?'

'Yeah.'

I wasn't getting anywhere fast. In my mind, to have a tattoo cured meant that the skin would have to first be taken off the person, as in cut off...

'Okay, buddy, let's take this one step at a time. Tell me more about this body art association.'

Karl looked relieved we were back on safe ground. 'We're affiliated to an American body. It's for people who dig tattoos. Basically, we swap designs and inking techniques. That sort of thing. There's not a lot more I can tell you.'

'Bear with me, Karl, because I'm having trouble understanding the process,' I said. 'Where do you actually source the...er...canvases from?'

'I told you, through the association.'

'So you get sent the artwork and frame it for your cousin?'

'Not just him.'

'Do you frame many?'

'No.'

'How long have you been doing it?'

'A while.'

'Be more specific, please.'

'Five, six months maybe.'

'Sorry, I still don't understand. Surely the tattoos have to come from dead people?'

Karl shuffled his big feet. It was like talking to Lurch.

'Mr Sweet?'

He shuffled again. 'Well, yeah. Of course.'

I didn't like the sound of the *of course.*

'You'd best explain, Sweet,' said Ely.

'It's simple. The EBAA helps those into skin art memorabilia,' he said as if we were half-wits.

'Which is?'

'Preserving tattoos, duh.'

'No need to be rude, Sweet. Can you explain what that actually means?'

'It's self-explanatory.'

'It's not. We need clarification.'

He sighed. 'Basically, we cure dead people's tattooed skin. It means loved ones can keep the tattoos rather than them going up in smoke or being fed to the worms.'

'There's a demand for that?' You could hear the disgust in Ely's voice.

'Yeah. Some people spend a heap of money on being inked and they don't want the art to be lost.'

'It's just a tatt,' said Ely.

'You don't get it. It becomes part of them, mate. A lot of thought goes into the type of tats they have. It reflects their characters. Tells their life story.'

'Blimey,' said Ely. 'Who would have thought?'

'We model ourselves on the American organisation.'

'Which is?' I asked.

'The National Association for the Preservation of Skin Art.' He gave me details, including a contact name and email.

'Thanks. Now tell me how it works.'

'I can't. It's a trade secret.'

'Give me the bones, Sweet.'

'I think you mean skin, boss.'

'Thank you, Ely. Mr Sweet?'

He wasn't happy but did as he was told. 'Basically, as soon as an EBAA member dies, we get cracking. Timing is crucial.'

'Why?'

'Basically, because skin begins to decay as soon as you die. We have to have a streamlined system in place so everyone concerned knows what's gotta be done. There're set procedures. Any loss of quality through decomposition gotta be avoided.'

'Go on.'

'When a paid up member dies, we get contacted as soon as. We then send their designated funeral director a kit to remove the tattoo that's been nominated and halt its decomposition.'

'How? Freeze it?'

'To begin with, yeah.'

'Then what?'

'The skin is sent back to us and we cure it. The family, or whoever has been bequeathed the tattoo, is sent a framed memento about six months or so later.'

'Lovely. So *not*,' said Ely.

'I don't like your sarcasm, officer.'

'Sorry. I didn't mean to be rude. So you do the curing?'

'Some of it.'

'And you have a pretty good success rate?'

'Not bad. We're still learning.'

'We?'

'I've a couple of apprentices.'

'Names please.'

'Tyson Smithson and Louis Ragnall.'

'I don't suppose you work with the Hammers' funeral home? Seeing they're so close.' It was a throwaway comment. I wasn't expecting a link.

Karl flashed me a guarded look. 'Sometimes. Not often. We're still growing the business. It takes time for the word to get out there.'

'But the Hammers are up for it?'

'Yeah.'

'So how many...er...skins do you do a week, say?'

'It varies. Sometimes one. Most times none. That's why I do the tattooing. It keeps the money coming in. Pays the sodding bills.'

'But the pieces for sale? How does that work?'

He lowered his eyes and kicked the dirty blue carpet with his plus-sized sneaker. 'Family might decide to sell. Especially if they don't feel comfortable having their relative's skin hanging on the wall. Or they sell to make some dosh. Some pieces fetch a good price because there's not that much available on the market.'

'Have you done much curing in the past few weeks?'

'A couple of pieces.'

'Local people?'

'Yeah. It's too expensive to access skin from elsewhere.'

'Can I have the names?'

'Yeah sure. It might take me a while. My filing system ain't that good.'

'We've got the time,' I said. 'We'll wait.'

You could tell he was having an inward tussle, as if he was going to protest but thought better of it. He then shuffled through a drawer, rustling papers, and handed me the names.

'Can we see your workshop?'

He did a shifty-eye thing, similar to his cousin. Then he silently took us out the back and showed us the stretched skin drying on boards. It looked like a tannery because not only was there human skin being cured, there were pelts too: cat, dog, goat, if I wasn't too much mistaken. And a large stuffed cat.

'You do animals,' I said.

'It's good practise and a bit of a side line if people want their pet's coat tanned.'

I couldn't visualise wanting to preserve Horace's moth-eaten fur, but then I wasn't that attached to the scabby mog.

'Well, one learns something new every day,' I said and wondered how many of the pelts belonged to pets that had been stolen off the street to be used for practise. There must have been 20 or so animal skins. I didn't reckon that many people wanted to preserve their furry companions. But, hey, I could be wrong.

But the pelts weren't my focus. I steeled myself to scrutinise the designs on the stretched pieces of human skin. There was an impressive Celtic dragon, a sultry woman with horns coming out of her wild locks and a skull and swords. While Ely talked to Sweet, I snapped a couple of shots to cross reference, just in case.

'Which are the latest ones?'

Karl indicated a couple of skins and told me the names of the deceased.

'Thank you for your co-operation, Mr Sweet,' I said ten minutes later when I'd had my fill of dead skin and wild art. 'That will be all for today.' And then I added. 'Actually, one last thing. Who owns the business?'

'Acropolis Holdings.'

'A name?'

Sweet shrugged. 'Dunno. I just run the place.'

'That guy gives me the creeps,' said Ely as we strode across the pink paving to our vehicles.

'You're not the only one. Who'd have your spouse's pickled skin hanging on your wall?'

I gave Ely the names from Sweet. 'You can check these out. Find out which funeral parlour was involved and talk to the families.'

'Right.'

'And see what you can dig up on Acropolis Holdings.'

'Got it.'

'And, as we're in the vicinity, let's go and see the Hammers again and ask them about the body skinning.'

Ely glared at the pavers as we waltzed into funeral parlour.

'Give it a rest, Ely,' I said. 'You're developing a complex.'

'Too late. I've already got it.'

The Hammers were more than happy to explain their role in the skin preservation business.

'It's a small niche but growing,' said Hammer.

'Have you done many?'

'No. To be honest, there's not big demand, DI Rock. But it's all above board and documented. I can show you our records.'

There had been five in the past six months, so not a rip-roaring business in the scheme of things. I was beginning to think my Operation Popsicle theory was dead in the water.

Hammer walked us through the foyer and on to the sun-flooded forecourt. 'Nice paving, Mr Hammer,' I said with a smile.

'Yeah, they're new. We got them for a good deal through a mate of Merv's. They even came and laid them for us during the public holiday at no extra cost so we wouldn't have our trade interrupted.'

'Oh really. Which holiday?' I took a punt. 'New Year's Day?'

'Yeah.'

'Fancy that.' I glanced significantly at Ely who wasn't looking at all thrilled.

'Yeah, a deal and some, don't you think.'

As we walked back to the car I tested the stability of the pink slabs. 'This one's rocky,' I said jokingly to my sergeant.

'Ha bloody ha,' said Ely.

'Might be worth a look underneath...'

'Don't even go there. I do *not* want to know.'

15

At the station, Rachel Gath had identified the final human remains in the freezer. Again they matched our missing backpackers. I also had a call from Mitch Sumner, the warden. He'd spoken to someone who remembered the advert. It was offering free tattoos by apprentice tattooists.

'I'm sorry, DI Rock, but the guy couldn't remember the address or name of the place.'

'Shame, but this is important nonetheless. Thank you for taking the time to find out.'

'My pleasure. If I hear anything else, I'll get in touch.'

I refrained from telling Mitch Sumner that four of his five missing backpackers were confirmed dead. He would find out soon enough.

'The chief wants to see you,' said Burton.

'Why?'

'As if I'm going to ask him that, boss. He's waiting for you in his office.'

'Eve,' said the chief. He smiled, which was never a good sign.

'Sir. You wanted to see me?'

He made basic small talk which was another bad, bad sign. I answered questions about my health, Chastity, my plans for rebuilding my house, and then, when he thought he'd lulled me sufficiently, he went in for the kill.

'I've got a country posting for you,' he stated.

'You *are* joking, sir?' Horror didn't come close to what I was feeling. The country? With all that space and sheep and trees and more sheep?

'As you are probably aware, humour isn't my strong point, DI Rock,' my superior officer said with more dryness than the Gibson Desert. 'You're going to the country, no argument.'

'You can't do this to me!'

'Oh but I can. I'm the boss. I'm in charge.'

'But why me?'

'You're the perfect choice.'

'Come again?'

'You're homeless.'

'Only temporarily.' *Especially in two days' time.*

'There you are then.'

'I'm not going,' I said flatly.

'You are.'

'You can't make me.'

'Don't be ridiculous, Rock. It's the most sensible solution.'

'Sensible for whom?'

'All of us. I need someone with experience to step into the position and you don't have a house, a vehicle, or anything really. The house and car will be provided.'

'No.'

'It's only for six months.'

'That's ages.' Goodness, I sounded like Chastity.

'It's nothing and I'm not going to argue with you.'

I argued with him anyway but to no avail. Short of giving in my notice, I was stuck.

I came out of the chief's office shell-shocked.

No house.

No car, except for the hired jam jar.

No clothes.

No hair.

The list was endless. But it didn't mean I had to go and be buried in some hillbilly backwater, far away from family and the two hunkiest dudes I'd had the pleasure of hanging out with in a long time. Actually, on second thoughts, I didn't mind taking a breather from my family.

'Who's rattled your cage?' said Quinn when he saw my face.

'The chief. He wants to send me away.'

'Where to?'

'Banjo country.'

'Might not be a bad thing. You've been under a lot of stress.'

'I'm fine,' I snarled.

'Which is why you keep pranging your cars.'

'I do **not** *prang* them. Someone is intentionally trying to make my life difficult.' My money was on Hugo Maine or one of his bully boys.

'You're more likely suffering from delayed concussion from the first accident. You should get checked out by a doctor.'

'No. The accidents were not my fault.' I was like a stuck record but I would keep saying it until someone – Quinn especially – listened.

'Babe, we all have our off days. You're just having an off week.'

'They weren't accidents, Quinn. I wasn't driving recklessly. It was the same vehicle that hit both cars. Dark sedan with tinted windows. Then there was that hoon incident the night before your car got smashed. Same car. Someone has it in for me.'

'You're sure of that?'

'Pretty sure.'

'Right.'

'Dammit, why don't you believe me?'

'I'm keeping an open mind.'

'Great.'

'Go home, Red. Have a decent night's sleep. You'll feel better in the morning.'

I felt like slapping him. Instead I challenged him. 'What about going for that drink? My new wheels are outside. We can go for a spin.'

'Sorry. I've other plans.'

'Great. Don't you trust me?'

'Don't be such a paranoid witch. Of course I trust you. With my life if necessary. Definitely with my body.' He slung his good arm around me, dragged me close and murmured into my shorn hair.

'Hip to hip, chest to chest; this is how it should be, babe.'

'Hah, you keep promising.'

'I'll deliver tonight.'

The fight went out of me and I almost had an orgasm there and then.

'But later. I've a snitch to see first.'

'Of course you do.' The heat was extinguished in a heartbeat. 'How much later? And where shall we meet? You can't drive and Adam will be on the boat so we won't be alone. So what's the plan?'

'Don't fret.'

'I'm not. But I need more than a promise to go on.'

'I'll book us a room.'

'You will?'

'I'll call you.'

'I'll be waiting.'

'Good girl.' He kissed me again before releasing me.

Giddy at the thought of finally spending time with Quinn, I cranked up my little car and sped to my temporary digs at St Immaculata's. I glanced in the rear-view mirror a few times to make sure no black car was on my tail. There wasn't and I reached the school safely.

I parked the car by the gym and sat there for a moment. If I was honest with myself, I wasn't terribly keen to be at the school, despite my bravado in front of Quinn. I didn't want any more drug-related incidents because, whichever way I looked at it, my wine had been spiked while in the kitchen and there wasn't a big cast of suspects.

I reckoned I should get out now, while the going was good.

But before I did anything else, I had a quick pampering session in readiness for my Quinn date, which was basically a shower and hair wash; I didn't believe in expending too much effort trying to be something I wasn't.

In deference to the special night, I pulled on a pair of black skinny jeans, blinding white t-shirt and new underwear – all crisp and crackling new and bought in the aftermath of my bombed home – and my new hand-tooled ankle boots. I swiped on some mascara to enhance my eyes, in spite of their tragic bruising, and then did the inconceivable, I carefully applied some foundation to take the shine out of the bruises and slicked on some lippy.

I felt positively buoyant.

Excitement fizzed in my veins as I anticipated the evening's entertainment.

I felt *good!*

Hell, I was on *fire!*

I then turned my attention to moving out. I didn't have a lot to pack. I threw my meagre pile of clothes into a black bin bag, my washing into another and the breakables into a cardboard carton that had once contained custard creams. I popped my leather jacket on top. I stripped the bed, dumped the sheets down the laundry chute, and cleared out. On the way downstairs, I knocked on Chastity's door. There was no answer so I shoved a note under her door to ask her if she was all right, tell her I was moving out and that I would let her know my destination once I did myself.

Sister Immaculata was nowhere to be seen, so I left her a brief note too, propped up against the now empty vase that had hosted Adam's Christmas carnations on the kitchen counter.

I chucked the bags and box into my white jam jar car. But I had one more thing to do. As it was getting dark, and the place deserted, now was an ideal time to suss out the basement.

In my teens, I'd used to use a small side door that led directly into the basement. Tradesmen had used it to deliver food and other essentials for the school. I'd found it a convenient way of getting in and out of the premises without being caught. For years it had been locked and effectively hidden by a giant plumbago hedge.

Through the now rapidly gathering gloom, I sprinted to the little green door. The plumbago hung heavy but I was surprised to see a newly trodden track had been worn parallel to the brick building. Some of the blue-flowering bush had been cut back too. Granted, not by a great deal, but enough to enable ready access.

I moved along the scuffed path to the door. Horace emerged

from the undergrowth and rubbed up against my jean-clad leg, leaving a rash of orange fuzz. I gave him a quick stroke, attempted brushing the fur from my sharp jeans, and then tried the door latch. It gave. My heart skittered. Should I go in?

I inched the door open and my heart skittered again. While I was debating the foolhardiness of going in solo – and without my gun, which was sitting on the front seat of the car under my bomber jacket – Horace beat me to it and shot into the dark, still room.

I decided not to follow. I felt I needed back-up. Just in case.

See, I *can* be sensible at times.

I whispered to Horace to come back. He didn't, so I left him there. I was sure someone – my mum or whoever was residing there – would find him soon enough. He wouldn't starve in the interim. He had enough fat to last a decade.

I sneaked back along the path and froze. There was a shadowy figure. I ducked down and scuttled under the plumbago, further dirtying my jeans. The hedge hadn't been significantly cut back in a long time and there were dead twigs and leaves. My nose twitched at the dry leaf mould. I prayed I wouldn't sneeze.

Whoever it was stood by my car. They pointed something at it. There was a series of thwock-thwocks. He then walked away. I stayed squatting down, imagining the worst. There was a slam of a car door, a rev of engine. They then drove off into the night. I untangled myself from the shrubbery and eased myself out, brushing off the sticky blue flowers and debris. I didn't feel quite so clean as I had twenty minutes ago.

Quietly but swiftly, I covered the distance to my car. I stopped. Was it my imagination or did it look drunk? I glanced down. The tyres were flat, dammit. I kicked one in frustration. Then I noticed the bullet holes in the paintwork.

With that someone grabbed me from behind.

16

WHEN I WOKE UP, I WAS BOUND LIKE AN EGYPTIAN MUMMY AND LYING on the deck of a launch. The wind was fresh, the stars bright, the moon a perfect silver comma in the black satin sky and that was where the night ceased to be pleasing.

'Good evening.'

I recognised that snake oil salesman voice: Hugo Maine. I would have answered him except I had duct tape stuck over my mouth.

'I trust you've enjoyed your week, DI Rock. I admire your resilience to keep on the road. You had some near misses. But here you are, still with us.'

I glared at him. So he had been behind the car accidents. I knew it! It was a shame Quinn wasn't here to hear the truth rather than thinking I was a demented, concussed woman driver.

'You know, I was disappointed you didn't want to be on my payroll,' said Maine. 'You have grit. But anyone who gets on my wrong side needs to be taught a lesson. And you have definitely been on my wrong side. You gate-crashed my party, upset the entertainment, had me arrested and got one of my favourite girls killed. Tut tut. Very bad. It's time you learned that I'm not to be messed with.'

Okay, let's get this straight: going to the party had been my neighbour's idea; the police raid had been nothing to do with me – although I *had* been responsible for catching the drug dealer; Maine had been arrested because it was his gig; and his favourite girl had tried to kill *me*. I don't think I should take personal responsibility for any of those things.

But he obviously held a grudge.

He got his minion to haul me to my feet. The boat was clocking a reasonable pace, slicing through the waves. I would have fallen over if I hadn't been held in such a tight grip.

We were on the Swan, heading towards the Indian Ocean. I recognised familiar landmarks. We were close to Royal Perth Yacht club and in yelling distance of Adam Fox's boat. Not that it was any good to me.

I wondered what Maine had in mind and then he said, 'Goodbye, DI Rock,' and I realised exactly what as his bully boy heaved me over the side of the boat.

The black river water was face-slap, gut-shocking cold. I went down, down, down. Though my legs were tied together, I kicked up hard anyway, caterpillar style. I didn't have enough air in my lungs to stay under long. I suppose I should have been grateful Maine hadn't loaded me with lead; instead I was manic with anger. How dare he do this to me!

I fought my way to the surface, the creepy sensation of jelly fish and weed sliding across my skin. I sucked against the duct tape and water seared up my nose before I was pulled back under by the launch's undertow, overpowered by the weight of water. I struggled to free my hands from behind my back and tried not to panic when I couldn't.

I don't want to be crab fodder. I don't *want to die.*

By some miracle I broke the surface. My lungs burned hell-fire. The launch was now way ahead. I presumed they wouldn't be returning. I attempted, not very successfully, to tread water, but sank, as did my new boots as they filled with water and heave-hoed away.

I frantically kicked again and got my nose a smidge above the surface. I snorted more water and gagged horribly against the duct tape. My sinuses and lungs roared with pain. Bile rose in my throat. I was done for. I gave up and sank into the foul blackness.

As I spiralled downwards I had the ridiculous thought that I shouldn't have bothered to shower and change. That there was no one to appreciate the new clothes, the lipstick, except the fish and crustaceans. What a waste.

Something latched on to me. Hands? A hook? I was dragged upwards. Water rushed past me and I collided with something hard; a boat hull. The next moment I was out of the water and being manhandled into a small aluminium dingy. My nose was full of water and mucus. Again I sucked hard against the duct tape, trying to get oxygen as my lungs screamed in agony.

'It's all right. I've got you,' said a man's voice. 'Stop panicking. You're safe.' The tape was ripped from my mouth. I greedily inhaled air in between coughing up brackish water and vomit.

'You're safe,' my good samaritan said again. He cut the duct tape binding my wrist and I wiped my hands over my face. My spluttering slowed but I began to shake and blubber like a baby. I wrapped my arms around my torso and rocked back and forth in the bottom of the tinny.

'Ssh, ssh,' he said, awkwardly patting my shoulder. 'You're going to be okay.' He dabbed a towel that smelled of fish across my face. 'There, let's dry you off a bit. It'll make you feel better.'

The rough, smelly towel stung my lips where they had been ripped by the tape. But I didn't care. I was out of the water. I was alive.

'Th-thanks,' I said taking the towel from him with shaking hands. My throat felt raw from the brackish water and vomit. My head pounded and chest heaved. My body shivered like a jack-hammer.

'Yeah, I saw you go in.' He flicked me a concerned glance as he sawed at the tape around my ankles while I dragged the towel around my shoulders to give me some warmth. 'Didn't think you stood much of a chance so thought I'd better help. I'd best get you to shore.'

'I c-can't th-thank you enough.'

I sat hunched in the bottom of the dingy, amid the fishing tackle and a bucket of goggle-eyed bream that glinted silver in the light of the waning moon, and shook and shivered with my teeth chattering faster than a flamenco dancer's castanets until we reached the club's jetty.

Reluctanctly, and at my insistence, the man left me on the jetty but only after agreeing to make a witness statement and pointing me in the direction of *Mermaid's Promise*, Adam's boat.

I limped along the jetty until I found the boat. It was in darkness. I boarded and half fell, half staggered my way clumsily down the stairs to the cabin. The cabin door wasn't locked. I moved cautiously, attempting to find the light switch when there was a slight scrape.

'Stop or I'll blow your bloody head off,' said a scary voice.

'Adam, it's me.' I sounded pathetic.

He swore and snapped on the light and then swore some more.

'Eve.' He pulled me into the circle of his arms. Oh it felt so good to be held, to be safe. 'What the hell's happened?'

I shivered in his embrace, river water pooling at my bare feet. 'Would you believe kidnapped and thrown in the river? By Maine.' I sniffed and tried not to cry. I didn't want to appear a sook, so I concentrated on Fox's bare torso squashed against me instead, which wasn't bad for a diversion.

'You poor kid.' He dragged the sheet from his bed and tucked it around me, cocoon like. It was still warm from his body but not enough to stop the tremors. He wrapped his arms around me again and held me a while and that was much more effective.

'You need a hot shower,' he said. 'Then you can tell me what's been going on.'

I dutifully took myself off to the shower.

'Do you need a hand?' he said.

Tempting.

'I can manage.'

'Well, don't lock the door and call if you feel faint.'

'My hero.'

'Yeah, right. Until Dad comes along.'

'Adam...' The guilts hit me and I felt a heel for lusting after both Fox men. But how could I choose between them? And now wasn't the time to decide.

'Go and have your shower, Eve.'

I clicked the door of the small bathroom shut and was brutally confronted by my reflection in the mirror.

Oh boy. Disaster time!

Gone were the remnants of my earlier attempt at looking nice. Long-lash black mascara and foundation had mixed with the low-down dirty river water. The result streaked my face. My bruises added to the Gothic image. My mouth was red from the tape, not from lipstick. To add insult, there was brown stringy weed in my hair. Some had also stuck to my cheeks, neck and arms. I resembled a grubby troll mermaid from the backwaters of a turgid sea.

I sighed and began the task of clawing back some vestige of civilised appearance by letting the hot needles of water do their magic. Once dry, I donned an old, soft, roomy t-shirt of Adam's, his jumper and a pair of trackie pants and crawled into his bed. He heaped the covers over me and gradually I began to lose the river's deep chill. Rhythmically, he stroked my damp hair, his eyes soft upon me. I grew nicely tranquillised by his ministrations. Warmth infused me in all the right places. I could get used to this scenario... *except I shouldn't.*

There was always a *but*, dammit.

'Can you call your dad to tell him where I am,' I said.

He stopped stroking and held my gaze. 'You've got to be kidding? You want him here too? Now?'

Yes, no, *yes...*

'I was meant to be meeting him later this evening. He might be trying to contact me and my phone is at the bottom of the Swan.'

He sighed. 'Okay. If I must.'

Quinn wasted little time in getting to me. He surged on to the boat so violently it lurched up and down. He clattered down the galley steps, looking like the wild man of Borneo, with his blond hair wayward and blue eyes sparking.

'What the hell's been going on?' He grabbed my shoulder that was peeking out from the covers and shook me without finesse. 'Where have you been? I've been out of my mind. I thought you were dead. God, Eve, I found your car shot up and you nowhere to be seen. Sniffer dogs and cops have been scouring the area. But no, here you are, with my son.' He scowled at Adam and then looked me up and down. 'In his bed, dammit.'

'It could have as easily have been yours, Daddy Bear, but his was already warm,' I said, awed at his anger and trying to defuse the tension with humour.

'Stop winding me up, Red. I've had a gutful already. Adam said something about Maine kidnapping you. Is it true?'

I told him what happened.

He said a fruity one liner. 'That bastard,' he concluded. 'He needs to be locked up for life.'

'He doesn't know I'm alive. It might be a good idea if I keep a low profile for a few days.'

'You can stay here as long as you like,' said Fox.

'Like hell she can.'

'It's my boat.'

'And she's my girl.'

Uh-oh. Awkward.

There was a static silence as the two men squared off.

'Perhaps it's time for you to leave,' said Fox and he wasn't talking to me.

'Not on my own. She's coming with me.'

Families. Don't you just love them?

'Get dressed,' said Quinn, turning to me.

'I don't have any dry clothes. I've borrowed Adam's.'

'Use the sheet.'

'For heaven's sake, Dad. Leave her be tonight. She's had a battering and needs to rest. I'll go instead.' Fox rammed some clothes into a rucksack. He flicked me one hooded glance and then left.

'Bugger,' said Quinn. 'I didn't mean for that to happen.'

'Go after him. Apologise. I'll leave and get out of your hair.'

'There's not much of it left.'

Did he mean my hair or the night? Both were dead short.

'It would be best if I made myself scarce.'

'I'll go after him, but you stay put. We're civilised enough for the three of us to survive the remainder of the night.'

But we weren't.

Quinn came back alone.

'He's gone.'

'Where?'

'No idea. I'm a helluva rotten dad.'

He slammed into the shower. When he emerged, damp, warm and bare-chested with just a dark blue towel hanging sarong-like off his hips, he looked a lot happier. And sexier. I felt a fillip of lust. Again. Good. It was nice to know the dunking in the river hadn't affected my libido.

Quinn then dropped the towel and climbed into bed.

'Time to warm you up, Red,' he said.

17

AND THAT'S WHAT QUINN DID. HE WARMED ME UP. THERE WAS nothing hotter, dammit. He said I needed to sleep, that I'd had a rough night. He had *no* idea of what I really needed and wanted. I'm a woman. I can multi-task along with the best of them. But would he oblige? No. He refused to be seduced by a bottom wiggle or smooch and I gave up, which wasn't all bad because I slept like the drowning dead, curled up under Adam's duvet in the sanctuary of Quinn's arms.

I awoke to the rattling of rigging against masts and the squawks of seagulls. The morning sun filtered through the small porthole. Quinn was deeply asleep, his blond hair tousled, his face in repose; such a rare, beautiful thing to behold. I almost reached for him, but decided to let him sleep.

I peeled myself away from his side but he caught my wrist. His eyes still closed, he said, 'Where d'you think you're going, honey?'

'Bathroom.'

He pulled me back towards him, his baby blues now regarding me through the whisper of sleep, and he kissed me, lingeringly and bone-meltingly slow.

I kissed him back, the memory of him last night, wrapped around me, branded on my brain as well as body.

A smile tugged at the corner of his mouth. 'Go on then.'

He was up and dressed by the time I came out of the bathroom.

He snaked his good arm around me and kissed me straight up and more than thoroughly. 'What we need is a good breakfast,' he said. 'Before Ely picks us up. He rang just now.'

He cooked bacon and eggs and then Ely drove us to St

Immaculata's with me still wearing my night time attire and clutching my wet togs in a plastic bag.

'We'll wait for you in the car,' said Quinn as Ely parked out the front of the school. 'We don't want to antagonise your ma any further.'

'What do you mean?'

'She wasn't happy with us last night. Called us a nest of vipers, or words to that effect.'

'Don't take it personally. She has a thing about the police.'

I legged it across the lawn. The sprinklers had been at work and the place looked dewy and serene. You would have been pushed to know there had been a car shooting, kidnapping and police search only a few hours before.

When I found her, the Iron Nun was sitting at her wide jarrah desk in her inner sanctum, looking grim and tight lipped; her habitual expression.

'I'm glad you're safe, Eve,' she said. 'But I resent having the police swarming over the school and invading our privacy.'

'I'm sorry but they were worried about me.' It was nice to know some people cared, if not my nearest and dearest. 'Is it okay if I stay here tonight? I'll find another berth tomorrow. Promise.'

'Will there be more trouble?'

'The man who kidnapped me believes I'm at the bottom of the Swan. So no.'

'I see.'

'Unless there is someone else out to get me.'

'Why would there be? Have you annoyed someone else?' Her eyes glinted behind her spectacles and I had the feeling she knew something that I didn't. I wasn't thrilled I had to stay at the school, but surely my own mother had no desire to dispatch me to the Valley of Death?

'Not that I know of. Is Chastity home?'

'No. I sent her to stay with a friend. She was upset about her parentage. She has no idea of your latest adventure, thank the Lord.'

'Good.' I had a flashback to my daughter's whispered phone call and flushed cheeks. 'I hope this friend is a girl?'

'Of course it is. Chastity, unlike you, isn't boy crazy.'

I hoped she was right.

'May I have a key to her room? I need to borrow some clothes.' I indicated my borrowed gear and she gave a disapproving sniff.

'Where are your clothes?'

'In the car that was shot up. I'm not allowed access to them until later. The car and contents have been seized for evidence.'

'Really, Eve, you need to take stock of your life. This is no way to live.'

'I know but stuff happens.'

She handed me the key and said, 'Not to other people. Just you.'

I couldn't argue. She had a point.

Chastity had posters plastered over the walls, photos, knick-knacks and most things any other teenage girl thinks essential to her well-being, including soft toys. She was a neat-nick and so everything had its place, unlike my more chaotic disposition. I did my best not to disturb her pristine order and carefully selected a few clothes for work, which wasn't easy as my daughter was slimmer and more feminine than me.

I ended up dressing in too-tight pale blue jeans and a form-fitting pretty pink top decorated with flowers. If I was going to make a habit of wearing my daughter's clothes I would have to cut back on the junk food and resume jogging. I rummaged around for any spare cash and left an IOU.

'Sweet outfit,' said Quinn as I got in the car.

'Hah. So not me. I need to spring my clothes from my car as soon as I can. And my gun.'

There was a buzz at the office over the shooting and a warrant out for Maine's arrest for kidnapping and attempted murder. Quinn jumped into the fray and began dishing out orders.

'We'll find the bastard,' he said, stalking about the incident room like a rampaging tiger. He was so different from the sleep-muzzed man of the dawn. Positively dangerous. I was glad he was on my side.

'For the record, Maine didn't shoot my car,' I said. 'Someone else did that a few minutes before I was grabbed.'

Quinn gave me a sceptical glance. 'Are you sure about that?'

'Yep. I was there, remember.'

'It could have been Maine doing the shooting and his henchmen that sprang you.'

'I didn't get a good look at the man with the gun, but I didn't get the impression either man was Maine.'

'It was getting dark. How can you be sure?'

'I can't,' I conceded.

I waited a beat. 'As we're talking about guns, I'll grab mine from the car. I feel naked without it. And my clothes. I need my clothes. I feel naked without them too.' I gave him a saucy grin.

Quinn's brows twitched ever so slightly. 'Behave,' he said, 'or there'll be a reckoning.'

'Oooh. I'm scared.'

'You should be. But as far as your gear is concerned, it's evidence and there's no gun listed on the car's contents. I checked. Are you sure it was there?'

'Yes. On the front seat under my jacket.'

'It shouldn't have been. You should have left it at the station.'

'Yes, in theory, but I was still on duty.'

'Red!'

'I was. That's my story and I'm sticking to it.'

I put in a request for a replacement gun and I called the insurance company for another car. I wasn't sure I'd be successful with either.

I wasn't.

In the meantime, I settled down at my desk, popped the waistband button on Chastity's incy-wincy jeans for comfort, and pulled up the computer file on our missing backpackers. I wanted to take another look at Charlie O'Toole's tattoos. I flicked through the pictures and stopped at the girl with the goat horns. Without my phone, I couldn't be sure, but I reckoned that was the same tattoo we'd seen curing at Karl Sweet's tattoo parlour.

Ely brought me in a coffee.

'Take a look at this,' I said. 'What do you reckon?'

He whistled through his teeth. 'A dead ringer,' he said. 'Let's go and arrest him.'

'We'll see if there are any other likely matches before we do.'

I contacted our opposite number in the UK and had a chat with the liaising detective. He promised to contact the murdered men's families and send me through any photos he could find of the victims' tattoos.

It was 9:15 and I reckoned it wasn't too late to ring America. I was keen to talk with someone from the National Association for the Preservation of Skin Art, the organisation Sweet had mentioned.

I got through to some guy called TJ Hogan who sounded as if he ate broken glass for breakfast, lunch and dinner.

'We're a non-profit group,' he rasped when I asked him to explain what NAPSA was about. 'We give advice and offer a service.'

'Like providing the kits for undertakers?'

'Yes, ma'am. The morticians flay the skin, arrest decomposition, then send it back to us.'

I thought about the examples I'd seen at the gallery and tattoo parlour. The largest piece wouldn't have been much bigger than an A4 sheet of paper. 'So we're talking about singular tattoos here?'

'Yes, ma'am but we're also experimenting on full body skins.'

Yewuck.

'Why?'

'Because some folk spend an exorbitant amount of cash on their skin art. They want it kept for posterity. It reflects their character. Tells their story. It's an historical pictorial record of their life.'

Hadn't I heard a similar line before? It must be the association's official pitch.

I had to ask, though I didn't want to. 'Tell me how it's done, TJ.'

'Sure thing, ma'am. The wet flayed skin is wrapped around a human-sized fibreglass mannequin. You can't do it if it's begun to dry out because the skin shrinks and we lose the picture. Once the skin is in place, we leave it to air cure.'

I had a horror vision of shop mannequins lined up in a row,

wearing dripping bloodied skins. 'Surely there's not much call for that sort of thing?'

'You'd be surprised, ma'am. The demand is growing as tattooing becomes more popular and people ink their entire bodies,' he said.

'Sorry to sound ignorant again, TJ, but it must be difficult to slice off a complete skin?'

'Yes, ma'am, it sure is. People are clambering on that bandwagon to have a go but it takes skill to skin a whole body. We employ an accomplished anatomist to do it. That's why you need a life-sized mould.'

I tried not to gag but my breakfast almost made a re-appearance.

'You know, ma'am, it's not that different from a taxidermist stuffing an animal.'

I had a flashback. Eek. There had been a stuffed cat in Karl Sweet's workshop. Was it a test piece? Was Sweet, or one of his workers, attempting to move on to bigger, human pieces?

Karl Sweet went to the top of the suspect list. He needed another visit.

'One last question, TJ, is there anyone who does full body preservation in Perth?'

'No, ma'am.'

I didn't believe him. I think the WA bandwagon had passengers.

While Ely was taking photos of curing tattoos in The Extreme Body Art Association's workshop, I flicked through a magazine in Karl Sweet's waiting room. Sweet fiddled about, shooting me furtive glances, giving the general impression of guilt.

'These are impressive,' I said holding up a spread of a well-oiled and colourful male torso.

'Yeah. He's one of the best and he's a local dude. How cool is that?'

'Really?' I had a closer squiz. How come I never got to see crumpets like this down the beach? 'Have you done any of his tats, Karl?'

'Nah, I'm not good enough for him. Not yet. But it's something to aspire to.'

'How long have you been at it?'

'A couple of years.'

'You're well-inked yourself.' Which was a gross understatement. There was hardly a patch of skin that hadn't been coloured.

'Yeah, we all ink each other to practise. It gets addictive.'

'Really?' I couldn't see the appeal myself. 'You mentioned apprentices?'

'Tyson. He's good but he only works here a couple of days a week. There's not enough money to pay him for more. Louis comes in sometimes.'

'I'll need their contact details.'

'Sure.'

'So this guy here.' I indicated the double-page spread hunk. 'If he wanted to have his whole torso preserved after death, could it be done here?'

Karl shrugged as his glance slid away. 'No. We haven't done a full one yet. We're still learning.'

Rachel Gath, her fish earrings swinging, came purposefully into my office. I can't say she was radiating her usual bouncy, benign energy. She was far more serious and businesslike.

'May I see you in private, DI Rock?' she said pointedly.

'Of course. Off you go, Ely.'

She snapped shut the door. 'I went through every Glock bullet found inside Terry Beard,' she said without preamble and gave me a significant look which I was at a loss to interpret.

'And?'

'Some had partial prints on them.'

'Good.'

Her look intensified.

'*Not* good?'

'I've two matches.'

'And that's *not* a positive thing? Won't we get some idea of who murdered Beard?'

'We got a guy called Harry Shorten. He's done time on and off over the years.'

'For?'

'Burglary, robbery, theft. He got out from his last stint two months ago.' There was a pregnant pause. 'And then there was another partial.'

'And it belongs too?' I prompted.

She blinked her Bambi eyes and I got the distinct feeling I wouldn't like the answer.

'You,' she said.

'What?' I sat there, pole-axed. 'Me? But how does that work?'

'I don't know but I'll have to tell the chief.'

'Yes.' My mind was reeling. When had I handled the bullets? Unless they'd been stolen from my stash and used to asphyxiate Beard. Was that why he was dumped in my skip? Was someone trying to frame me? *Maine?* The bastard. I wouldn't put it past him.

'Sorry, pet.'

'Don't be. You're simply doing your job.'

'You don't have a credible alibi,' said the chief.

'It was Christmas Eve. I was at St Immaculata's, asleep.'

'But by your own admission, you were alone. No one can vouch for you. It would be best for you to stand down until this case is resolved.'

'You think I had something to do with the murder of this man? Really?'

'It needs to be investigated without prejudice, DI Rock.'

'But sir!'

'Why do you always argue, eh? Go home, DI Rock. You're suspended on full pay. Take a well-earned rest. Get yourself in good health. You haven't fully recovered from last night. Or, indeed, from the last case.'

'Does this mean I don't have to go to the country?' I was grasping at clouds, silver linings and all that jazz.

'I didn't say that.'

'But I might not be well enough to go.'

'Or you might be in jail,' he dead-panned.

He had a point.

'But I never met this Beard!'

'So you say. But he was found in the skip at your property with your bullets inside him. There must be some connection and I don't want the Force compromised by having you involved, however remotely, with the investigation. You will stand down until further notice.'

I marched out of his office and took the stairs down to our floor rather than the lift. It gave me time to cool down and get myself in hand.

But there weren't enough stairs to get a good result. Ely took one look at my stormy face and said, 'What?'

'I'm suspended.'

18

'LET ME GET THIS STRAIGHT,' SAID QUINN. 'YOUR BULLETS WERE THE cause of Beard's death?'

We were sitting at the funky hipster joint that was rapidly becoming my local. We were having a coffee. There wasn't a dolphin in sight but there *was* the tattooed waiter. He gave me a warm smile of recognition and I had a bolt of panic. I hoped Quinn and Ely hadn't seen his friendly smile. I didn't want to explain I'd been to Jinxed twice before, and with whom. I didn't think either of them, for their various reasons and prejudices, would approve of my drinking companions.

'Yep. My ammo did for him. That sums it up succinctly.'

'And you didn't do it?'

'You're a brave man asking that, mate,' said Ely. He'd driven us there to have a pow-wow on our strategy for the next few days – or weeks – until we found the culprit.

'Of course I didn't do it!'

'I had to make sure.' Quinn grinned. 'So how come your prints were on the bullets?'

'Not all the bullets. Just three.'

'But they still helped kill the guy,' pointed out Quinn.

'Out of interest, where do you keep your ammo, boss?'

'In a tea caddy by my bed. Or I did once upon a time, when I had a house.'

'Really?' Ely was sceptical.

'Yes, really. Then they're easy to reach in an emergency.'

'So where do you usually keep your gun?' he said.

'Under my pillow.'

'Blimey. That's dead against regulations.'

'It works for me.'

'Let's go back to the tea caddy,' said Quinn, refocussing the conversation. 'Do you still have it? Or did it get destroyed along with the house?'

'Annihilated except for its lid.'

'So the bullets weren't from your stash. Where does that leave us?' asked Ely.

'Perhaps the bullets came from work. It's feasible I may have handled some there.'

'Really? So now you're saying someone on the Force pinched some bullets and killed Beard?' said Quinn.

'Okay, no. That's unlikely. But then so is my family filching my ammo and making a bloke swallow them. And it doesn't explain how this Shorten guy comes into it. Did he murder Beard or did he have his ammo pinched too? I admit, my money's on Maine. Maybe he or his bully boys stole the ammo from my house before they bombed it. Maybe one of his boys is Shorten?'

'That's more likely. Maine needs to be found.'

'Leave Shorten to me and I'll see what I can find out about him,' said Ely.

'So we agree that Beard was left in your skip on purpose,' said Quinn.

'Yes, I suppose, but why? I didn't have any connection with him. He was never one of my collars. He was way before my time.'

'Maybe to frame you? Or at least make life difficult for you?' said Ely.

'Which brings us back to Maine, Shorten or an unknown person. Here's an idea – if Rachel had checked the bullets earlier, I would have been suspended or arrested on Boxing Day.'

'Which means?' said Ely.

Quinn and I exchanged a glance.

'What am I missing?' said Ely.

'We think St Immaculata's is being used as the Wisteria Place gang's hideout,' said Quinn.

'Good one.' Ely shook his head in disbelief.

'Don't diss it,' I said. 'Stranger things have happened. In fact, to help back up the theory, I need some tests done on some cigarette butts I found at the school.'

'You have the butts here?' asked Quinn.

'No. They're in your Holden's glove compartment.'

'I'll get on to it.'

I was edgy and couldn't settle. I would have preferred to be snuggled up with Quinn but that wasn't going to happen while he was staying on Fox's boat.

Because I was feeling sooky, I'd decided to sleep in Chastity's room rather than make up a bed in my old one. Hers was cosy and lived in, unlike the other barrack-like, run-of-the-mill student rooms. I'd locked the door and shoved the chest-of-drawers in front of it as an extra precaution against intruders, because my mother *did* have the master key and I *didn't* know who had shot my car, or why. *Not that I thought it was her...*

I messaged Chastity before I got into bed, to make sure she was okay, but I was still *parente non-grata* and got no reply.

The night was a nightmare tussle between sleep and wakefulness. I tried to relax but every single noise shot a surge of fight-or-flight adrenalin through me. I was more affected by Maine's attack than I'd thought. I tried deep breathing but it made me light headed. I mentally sifted through the information on Operation Popsicle and the heist, but that made me want to go into work and look things up to clarify my lines of thought. So I lay on the single bed, clammy, hot and fed up, waiting for the morning to roll in and rescue me.

When it finally arrived, I dropped off to sleep. Go figure. About eleven, I re-surfaced and I trotted down to the kitchen to make myself a late breakfast. I stopped on the threshold because a man was standing with his back to me at the sink.

I had a flashback to the other night. Was it the guy who'd wanted to make out with the resident nun? He looked similar: old and barrel shaped. He appeared comfortable and domesticated in our kitchen as he filled the kettle from the tap, which begged the question that he'd been here before.

As the man turned with the kettle in his hand, he caught sight of me. I don't which of us was more surprised.

'Eve!' he said.

'Henry! What are you doing here?'

He flushed and flicked the kettle's switch. 'I came to see your mum. I'm just making her some tea. Want some?'

I declined, though it did seem churlish, because Henry wouldn't have been involved in the drugging. He'd been nowhere near.

Or had he?

Goodness, I was getting paranoid.

'And what are you doing here?' he said. 'Your mum said you'd moved out.'

'I did but came back for one last night. I'm leaving today.'

'I see. Not going into work then?'

'Yes. Any moment now.' I didn't tell him about the suspension. I thought it best not. 'I'm glad you two are getting on better, Henry. That's nice.'

'We have our moments.' He dunked a peppermint teabag in a chunky white mug. I almost pointed out that Mum preferred one of Chastity's pretty poppy-patterned china cups and saucers from the kitchenette, but I decided it wasn't worth it. Mum was more than capable of putting him straight.

'Anyway,' said Henry. 'I'd best go. She's waiting.'

I used the landline to call Ely for a lift and went outside to wait. While I waited, I wandered towards the plumbago hedge and decided, as it was daylight and my parents were ensconced in the office drinking herbal tea, I would have a quick stickybeak. I jogged down the path, lifted the door latch and pushed. Unexpectedly, the door opened. I cautiously peeped in.

The basement was empty but, like before, it had the trappings of habitation, though even more so, as if someone was getting comfortable. Two of the school's utilitarian white mugs were on the table, along with a full ashtray. There was bedding, magazines and a jacket slung over a chair. There was the pong of sweat, tobacco and whisky. The room could have done with a good airing.

The four wheelie bins were still lined up along the back wall. The place was quiet. It was now or never, but I'd have to move fast. I didn't want to be caught. I swiftly strode to the bins and lifted the lid of the first one. It was full of calico bags, like the ones you get rice or lentils in. I unzipped one that had *Polished Jasmine Rice* printed in red and blue on the sack and parted the material.

I stared inside the bag and resisted the temptation to whistle.

A slight noise from along the basement corridor caused my blood to surge. It was the sound of a door being unlocked. Quickly, I zipped the bag, catching the frayed hem in the zip halfway. Darn. I shoved the bag under another one so it wouldn't be immediately discovered.

I would have loved to check the other bins but I'd seen enough to satisfy me.

On my way out of the basement, I snatched up the two dirty mugs, using the hem of my t-shirt to hold them so I wouldn't smudge them with my prints. As I closed the door I heard the beep of Ely's car horn. For once, he had excellent timing. I emerged from the hedge, cradling the mugs to my body.

'Been rolling in the garden, boss?' said Ely, flicking a blue flower off my top.

'Something like that. Have you a couple of evidence bags?'

He pulled a handful from his jacket pocket. 'What's with the mugs?'

'I want you to get them fingerprinted for me.'

'Why?'

'Curiosity and a hunch.'

'Can't say fairer than that. Is this to do with the gang's hideout?' He chuckled, obviously thinking it a jolly joke.

'Yep. At least two people are hiding in the cellar. Hopefully these mugs will help determine who they are.'

'Your call.' Ely placed the bagged mugs on the back seat. 'Now where to?'

'I need to find a nice cheap motel for a few days until I can work out my finances with the insurance guys.'

'How about the backpacker hostel?'

'Oh, come on. Can't you do better than that?'

'It's cheap, public transport on tap and walking distance from the cop shop. What more could you ask?'

'Comfort? Privacy? My very own place?' I missed my little house, damn Maine and his fire-bombing mates.

'Now you're getting picky, boss.'

'Okay. The hostel it is. I haven't got time to find anywhere else.'

'You've stacks of time,' said Ely. 'You're effectively on holiday.'

'If you think I'm going to sit back and twiddle my thumbs, you're way off.'

As Ely navigated the traffic, he told me his pavers had turned up. 'You know, I'd presumed they would be individual paving bricks,' he said. 'But they come in slabs of a metre square with the zig-zag designs already imprinted on them.'

'Interesting,' I said.

'I wouldn't go that far but it did show my ignorance. I thought it would take the guys ages to lay them but they just plonked down these big sheets on the sand pad.'

I frowned, thinking. 'Actually, it *is* interesting. Ely. It would have made it easier to hide bodies under the driveway at Cranberry Court. Just lift a couple of slabs and dig a hole... It's possible.'

We drove on in silence for a minute or so.

'Think where else we've seen those pavers,' I said, warming to my idea.

'Don't worry. I have been,' said Ely, fed up.

'I wonder,' I said.

'Please don't, boss.'

'But it *is* a possibility. Maybe we should get a warrant to dig up the tattoo parlour's forecourt? Maybe the funeral home's too. After all, the Hammers got their new forecourt on New Year's Day, two days after the paving went missing from Duggins' driveway. They could have reburied the bodies, if there were bodies, under those slabs.'

'Your imagination is running away with you.'

'Maybe, maybe not. I might hold off on any action until we've heard from the British police.'

'You're not allowed to do anything. You're suspended.'

I ignored him. 'Let me know when they email through the backpackers' tattoo photos. If there are any matches we should start digging. I think we're on to something.'

'Great. I've really, *really* gone off those pink bloody bricks.'

'Never mind. You'll forget what they were used for in a decade or two.'

'Thanks.'

'And let me know about the mugs' prints.'

Mitch Sumner was surprised at my request for a berth. He allocated me a room on my own, bless him, but then I wasn't sure of his motives. Was he doing it for my comfort or the other hostellers? Serving police officers did tend to put a dampener on party venues.

'Where did you get those mugs from?' Quinn asked as he sat on my hard, narrow bed late that afternoon. The hostel room wasn't much bigger than a police cell and had as much chic luxury.

'Tell me first if there were any significant prints.'

'Harry Shorten's.'

'Him again? Interesting. Do we have a photo of him yet?'

'We're trying to find one.'

'Anyone else?'

'Felix Spalding. He's another old lag from the past.'

'Oh.'

'Who were you expecting?'

'Not him.'

'That doesn't answer my question, Eve.'

I sighed. 'Henry and I'm not proud of it.'

'Your dad? Grief.'

'I don't look on him as my dad. There's no connection between us.' And, if I was right with my theory, I would prefer to put as much distance between him and me as possible.

'Relationships take time,' said Quinn.

'Hmm. I can't really work out why he's come back into our lives.'

'He's getting older and wants to make amends?'

'I suppose.' I wasn't convinced.

'Okay, I'll ask again: where did you get the mugs from?'

'St Immaculata's cellar.'

'Interesting.'

'The wheelie bins are there too.'

'Of course they are.' He grinned

I did too. 'One bin was full of bags. I only got the chance to look in one bag and it was full of jewellery. I reckon we've got the Wisteria Place booty.'

Quinn whistled. 'Well done. But you shouldn't have been there without back-up.'

'The opportunity presented and I took it. You would have done the same, Quinn. Admit it.'

'Point taken. I'll get a search warrant.'

'As soon as you've got it, tell me.'

'But you're suspended.'

'I want to be there.'

'*Red*.''

'Please.'

'Okay but keep a low profile. We don't want the lot of us getting into trouble with the chief.'

Ely called me later. 'We've got the warrant,' he said. 'Quinn said you're coming along for the ride. Is that wise?'

'Try stopping me.'

'I wouldn't dare.'

'Don't worry, Ely. You won't know I'm there.'

He came and collected me from my hostel cell and on the way

to the school he filled me in on the latest findings. It turned out that Felix Spalding's DNA was on all three butts which, along with the mug fingerprints, put him firmly on the school precinct. Spalding, like Beard and Shorten, had been away at Her Majesty's pleasure on and off for years for burglary and armed robbery. Similarly to Beard, he had been released just before Christmas.

'Did these guys know each other?' I asked. They were before my time on the Force. I didn't know much about them.

Except that one of them had been game to chat up my nun mum.

'They've been in the same prison,' said Ely.

'Did they work together at all? As in robberies?'

'Spalding and Beard have history. There's no link with Shorten at this stage.'

'It's a significant coincidence they were all in Perth at the same time. Were they all members of the Wisteria Place gang, I wonder?'

'Beard was dead before the heist.' Ely pointed out.

'Murdered and mugged before the heist, which may point to a falling out between thieves?'

At the school, we came face to face with my mother. Not a pretty sight in the scheme of things. She was at her desk with a Bible open in front of her. When I say a Bible, I mean a *Bible.* It was one of those big old fashioned tomes with impressive brass hinges and fastenings that smacked of reverent gravitas.

'We have a warrant, Sister,' said Ely. He was apologetic and awkward, bless him.

Sister Immaculata wasn't.

'This is an outrage. How dare you allow this, Eve?'

'It's my job. If you've nothing to hide, it'll be painless.' She didn't need to know I'd been suspended and had no official clout. 'Come along,' I said and gestured to the door.

'I'd prefer to stay here, thank you.'

'No. You come with us. Then you can witness everything is above board.'

'I trust the police.'

'Well, that'd be a first.'

'Don't be ridiculous, Eve. I've always had a high regard for the police force.'

I didn't deign to reply.

'Ely, you stay with her,' I said to my sergeant.

'That won't be necessary,' said Sister Immaculata.

'This will be done by the book, Mum.' I was such a hypocrite! 'Ely is staying.'

In a very unreverent way, she thumped shut her Bible and sat there glaring.

Officers, led by Quinn, scoured the school grounds and buildings but found zilch. St Immaculata's School for Girls was squeaky clean. Especially the basement, dammit, where the bins were gone and all signs of habitation had been wiped out. It was as if the place had never been lived in.

'Well, what do you know,' said Quinn. 'The place has been swept clean.'

I said a rude word. 'I'm not giving up yet.'

I knew Sister Immaculata was hiding something. She was too confident.

'I didn't think you would,' said Quinn. 'How do you want to play this?'

'Follow me.'

Back in her office the Iron Nun was sitting in state, eye-balling Ely, giving him the jitters. She had re-opened the Bible. I glanced at the marked verse. It was Matthew 6, 14-15: *'For if you forgive other people when they sin against you, your heavenly Father will also forgive your sins. But if you do not forgive others their sins, your Father will not forgive your sins.'* And I wondered which of us that was aimed at. Take your pick, I suppose.

'Have you quite finished?' she now said with icy politeness.

'No,' I said. Something was bugging me. In the recess of my mind, a memory niggled away.

What the hell was it? And why did I think it had something to do with camels? I stared at the old Bible. Camels? Old Testament. Then it came to me in a flash. Thank God for Sunday School.

I hustled Quinn out of the office. 'We need to get a woman officer,' I said.

His brows rose. 'Because?'

'I want Sister Immaculata searched.'

'Eve, babe, really?'

'Trust me on this, I know my mum. I understand how her mind works – to a degree at any rate. I want her searched.'

He gave me a steady, searching look. 'Okay, I trust you. But for the record, I don't like it.'

'You don't have to. I'll take the rap if I'm wrong.'

As luck would have it, we had two women officers on the team and they dealt with the cantankerous nun and struck gold, literally. And gems.

There was a calico bag of jewellery stashed under her chair, hidden by the folds of her black habit.

'Well, well,' I said to Sister Immaculata. 'And where did these trinkets come from, hmm?'

'I found them,' she said.

'I don't believe you.'

'Why would I lie?'

'Okay, then, where did you find them?'

'They were in the bag lying on the ground in the school car park.'

Which was where Chastity had found the ring. A coincidence?

'When.'

'Just before you arrived.'

'Why didn't you give them to us straight away?'

'I didn't know what you were looking for.'

'Why hide them?'

'I panicked.'

'Really? You honestly expect me to believe that, Mum?'

'Yes.' She folded her hands over her stomach and put her nose in the air as if that was the end of the story. Regardless of what we said and how we said it, she wouldn't budge on her story.

She also emphatically denied that anyone had been sleeping in the basement. But I knew different; I'd seen the evidence and I wondered what had happened to the two men. They must have cleared out not long after I'd left the school the day before.

We had a description out on Spalding but still no image of Shorten. I'd also given a sketchy description, with a partial reggo, of the van that I believed they were driving.

As for the Iron Nun's cache, it didn't take long to cross reference the jewellery. It was part of the haul from Wisteria Place, along with a couple of items that had come from the jewellery shop on the mall, which meant that either the two robberies were linked or someone at St Immaculata's was the fence.

The Iron Nun?

Hmm...

19

LATER QUINN, ELY AND I SHARED FISH AND CHIPS DOWN BY ELIZABETH Quay.

The sun was setting, sliding like liquid gold into the Indian Ocean. The air was still thick and hot from the scorcher day as Cyclone Clarry was still doing its damnedest up north. It would be a relief to kiss the cyclone goodbye, once it got around to dumping its load on Darwin and dispersing.

I wiped a stream of sweat that was waterfalling down my neck. If I'd possessed any bathers, I would have gone in for a dip, but they were another item to put on the ever-expanding list for when I had time and inclination to shop.

'How did you know Sister Immaculata was hiding something?' Quinn asked. 'I wouldn't have suspected.'

I dipped a chip in the tomato sauce. 'I was brought up reading the Bible.'

'The inference?'

'Jacob's wife Rachael stole her family's religious icons when they left her father's camp. When her father Laban came to search the tents, Rachael stayed seated on her camel's saddle, saying that she was unwell. But in fact she was sitting on the booty.'

'Good one,' said Ely.

'The story always bugged me. If I'd been her dad I would have demanded she was searched along with everyone else.'

'And that's why you make a good cop: your strong sense of justice, even as a kid. You were destined to become a cop, Red.'

'But this is an empty triumph. I'd have preferred Mum not to be involved.'

We finished our food and Ely dropped Quinn off at the station to further interview Sister Immaculata. Ely took me to the hostel to collect my things. With my mother in a cell, the basement visitors flown to another hideout and my daughter away, I decided I might as well take up residence in the school again. It was marginally better than the hostel accommodation and a lot jolly quieter.

Mitch Sumner was philosophical when I told him I was moving out. He was used to seeing folk come and go.

As Ely and I lugged my two black plastic rubbish bags of meagre belongings through the common-room, I caught site of the young bloke I'd seen on my initial visit to the hostel. He was deep in conversation with a highly tattooed Vietnamese lad. This time I remembered where I had first seen him.

I purposefully didn't make eye contact but as soon as we were outside I mentioned him to Ely.

'Can't say I noticed,' he said.

'Go back and have a gander, but discreetly.'

He did and came back none the wiser. 'So who is he?' he said.

'Danny Pike's assistant. He was on the market stall the day we interviewed Pike. I saw him at the hostel the first time I met the warden.'

'So?'

'Did you see who he was talking to?'

'Some guy.'

'With tats.'

'And?'

'There was an ad on the noticeboard for free tattoos. It was taken down after I'd been at the hostel, the same evening I'd spotted Pike's assistant. I believe at least two of the dead backpackers had taken details from that same ad. What if this lad is touting for business for Sweet? Or even for himself?'

'If you're thinking what I think you're thinking, you have one sick mind, boss.'

'But it's feasible.'

'Yeah, I guess it is.'

'Go and see Karl tomorrow and ask him if the guy is one of his tattooing mates.'

Ely dropped me at St Immaculata's. We did a quick sweep of the school to make sure everything was secure and that there were no nasties lurking. We didn't find any, which boded well for a stress-free night.

'Will you be okay on your own?' He asked doubtfully.

'I'll be fine.' At least, I hoped I would be.

In a perfect world, Quinn would come and stay with me.

Or Fox.

But I had long ago given up on perfection. I'd be lucky if Horace appeared and deigned to hang around for company.

'You go home and enjoy a Saturday night with the wife. I'll snuggle up with a bottle of wine and the cat.'

Ely left and the heavy weight of the empty school bore down on me. I filled Horace's bowls with fresh biscuits and water and then I took my bags up to Chastity's room. I locked myself in, going through the routine of manhandling the chest-of-drawers in front of the door. I didn't feel confident being in the main body of the school. There was too much space, too many rooms with dark corners, too many cranks who had it in for me.

Lying on the bed, I messaged Chastity but she was still stonewalling me. Don't you love teenage daughters?

At midnight my phone went off, almost giving me a heart attack. I'd fallen asleep on top of the covers, still in my clothes, with my wine untouched on the bedside cabinet.

'Red.'

'Quinn?'

'We've fished a body from the Swan. Looks like it's Felix Spalding.'

Goosebumps crackled over my skin. That could have been me, if that kind fisherman hadn't pulled me from the water. I shut down on the thought. I didn't want to waste energy on negative emotion. I was highly strung enough, imagining nasty outcomes.

'Send someone to pick me up.'

'You're suspended.'

'Then *why* call me?'

'Because I thought you wanted to be kept in the loop.'

'I do. So get Burton or Fox over here now.'

'No.'

'Quinn!'

'And another thing, Spalding was shot with a Glock. It was found in a rubbish bin on the foreshore.' He paused with what I can only describe as dramatic timing. 'It's your gun, babe.'

'Bugger.'

'Yep. That just about sums it up.' And he hung up.

I lay there in the dark wondering why first Beard and then Felix had been dispatched and why the connection to me. Not only was it bizarre, it was annoying. Why should I be a suspect for someone else's crimes? It was preventing me from doing my job.

Was that the reason? To get me off the case?

Or was I up myself for thinking I was really that important?

Hmm.

Now, thanks to Quinn's call, I was wide awake and antsy. I was tempted to break out of my self-imposed dungeon and make myself a cup of tea. The salty fish and chips had made me thirsty. The more I thought about it, the more I wanted a drink. The urge grew stronger with each ticking minute.

I eased the chest-of-drawers away from the door, unlocked it and peered out into the dark corridor. I tiptoed along, feeling a right narna, as, realistically, who, apart from me, was going to be in the school tonight?

Of course, Hugo Maine or his men could be lurking in a dark corner, waiting to pounce. But I didn't think so. They believed I was lying at the bottom of the Swan River, feeding the local crab population. I was old news.

And the guys from the basement? Well, one of them was dead, the other long gone. I didn't think they wanted to be in cooee of the place.

Mum was locked up and Chastity was away.

Still, I took precautions, using silence and darkness as my invisible cloak. I inched down the back stairs in the dark, feeling my way carefully, and almost fell to my death when Horace ran between my legs, causing me to screech as I tumbled down the last few steps and hit the floor.

I writhed around, groaning and swearing. The kitchen light snapped on and I froze in my agony.

'Henry!' I staggered to my feet, using the wall to prop me up, clutching my knee with my other hand, my heart pounding. 'What are you doing here?'

He looked as shocked as I felt. 'I could ask you the same thing, Eve.'

'I was thirsty. I came down for a drink.' I rubbed my knee to ease the pain, not that it did much good.

'But you'd moved out.' He sounded accusing. Where was his usual diffident, benign manner?

'Yes, but I moved back.'

'Does your mother know?' There was that strident tone again. Interesting.

'No, she doesn't. She's away. But why are *you* here?'

'I've misplaced something. I came back to see if it was here.'

'In the middle of the night?'

He hesitated. 'I didn't want your mother knowing.'

'Because?'

'We had a row.'

'I see.' I didn't, but I decided to suspend belief. 'What have you lost?'

'Nothing important.' He did that slight eye-shift thing that people did when trying to avoid answering a difficult question. I knew the tic. I saw it often enough in the interview suite. Henry was hedging.

'But important enough to sneak in at midnight to look for it, Henry?'

'I happened to be passing.'

And he just happened to have a key.

I didn't know if I trusted him, but maybe that was due to my dark suspicious police mind.

'Want some tea?' I said to defuse the tension.

'Sure. Peppermint would be nice.' He glanced at his watch.

'Do you have some place to be?' I switched on the kettle and got out two of the chunky white mugs and a couple of herbal teabags.

'No, no. It's all good. It's not as if I've anyone waiting for me.'

'Where are you staying?' I realised he'd never said. True to form, he didn't this time either.

'Here and there. Friends, acquaintances, the odd motel room. I haven't got a permanent base.'

'Because art doesn't pay?'

'Sorry?'

'Your art. It doesn't bring in enough to afford rent? And the department store Santa gig is over for another year.'

'Oh. Well, yes.'

Hah, I reckoned he was as much an artist as me. He'd been spinning a line for whatever reason.

'Did Mum let you stay in the basement?'

His eyes narrowed, his face hardened. Was it my imagination or was I picking up a sinister vibe here? Surely not. He might be shonky, but he was still my dad. We shared blood.

But that didn't stop the trickle of something akin to fear go down my spine.

'Why do you ask?' he said. 'And where *is* your mother?'

'She's helping us with our inquiries.'

'You've arrested her?' He sounded outraged. 'But she's your mother!'

'And I'm a police officer. I uphold the law. If someone breaks it, they suffer the consequences. Family included.'

There was a strained pause.

'You're a hard woman.'

'You didn't ask why she'd been arrested.' I set his tea in front of him. 'Biscuit?'

He shook his head. 'Your mum said I was wasting my time but I thought you'd be your father's daughter. You're not. You're a sodding pain in the arse.'

'Daughters can be. Chastity gives me plenty of grief.' I blew on my tea and took a disgusted sip; I detested all herbal teas but especially peppermint. I watched Henry over the rim. I wished I had a gun. I wished I had my damn phone. I only had the mug. It was a poor substitute. 'Were you hoping to get me on side? To turn a blind eye to your exploits?"

'I don't know what you mean.'

I let it slide. 'Do you want to know why Mum was arrested?'

He remained schtum.

'She had a stash of jewels that had been stolen over Christmas.'

His eyes flickered.

'I doubt she was involved in the two thefts but I do think she gave house room to the thieves, for whatever reason, and then she helped herself to the contents of the four wheelie bins stored in the basement.'

Henry sucked in a breath.

'Yes, I found them, Henry. Well done for trying to deflect me with the rubbish dumping. It fooled the others, but not me.'

'You're delusional.'

'Was it you who drugged me?'

'Don't be daft.'

'Were you part of the gang who originally stole the gear from Wisteria Place?'

He snorted. 'I'm an old man. That's a young punk's game.'

'I believe Terry Beard, Felix Spalding and Harry Shorten were part of the gang too.'

'You're way off.'

'Why was Beard killed?'

'You're asking me? As if I would know!'

'I think you do.'

'I don't and I'm not staying here to be insulted any longer. You're a big disappointment to me, Eve.'

I could have said the same but I wasn't into petty point scoring. I wanted hard facts.

'I'm just doing my job, Henry.'

'Your job sucks.'

'I'll need to speak to you again.'

'Go to hell.'

Was that any way for a father to speak to his daughter? I didn't think so. But I didn't feel compelled to tell him so. He could go to hell too, but I would still come looking for answers.

As Henry wrenched open the door he was confronted by another man standing on the step. So much for me being alone in the school. It was turning into visiting hour!

Henry reared back. 'Hugo!'

'Hello, Harry. How are you, mate? It's been a while.'

And Hugo Maine strode into the room as if he owned it, urbane and smarmy as usual. 'DI Rock, ah, I didn't expect we'd have to meet again this side of the veil, but here we are. What a jolly party.'

I gawped from my spot by the kitchen counter and again rued the fact I only had a mug of tepid tea as a weapon: but golly, I would make it count if I had to.

And then I computed what Maine had said.

'Harry?' Omigod. '*You're* Harry Shorten,' I said to Henry.

Why hadn't I clicked? Henry Talbot, Harry Shorten. A play on names.

Henry shrugged and didn't deny it.

'You didn't know?' said Maine. 'Tut, tut, you're losing your touch, DI Rock.'

I scowled at him. I didn't care. What did concern me was two dangerous men in my kitchen and only a stainless steel counter and china mug to protect me.

'I've been watching you all pussy-footing around the school these last few days and nights. It's been very entertaining,' said Maine. 'It occurred to me that Harry here was going to eliminate you but he only managed to shoot your car.'

I glared at Henry. '*You* shot my car? Why?'

'Why not? It was there. I had a gun. It would annoy you.'

'Gee, thanks.'

'Why are *you* after Eve, Hugo?' said Henry. He didn't look exactly thrilled seeing Maine. I wondered if they'd had past dealings that hadn't gone so well.

'Your daughter and I have unfinished business. Isn't that right, DI Rock?'

'You're still at large, so yes. Once you're in jail, my job will be complete,' I said. Challenging him wasn't sensible, but I did it anyway.

'You're so funny, Detective Inspector. But tell me, am I interrupting anything important? Or have you finished your father-daughter chat?'

'I was just leaving,' said Henry. 'She's all yours, mate, and good riddance.' He went out into the night, slamming the door.

It was nice to know where you stood with family. Henry didn't feel the urge to protect his daughter. But then, why would he? I would arrest him given half a chance. There was no love lost.

'Oh dear. Daddy issues. He seems annoyed with his little Evie.'

'Shut up, Maine.'

He gave a superficial laugh and then grew serious. 'You're proving to be a pain in the butt, DI Rock.'

'That's old news, Maine. But feel free to join the consensus. What do you want?'

'You.'

I clenched my jaw, hoping I didn't look as scared as I felt.

'And you've found me. Now what?'

He took out a gun and gave a crocodile smile.

I was done for. But I wouldn't do down without a fight.

'We'll try again, shall we? Hmm? Move.' He reopened the door Henry had exited and stepped sideways.

I limped towards it, my knee giving gyp. But as I got within reach, I threw tea in Maine's eyes and swung the mug upwards. It connected with a satisfying crunch to the throat. Maine's gun discharged as he crumpled to the floor with a grunt. Gasping for breath, Maine raised the gun, his face contorted with rage. There was no vestige of the suave businessman; he was stripped back to his vicious, feral self.

I kicked out and sent the gun spinning. He lunged for my foot and yanked me on top of him. I gouged at his eyes, clawing desperately while he fought for supremacy. He was stronger than me but I was quicker. We were both fuelled by rage, but I had fear too. I prayed it would give me the edge.

Behind me I heard someone yell.

The gun went off again and Maine yowled like a coyote. Had he been hit? Had Henry returned to save me?

Maine cursed and spat obscenities as he held his thigh. Blood seeped from between his fingers and stained the floor.

'Stop! Police!'

It wasn't Henry but Adam Fox standing over Maine with his gun poised in a very Dirty Harry pose. I hadn't seen Fox since the attempted drowning. He was a very welcome, if surprising, sight.

I peeled myself off the floor with the greatest of difficulties, as my limbs were shaking like blancmange.

Fox remained focussed on Maine. 'You okay?' he said to me.

'Yes.'

'You'd better check your dad,' he said. 'He's been hit.'

Henry?

A pair of legs was poking through the doorway. As I moved closer to him, Henry propped himself up with difficulty on his elbow. Before I could stop him, he raised a gun. There was a loud report. I ducked, with my arms crammed over my head. Maine jerked and slumped, his skull cracked on the stone floor and his mouth fell open. Fox cursed and spun towards the door. Henry dropped his gun and collapsed flat on his back.

Fox called for ambulance and back-up teams as I limped towards Henry. He was copiously bleeding from the stomach. I grabbed a questionably clean tea towel and tried staunching the blood flow. There was so much of it.

Fox came over with more tea towels, clean ones this time.

'Maine's dead,' he said using one as a thick wad over the bleeding wound.

'Good,' Henry said in a weak voice. 'He was an evil sod. I need to make a statement.'

'Save it for later,' said Fox.

'I might not make it, kid.'

'We'll take that risk.'

20

Fox slung an arm around me as we sat in the hospital waiting room. He gave me a squeeze.

'Going okay?' he said.

'Yeah, but it's been one helluva night.' I was hurting in all these different places and shattered to the core. Once all this was over I vowed to get myself in shape and do some serious self-defence classes. My current training was inadequate. My physical fitness, zero. I had to do better if I was going to survive my life.

We were waiting for Henry to come out of surgery. Maine was on ice downstairs in the hospital morgue. His two minions, who had been sitting in the car outside the school waiting for us to appear, had been arrested and were at the nick.

'How come you were there?' I asked. 'You've been conspicuous by your absence.'

'The team was worried about you. Dad organised a round-the-clock roster. I've been doing night shift.'

'I'm touched. But why didn't anyone tell me?'

'Because we thought you might try and give us the slip.'

'As if.'

'Yeah, right.'

'How long has this been going on?'

'A while,' and he gave one of those faint smiles that meant he wouldn't be letting on exactly how long. I wondered if my drink with Gorgeous Georgio had been clocked by the boys. If it had, there wasn't much I could do about it.

'Maine's attack on you had us rattled.'

'Rattled me too.'

'So we decided to shadow you.'

Ah, so after my Gorgeous drink. I could rest easy. Phew.

'Well, I should be safe now Maine has gone. You can all stand down.'

'Yeah. Maybe. If you're ever safe, Eve. You have a tendency to attract trouble, you know.'

'Only sometimes.'

'All the time.'

'I can't help it and I don't court it. Thank you for saving me. I don't think I would have walked out alive otherwise.'

'Oh I don't know. You were doing a pretty good job, pummelling Maine into the ground.' He gave a low chuckle.

'No technique but pure, raw fear.'

'Don't knock it. It's hard to fight someone who's using every dirty trick in the book.'

I looked down at my broken, bloodied nails and then curled them into my palms. It had been a damn close call.

'You should thank Henry, too,' said Fox.

'I hadn't expected him to come back and help.'

'He confessed in the ambulance to killing Beard and Spalding. You're off the hook. Not that you were really on it.'

'I wonder why he killed them.'

'If he pulls through, we'll find out.'

Henry survived surgery but was unconscious. I was taken home in the grey dawn by Fox, leaving Officer Clark on duty.

'This time,' I said to Clark with a stern frown and my index finger planted firmly on the centre of his chest. 'Don't let any unauthorised people enter the room, even if they're bringing grapes. Remember what happened to Duggins.'

'You got it, DI Rock.'

Fox pulled into the school car park. 'Like me to stay?' he said. There was a challenge, if I wasn't too much mistaken, in his angelic baby blues.

'Yes. No. Better not.'

He laughed. 'That covers all bases.'

'Go home and sleep, Adam. You deserve it.'

'I reckon I deserve other things too. But, as I've said before, I'm a patient man. I'll wait for as long as it takes.' He leaned over and brushed his lips over mine, causing tingles where there shouldn't be any. 'I'll walk you in just to make sure everything is secure and then I'll shoot through.'

Which he did, with the kookaburras cracking their sides in noisy abandon.

'Two wheelie bins were found last night, full of stocks, bonds, gold bars and jewellery,' said Ely. He'd brought coffee and croissants for breakfast. We were sitting in the sun in the school quadrangle amid the scarlet geraniums and blue agapanthuses. The wattle birds were bickering in the peppermint trees while the New Holland honey-eaters squabbled over whose turn it was to dunk in the birdbath. I'd filled the blue ceramic bowl with fresh water earlier that morning while limping the rounds of the school to check its security. I didn't want another evening with people wandering into my temporary domain at a drop of a hat. It gave me the heebie-jeebies.

I was wearing one of Chastity's frilly floral skirts, so I had easy access to my knee. My leg was propped up on a stool with an ice pack on the swollen and bruised joint. I had another ice pack on my elbow where I had brutally connected with the stainless steel counter while wrestling Maine.

It would have been a nice day, except for my family's criminal activity.

'The gear was in the back of a van that matched the description you gave us.'

'Where did you find the van?'

'Around the corner from here, in a residential side street.'

'Henry must have parked it there.' I took another bite of croissant, savouring the rich food as the melted cheese and bacon dripped down my chin. Blow the need to diet. I was happy to be alive.

'The team is pulling out all stops trying to find the other bins.'

'Perhaps Henry can tell us once he's well enough to be interviewed.'

'That was a turn up for the books. How do you feel about him being involved?'

'Disappointed but not surprised. Hopefully we can get a full statement from him about the mall jewellery theft and Wisteria Place.'

'And maybe Beard and Spalding's murders if we're lucky. Then you can come off the suspect list.'

'I'm already in the clear. Henry confessed to DS Fox last night. I should be back to work any day now.'

We finished our food and Ely stood to leave. 'I'm off. Do you need anything before I go?'

'No. I'm fine. Thanks for breakfast.'

'Quinn's orders.'

'Thank him too. And remember to see Sweet about Danny Pike's boy.'

'Anything else?'

'Keep me informed.'

'You got it.' He hesitated. 'You sure you're going to be all right on your own, boss?'

'Get the hell out of here, Ely. I don't need babysitting.'

'Okay, but call if you need anything.'

'Thanks. I will, now split.'

The day stretched in front of me. I wondered how I was going to fill it. I shouldn't have worried. I slept, I ate, I ice-packed and deep-heated my joints, I messaged Chastity to tell her Henry was in hospital but not receiving visitors, and then, with nothing else to do, went meticulously over my case notes.

Until Quinn turned up.

'What are you doing here? Shouldn't you be working?'

He cupped my face with his hands and kissed me firmly on the lips. 'I've earned some time off.'

'So you're on your own?'

'I'm on my own.'

A quiver of lust laid hold of me.

'Good.'

'I thought so.' He picked up the blue ice pack and regarded my knee. 'Adam said it had been a wild night. You were lucky he was there.'

'Very. Thank you for organising my bodyguards.'

'Don't give me too much credit. It was a way of finding Maine. You were bait, sweet cheeks.'

'Oh.'

He chuckled at my expression, flicking the silly frilly skirt to reveal some thigh. 'And we didn't want Maine trying to despatch you again and actually succeeding.' And he dipped down for another, longer, fuller kiss, this time with his hand sliding up my thigh, causing a serious heart flutter or six.

When we ran out of oxygen and unlocked our lips, I said, 'How did you get here if you're on your own?'

'The arm is back in business. Or at least good enough. I'm back to driving.'

'You've wheels? Lucky you.'

'Yes, and you're going nowhere near them.' He scooped me up, swung me around and then settled back in my seat with me on his lap. I snuggled into him and we did some more lip synchronising.

'This is the life,' he said, linking his fingers with mine, his lips on my hair. 'As soon as *Wild Thing* is back on the water, we should head off, away from all this.'

'And not work? That's all well and good but what would we find to talk about?'

'We won't be talking, Red.'

'Oh.' I gave a snicker. Actually, it was more of a dirty laugh.

He slapped my bottom. 'My woman.'

I approved of the endearment but then something, someone caught my eye.

'Perhaps we should head off now.'

'You're one impatient chick, sweetheart.'

'Not really. Sister Immaculata is back from the nick.'

'Of course she is.' Quinn raised his head and looked over the lawn. 'Oh yeah, the woman herself. Bad timing.'

We watched in silence as the Iron Nun stomped across the grass like an angry crow.

'Hello, Mum.' I went to wriggle off Quinn's knee but he held me firm.

'You're disgusting!' she said with brutal bluntness. 'This is not appropriate behaviour for a girls' school.' I felt about twelve again.

'School is out and we're consenting adults,' said Quinn mildly.

She harrumphed. 'I hope you're not intending to stay? Because you're not welcome. Either of you.'

'I'll move out now,' I said. 'Can you help with my bags, Quinn?'

'Sure.' He let me slide off his lap and then he stood tall and solid beside me, his arm around my shoulders. 'Did you know Henry is in hospital, Sister?'

'Don't talk to me about that man. He's bad news.'

'He's in critical condition. Do you want us to take you to see him?'

'No. I have no wish to set eyes on him again, thank you. I want to be on my own.'

'Where to?' said Quinn ten minutes later. He slung my plastic bags into his new vehicle, which was actually an old shabby buggy; there was nothing new about it.

'The city hostel.'

Afterwards we had dinner at the hipster restaurant and I was happy that both the young tattooed waiter and Gorgeous Georgio were nowhere to be seen.

Because of family connections and complications, my sergeants Ely and Burton conducted the interviews with Henry Talbot, or Harry Shorten as he was now referred to.

'Shorten admitted to being Terry Beard's partner in the jewellery store robberies,' Ely told me the next day as he followed me through the crew room, filling me in on the latest in the Wisteria Place case.

I stopped short at my office door. The room was full my

colleagues grinning from ear to ear. There was a huge vase of red, yellow and white roses on my desk, along with a bottle of champagne and a box of Margaret River deluxe chocolates.

'Welcome back, Red,' said Quinn coming forward and kissing my cheek in a very un-Quinn-like chaste way.

My fellow cops didn't often make me feel loved but I admit to a rush of emotion and becoming a little damp-eyed.

Quinn grinned as I swiped a tear. 'Crying, Red? That's not like you.'

'Yeah, must be getting soft in my old age. Thanks, everyone. Much appreciated. I'm glad to be back.'

'Don't open the choccies without us,' said Rachel Gath, giving me a hug.

'Or the champers,' said Burton, who didn't.

'But I *can* keep the flowers?' I said with a laugh. 'Thanks!'

While the chocolates were shared out, Ely resumed his run-down on Shorten with Quinn sitting on the corner of my desk, his leg swinging back and forth, his warm gaze resting on me, making it hard to concentrate.

'Right, where was I?' said Ely. 'Oh yes, Shorten and Beard's first attempt at a heist went wrong, which was when Beard last landed in jail. That's where he met Felix Spalding and recruited him for the Wisteria Place job.'

'Were there only three people in the gang?'

'Yes. But they had it planned with military precision. They'd chosen to do the robbery during the Christmas holiday break, when the CBD was dead quiet.'

'Sensible.'

'It was. They sprang into action literally a couple of minutes after the staff locked the doors of the facility on Christmas Eve. The three of them went down the elevator shaft in the next-door Ramosa building, taking their wheelie bins with them. They'd paid some homeless punks to light fires around the CBD to act as diversions while they drilled through the wall during the night and then left by the shaft early in the morning.'

'But Beard was murdered early that morning?'

'Yes he was. He'd run foul of Shorten when he'd done that solo, one-off job in the mall on Christmas Eve,' said Ely. 'He was bragging about it in the vault. Shorten felt he needed reining in or he'd compromise the Wisteria Place job, like he'd done on the first heist attempt.'

'So before they left the vault, they made him swallow a shed-load of bullets, including some of yours that Shorten had snitched from your tin when you lived in Subiaco, hence your fingerprints. They put Beard in one of the wheelie bins and took him out and dumped him in your skip.'

'But why my bullets and my skip?' I was still annoyed about that.

'Several reasons, apparently. He knew the layout after all that Santa stalking. He knew the house next-door was empty. He knew that an old guy lived on the other side who was deaf and dogless. And he knew the skip bin was *in situ*, whereas most people had got rid of their bins before Christmas.'

'Sounds logical, I suppose.'

'There's more, boss. He was more than happy to frame you to get you off the case and potentially arrested so you wouldn't be snooping around the school. He was angry with your mum when she invited you to stay there.'

'So that was why she changed her tune and wanted me out. What about Spalding's murder?'

'The two of them discovered some of the gems were missing. Spalding thought Shorten was cheating him out of his share. They had a fight. Shorten used your gun, which he'd taken from your car after your kidnapping. He hoped that by implicating you again it would keep you out of the way for longer so he could get clear of Perth.'

'But I can't understand how my mum got involved in the first place, except for her history with Henry.'

'I asked him that. He reckoned she owed him. He'd paid for, quote, *this sodding white elephant of a school for years.* Apparently since you were born. He thought the least she could do was let them use the place as a hideout while they divvied up their booty.'

'There's still no sign of the other two wheelie bins?'

'No. And Shorten's had a relapse. He's not well enough to be interviewed at the moment. But we're monitoring him closely and we'll get a statement as soon as we can,' said Ely.

'One last thing,' said Quinn getting to his feet. 'You're free to collect your car and clothes. They're no longer needed for evidence.'

'Hallelujah,' I said. I was so over cute florals and frills.

21

While I'd been suspended, the media had got hold of the Operation Popsicle case. It had sparked a rash of crank calls. Burton was put on crank-call duty to filter the dross from the silver.

Now he came to me scratching his head. 'There's been a complaint from a Nedlands family whose dead son had his tattoos removed without their consent. It was noticed when his granny had an unscheduled viewing.'

'Any evidence?'

'No, granny only mentioned it at the wake and by then the boy had been cremated.'

'Can they remember what the tattoo was?'

'A skull with three swords pierced through it.'

'Check with Ely, but I reckon we've seen a similar design curing at Sweet's parlour. Go see the family. If it's a visual match, we need to get a statement and DNA check.'

On the way to see Karl Sweet, I asked Ely to drop by the school. I decided to pay my mother a visit, to see how she was travelling. You see, I can be dutiful on occasions.

I walked through the quiet, cool building, my sneakers squeaking on the jarrah floors and leaving tracks in the fine dust that had settled since the start of the holidays. I absently wondered when the cleaning staff would reappear for their spit and polish blitz before the new term.

The Iron Nun was in her inner sanctum, standing at her desk, hunched over her old Bible. She slammed it shut as I came into the office with a perfunctory knock on the open door.

'What are you doing here?' she said.

'I came to see if you were all right.'

The fact she was reading scripture suggested she wasn't.

'I'm a survivor,' she said. 'You don't have to worry about me.'

'I do anyway, Mum.'

I leaned against the door jamb and folded my arms over my chest.

'Is there something else you wanted?' she said. 'Because I have things to do.'

'Why did you let Henry live here?'

'He asked for a place to stay. He was homeless and broke. What could I do?' Her eyes flashed behind her glasses. 'I don't regret it. Everything would have been fine if you hadn't poked your police nose into things. It led to complications.'

'Did you know he was involved in criminal practices?'

'No. Of course not.'

I didn't believe her. They had both operated on the flip side of the law. She would have recognised the signs. 'Come on, Mum, he must have said something to alert you?'

Her nose rose skywards. 'I knew there were certain activities going on. I didn't inquire what. When things got difficult, he blamed me for allowing you to stay.'

'He could have moved out.'

'It was easier for you to.'

In whose opinion?

'He was my former lover, the father of my child. I had a duty to help him. Wouldn't you have done the same?'

I sighed and thought of Quinn.

And Fox.

'I guess.' We Rock women were suckers for their men.

I stepped over to the desk, my eyes automatically dropping to the Bible. I don't know when she'd acquired this version but it had always held an aura of reverence. It was chewed around the edges through moth and silverfish activity. The thick leather-bound casing was cracked and pitted by years of wear and tear. But the gilt-edged pages and the brass hinges and catch had never failed to impress me. I absently reach out to touch the book.

'Stop!' said the nun. 'This is an antiquity. You need to wear cotton gloves if you want to touch. I don't want you damaging the pages.'

'You're not wearing gloves.' I pointed out.

'*I* don't handle guns.' She countered.

'Are you saying my hands are contaminated because I carry a gun?'

Her lips pursed. 'It's sinful.'

'Cast the first stone, why don't you,' I said and walked out, anger coursing through me. She was such a bloody hypocrite.

'How is Sister Immaculata?' said Ely.

'She's an old bat,' I said.

'On form, then.'

'You said it.'

As Ely pulled into the traffic, my phone rang.

'Yes?' I said curtly, still cross with the self-righteous nun.

'DI Rock?' The English accent was a dead give-away. My British police liaison was on the phone.

'Sergeant Miller.'

'Andy.'

'Andy. Have you got anything for me?'

'Professionally or personally?'

Okay, we had a wide boy.

'Let's start with the professional, shall we?'

He laughed. 'I've managed to get images of all three lads' tattoos. I'll email them through.'

'Excellent. Thanks.'

'Now for the personal. You can buy me a drink when I come over for a holiday.'

'You bet.' But I hoped the holiday was a pipe dream. I didn't need further complications in my private life.

I accessed the emails and showed them to Ely when he parked outside the Extreme Body Art parlour. He scrolled through his own file of pix he'd taken at the tattoo parlour.

'Looks like match after match after match,' he said.

'Shall we go and chat to the accommodating Karl X?'

Sweet looked about as pleased as a cat with lactose intolerance.

'Not again?' he said. 'I told you everything I know.'

'This isn't about your trainees,' said Ely, who had established the day before that Danny Pike's boy Tyson and Louis Ragnall regularly offered free tattoos to hone their skills.

'What then?'

Ely showed him the pix on his phone. 'Seen these before, Karl?'

'They're generic designs. Dime a dozen. Lotta guys have them.'

'So you *have* seen them before.'

'Well, yeah. Or similar.'

'Which are curing out the back of your place.'

'Yeah, and?'

'We need to take DNA sample to eliminate them from our enquiries.'

He wasn't happy about it.

'I should have my lawyer present.'

'If you think you've done wrong, sure.'

'I haven't.'

'Then why are you sweating, Karl?'

'I'm hot.'

'It's not a guilty glow?'

'No. I want my lawyer.'

'Who is…?'

'Georgio Papadopoulos.'

Which gave me an awful sinking feeling.

'Gorgeous Georgio. Who would have thought?' said Ely. 'Go ahead and give him a call but we'll still be sending someone to collate DNA from your drying skins.'

'The bloke from the funeral parlour is on the line,' said Burton as soon as we got back to the nick. He transferred the call through to my desk phone.

'DI Rock.'

'Barry Hammer here. I'm at the crematorium. I need you to see something.' He spoke in a conspiratorial tone and refused to elaborate.

Ely and I retraced our steps to the car and drove over to Karrakatta Cemetery. We navigated our way through groups of mourners who were at different stages along the funeral conveyor belt. Some were waiting for the service to start, some had already farewelled their dearly departed and were now catching up with friends and family, others had that shattered look of an emotional deluge, some were crying, some taut faced, and some hunched in tight huddles away from the others. I guessed they were either strangers or the estranged.

Hammer met us around the back of the crematorium looking splendid in a black frock coat and pinstriped trousers. All he needed was a top hat to be a Dickensian character. He took us inside where four other similarly dressed men stood around a coffin.

'This is Mrs Booth,' said Hammer. 'But look.'

And we did.

I hadn't particularly prepared myself for a viewing but the waxy-faced corpse was serene in her final repose among the hot pink satin. The discordant note was the extra body parts packed neatly around her.

'Oh dear,' I said.

'Blimey,' said Ely.

'The family don't know,' said Hammer.

'That's a good thing,' said Ely.

'How come you noticed?' I said. 'Is it normal to flip the coffin lid before cremation?'

He looked at us from under his bushy monobrow. 'It's routine.'

'Really?'

He glanced at his cohorts and said with a grave-deep sigh, 'We have a special service for those who can't afford a coffin.'

'What sort of service?' Ely asked.

'A rental service.'

'You rent out the coffins?'

'It's standard practise. We remove the bodies before cremation and put them on a tray so the coffins can be reused by other guests.'

'Guests?'

'The deceased.'

'What sort of trays?'

He showed us one. 'It's called a cremation tray in the business.'

'It's a sheet of sodding plywood,' said Ely.

I stared closely at the butchered body parts. They seemed to be dusted in sand. Black sand. My guess: it was the same dirt from Cranberry Court.

'We need to get forensics here.'

'Is it possible we can return to the funeral home to deal with it? We don't want to hold up the other customers.'

'You don't want to be seen surrounded by the police, you mean,' said Ely.

'It wouldn't be healthy for business.'

'The coffin will be taken to your premises when we're finished here and not before. We'll need to talk to every member of your staff as well as the crematorium employees.'

Later we interviewed Barry Hammer at his funeral home. He'd changed into his overalls and was looking far more morose then ever Boris Karloff had in the most grim of Hammer House of Horror flicks.

'This has never happened before?' I asked him.

'No.'

'And you oversee every cremation?'

'Those from our Home, yes. We're not a big unit.'

'Out of interest, have any of your clients been missing bits just before cremation?'

'Why would our *guests* be missing *bits*? And what sort of missing bits are we talking about? Not the eyes and stuff you asked about before? Because we don't do that sort of thing. Duggins may have on the quiet, but we don't. Honest to God.'

'This time I'm talking skin.'

He stared at me from under his single thick brow. 'Do you want to be more specific?'

'Tattoos?'

'Only if the removal has been authorised. We don't go around hacking bits off for the fun of it.'

I ignored his sarcasm. 'Was Toby Court a *guest* of yours recently?'

'Young Toby? Why, yes.'

'Did you flay his skin?'

'No.'

'I think you did.'

'You're mistaken.'

'Toby's family contacted us to say his grandma had an unauthorised viewing and noticed his tattoo, which she had paid for as an 18th birthday gift, had been removed.'

'That's crazy. The Courts hadn't requested a flaying.'

'Would any of your staff have taken it upon themselves to remove it?'

'No!'

'Are you sure?'

'Yes.' And then his thick brow descended. 'No. You should talk to Merv Turner. Toby was a mate of his.'

'We'll interview all your staff. But back to the coffin swapping. Was Duggins involved in that?'

'Yes, all the guys are. We're a team. And, DI Rock, the coffin recycling is all legit. The families are all for it. It knocks a couple of grand off the funeral. That's worth having.'

'I'll bear it in mind for future reference.'

'You do that.'

'Did Duggins do the swaps on his own?'

'Nah, you need a couple of you to do that. Bodies are heavy.'

'Who did he work with?'

'All of us but mainly Merv.'

Merv Turner again.

Merv Turner was a buffed young man with bulging muscles and colourful tattoos. He readily admitted to removing Toby Court's tattoo.

'Yeah. I did. Toby was a mate. He loved his tattoo. I thought it would honour him if I took it off and cured it,' said Turner.

'Have you removed tattoos before?'

'No. It was my first.' He held our gaze, defying us to challenge his statement.

'It was well done.'

'I've watched Mr Hammer.'

'So you knew about the practice?'

'Yeah. It's not secret.'

'So you took the skin to Karl Sweet?'

'To his place, yeah.'

'You're well inked. Do you spend much time at the tattoo parlour?'

'A bit.'

'Have you had a go at tattooing?'

'Nah. I like bigger canvases. That's why Mr Hammer lets me paint the coffins.'

'But you're friendly with the blokes at the tattoo parlour?'

He gave me a sharp look. 'They're mates, yeah,' he said, less than enthusiastic.

'Which one of them does the paving work?'

'That would be Louis. He works part time for the company near the Hammers. He does a bit on the side too.'

'Have you worked for him?'

'Nah. I work full time.'

'How can you explain the human remains in Mrs Booth's casket?'

'Anyone could have put them there,' he said promptly.

'You?'

'Nah, not me. Ask the other blokes.'

'We have. They deny it too.'

We asked him if he knew about Duggins' sideline of providing body parts for Lucy Drew.

'Yeah. But only because I found him mucking around in the morgue out of hours.'

'Did you help him at all?'

'Nah. He was mental. I didn't have much to do with him if I could help it.'

I could understand completely where he was coming from.

'Thank you, Merv. We'll be in touch.'

22

'DI Rock! How is my favourite lady?' Georgio Papadopoulos strode over to me with his arms outstretched. In a flourish, he took me by the shoulders and kissed me on both cheeks before I could say or do anything to dissuade him and out of the corner of my eye I saw my sergeant's eyebrows flick in surprise.

We were at the cop shop, having brought in Karl Sweet for questioning.

'Is it my imagination or have you increased your bruise ratio?' said Papadopoulos, giving me a comprehensive once-over.

'I've had a little trouble these past few days.'

'Poor Evie. Need some more R&R?'

Ely's brows hit his hairline and beyond. He gave me an incredulous glance, which I resolutely ignored.

'I'm fine, Mr Papadopoulos. It's all good. Have you spoken to your client?'

'He has nothing to hide, Eve.'

'We'll be the judge of that.'

He gave me an indulgent look which I found more than irritating.

'We have a problem, Karl,' I said to Sweet. 'The tattoos curing in your workshop have been linked to five dead men.'

'Yeah. But you know that. I showed you the paperwork.'

'Yes, Karl. I have identified those, but there are five others who aren't in your files but they are on ours.'

His eyes flicked to Papadopoulos. 'I don't understand.'

'DI Rock means that you have skin belonging to four men who have been on our missing persons file. What do you say to that?' said Ely.

'I'm confused.'

We showed him pictures. 'Do you recognise the tattoos?'

'They look familiar, yeah. But they're regular designs, like I said before.'

'They're photos of tattoos currently curing in your workshop.'

'Okay. But I'm not the only one who cures them. The lads do too.'

'There's also a tattoo that was taken off a dead boy without permission.' We showed him a photo of that one too.

He looked directly at Papadopoulos. 'I don't know anything about that one.' It was the first and only time he sounded sure of himself. 'You should ask Tyson or Louis about that one. And those other tats. They have nothing to do with me. I only do ones with paperwork.'

The interview got us nowhere. Sweet might as well have played dead for all that he contributed. Papadopoulos sat next to him, silent, his pale green eyes watching us intently.

We suspended the interview and left the room. Georgio Papadopoulos followed us out.

'If you no longer need my client, may I suggest we terminate the interview?' he said.

'I don't have a problem with that, but we will need to interview him again.'

'Of course. Keep in touch, Evie.'

'Evie?' said Ely in disgust as the lawyer returned to his client. 'Really, boss. You should slap him down.'

'Yes, well, it's easier said than done.'

'He's a jerk.'

'Forget him. We need to talk to Karl Sweet's trainees.'

'I'll get uniform to round them up and bring them in first thing tomorrow.'

I had a message to ring Barry Hammer. I returned his call.

'I've been thinking and I don't know if this is relevant, DI Rock,' said Hammer. 'But I hadn't told the boys that Mrs Booth's family had requested a cremation tray. I'd forgotten and sprung it on them after she'd come through the curtains.'

'So there hadn't been a chance to remove the extra body parts,' I said.

'And if I had told them earlier, I'm guessing they wouldn't have put them there in the first instance.'

'I wonder if they've done it before.'

'There would be no way of telling. We don't open the coffins of those who have paid for their box.'

'Which brings us back to Duggins. He could have been stealing parts and you didn't know.'

He sighed. 'I guess. Taking things off dead people is one thing, but where did those extra body parts come from?'

Where indeed? And how many times had this method been used to get rid of unwanted remains? I shuddered. As Barry Hammer had said, there was no way of telling.

I checked with the guys who were following up the cannibalism link. There didn't seem to be an outlet in Perth. That didn't explain the body parts in Duggins', or more specifically Danny Pike's, freezer. Frustratingly, we still had no clue why Duggins' finger was lopped or why he was murdered and by whom.

Quinn and Fox were off seeing their lowlife contacts in an attempt to find the outstanding booty from Wisteria Place.

Quinn had left me a note with the keys of my hole-riddled car to say that, although it looked like a piece of Jarlsberg cheese, it was mechanically sound, the tyres had been replaced, my clothes were in the boot and the vehicle was parked in the staff car park.

Ely had also left me a note. It had the contact number and address for Acropolis Holdings. As it was after business hours, I took the details with me to ring the number in the morning.

But now, even if it was late, I decided to take the car for a spin before I went home, home being the city hostel. I headed for Subiaco and parked in the street by my derelict property. Someone, presumably my builder, had propped up the listing dunny with a couple of pieces of 4x2 to prevent it from falling over. My letterbox was still defying gravity without assistance. Everything else looked dead.

Depressed, I drove to the noisy hostel, promising myself that I would get back on to the insurance company and bug them as soon as possible: I needed a house. I needed a home. I needed a life.

I was woken early the next day by a phone call from Fox to tell me Henry had died. I messaged Chastity and the Iron Nun and then took off to the hospital. Fox met me there.

'He didn't regain consciousness. I'm sorry, Eve.'

I grappled with my emotions.

Or lack of them.

I wasn't sad, exactly. I don't know what I felt, really. Probably guilt more than anything, because of the relief he had gone and I didn't have to face the full fall-out of the heist and three murders.

'Were you here with him?'

'Right until the end. He died on my watch.'

'Good. It would have been horrible if he had been alone or with someone he didn't know.'

Fox followed me to St Immaculata's where a tired and pale Chastity was back in residence.

'This is your fault, Mum,' she said without even a *hello*.

'Not completely. Are you okay?'

'Yes, I'm fine. But I'm cross with you. People die, lives are destroyed, things get broken. You're jinxed.'

'Whoa, back off with the histrionics. Henry was already a career criminal. I didn't make him turn to crime.'

'But he didn't have to die. I'd only just got myself a granddad.'

'Henry could have kept walking and not come back, but he redeemed himself at the end. He saved your mum from Maine,' said Fox wading into the debate.

He made Henry sound noble. He hadn't been, but it was what Chastity needed to hear.

Or did she?

'What do you know,' she said scathingly.

Fox had been relegated to big brother status, which was a good thing in my book.

'I was there, Chastity,' he said.

'Adam saved me too,' I added and gave him a smile which, unfortunately, she intercepted.

'Sure he did. He's always trying to saving you.'

I couldn't argue with that.

'Adam already had Maine covered. Henry took it one step further,' I said.

'And killed him. Why can't I have a normal family? It's so unfair.'

'I'm sorry but that's how we are.' I tried to steer the conversation towards a more everyday subject. 'How was your sleepover?'

'I don't want to talk about it.'

So we didn't and I left Chastity banging about in the kitchen making cookies to appease her anger and grief with Fox, looking less than comfortable, in her firing line. I went in search of Sister Immaculata. The door of her office was firmly shut. I knocked and called through the wood panelling to see if she was all right. She said she was and told me to go away. I did. None of my family wanted to have anything to do with me. I can't say I blamed them.

Fox escaped the kitchen and followed me out to where our cars were parked.

'It's a shame Henry didn't have a chance to tell us where the rest of the jewels were stashed,' he said. 'Dad won't be happy. The Wisteria Place hot shots have been giving him a hard time.'

'The thing is,' I said, leaning against my car. 'There wouldn't have been that much time to hide the gear. They were sharing a vehicle. From our investigations, they'd been in jail a lot and had spent time in the Eastern States, so their network of friends and colleagues would have been minimal here. They didn't appear to have a Perth base other than St Immaculata's. They'd only really spent time in the western suburbs.'

'But we've searched all the likely areas.'

I had a light bulb moment.

'But have you? I have an idea. Follow me.'

We drove in convoy to my sad Subiaco patch. Fox parked behind me and we both got out and stared at the derelict site.

'Why are we here?' he said.

'The dunny.' I marched over to it with Fox traipsing along behind me, declaring I'd finally lost my marbles.

'See that?' My hunch looked as though it had legs. The toilet door was bolted and padlocked shut with heavy duty locks; something I'd failed to notice the night before.

'The builders may have locked it because it was dangerous.'

'My builders have been on holidays since Christmas. They still have another two weeks of vacation to go.'

'They may have locked it before they went.'

'Just get some bolt cutters and stop trying to second guess. I reckon the missing bins are inside.'

I hung around waiting for Fox to locate some bolt cutters. The Scotty dog man walked by and gave me the scowl.

'What are you doing here?' he said.

'Shooting the breeze.'

'We don't want any more shooting around here.'

'It was a figure of speech, mate.'

He left, grumbling about my sick humour, and saying how I should sell and move on and do everyone a favour.

'You took your time,' I said when Fox finally returned from the hardware store.

'These,' he held the bolt cutters up. 'Aren't something I tend to carry on me.'

'But now you can add them to your arsenal.'

He cut through the padlock with a lot of straining, grunting and swearing. We prised open the door and *voila!* The bins were stacked one on top of the other. We pulled them out of the leaning tower of dunny, giving a great deal of respect to the teetering masonry. I lifted up each lid to check the contents and smiled at Fox.

'Good result,' said Fox.

'I reckon. Call it in,' I said.

I left him dealing with the bins while I made an appointment with Acropolis Holdings to call by on my way to the station and have a chat with the tattoo parlour's owner.

23

'MR PAPADOPOULOS IS EXPECTING YOU. GO STRAIGHT IN,' SAID THE receptionist.

The lawyer Papadopoulos? Well, I hadn't seen that one coming. I schooled my expression and knocked on his office door.

'Come in,' he called.

Georgio Papadopoulos was standing by his desk, which was fine in the scheme of things, except he was magnificently bare-chested and holding a crumpled white shirt in his hand.

'Oh, I'm sorry.' I backed out fast.

'Don't be,' he said with a laugh. 'Come back in, Evie. Don't be shy. I'm doing a quick change before I head into court.'

I tentatively re-entered the office. Papadopoulos slung the soiled shirt on his chair and ripped the cellophane packaging from a new one.

I couldn't help but take another peek. I'd had no idea what had been going on under his ubiquitous white business shirts. Golly. It was a crime to hide it. I should arrest him now...

As he put on the crisp new shirt, he said, 'Like what you see, Eve?'

I would be blind not to appreciate Georgio's hunky attributes. He was ripped. Most lawyers of my acquaintance were corpulent and unhealthy. In fact, most men of my acquaintance were, excluding the Fox men, and possibly Ely, though perhaps I should have a second glance at his abs to make absolutely sure.

But I wasn't just surprised Georgio Papadopoulos worked out to such terrific effect. It was his body art that snagged my attention – *okay, along with the impressive six-pack* – because I had seen the work before.

Splashed over the centre pages of a magazine.

'You're staring,' he said with a self-satisfied chuckle.

'Sorry.'

'Don't be. I like an appreciative audience.'

'You'd best get your shirt on so we can both concentrate.'

He buttoned up the shirt and I was sure he was taking his time for my benefit. He should join the Chippendales or go solo as he obviously liked to perform to an audience. 'What did you want to see me about?'

His fingers were hypnotic to watch and I pulled myself into gear. It was time to be professional. 'Your connection with Acropolis Holdings.'

'I see.'

'It's your company.'

'One of them. I have many investments. I'm worth knowing.' He did one of his irritating winks.

'You own the Extreme Body Art Tattoo Parlour?'

'I do.'

'Do you have much interest in its daily running?'

'No. I leave that to the manager.'

'Karl Sweet?'

'Yes.'

'What's your relationship with him?'

His white teeth gleamed a smile through his dark beard. 'Relationship? He's the manager of that particular business, Evie. He's also my client. We don't hang out together, if that's what you mean.'

'Do you know his trainees?'

'I've met them on occasion, yes. I don't hang out with them either. Are you interviewing me, DI Rock?' He sounded mockingly incredulous.

'Not really. I'm just getting my head around things. That'll be all for now. Thanks for your time.'

'You're welcome. We must go out for another drink. I enjoyed our last one.'

'Not until this current investigation is over.'

'Which investigation is that?'

'The one connected to your clients Lucy Drew, Karl Sweet and the late Lionel Duggins.'

'Ah.'

I left him looking thoughtful. And, thankfully for my piece of mind, fully clothed.

'Good work, Red,' said Quinn as I strode into the incident room. 'I owe you.'

'That's what I like to hear.' I waggled my eyebrows at him. I would have done more but I didn't want to embarrass the other officers. 'So the Wisteria Place big bosses are happy now?'

'Nope, unfortunately not. There are some choice pieces still AWOL.'

'Like?'

He gave me a list. It wasn't long but the half a dozen items or so were worth a packet.

'These must be the missing jewels that caused the grief between Henry and Spalding.'

'One of them must have sorted the stuff away somewhere with the idea of collecting it once things cooled down,' said Quinn.

'Has the van been taken apart?'

'Thoroughly. I reckon it's hidden at the school.'

'But where? The school was turned over pretty thoroughly during the raid.'

'We missed something. You know the place like the back of your hand. Can you think of anywhere that a handful of jewellery could be hidden?'

'I'll give it some thought, but I can't think of anywhere off the top of my head.'

'Rachel has matched the Booth coffin human remains with the cured skin samples. She also found traces of sand and dirt from Cranberry Court,' said Ely.

'Which means the remains were dug up, as we suspected. But who did it?'

'The boys who laid the Hammers' paving were Merv Turner's mates, Tyson Pike and Louis Ragnall. I wonder if they did the original work at Cranberry Court, too?'

'And then used the same paving slabs to do the funeral home after digging them up from Duggins' house.'

'That's feasible,' said Ely.

'Weren't you going to get them in for questioning?'

'I'm on to it. One last thing. Rach said the remains had been professionally butchered. It hadn't been a hack job.'

'Add Danny Pike to the list for interviewing,' I said.

The three young men were proving hard to find but Danny Pike was hauled in.

'You kidding me?' said Pike. 'I told you before, no way would I jeopardise my business by butchering boys for their tattoos. The only wrong thing I've done is threaten that Sweet art git to give back Miss Drew's work and even then I reckon I was well within my rights.'

'What about Tyson?'

'What about him?'

'He's your son?'

'Nephew.'

'Is he much of a butcher?'

'He's almost finished his apprenticeship, so not too bad.'

'Is he a good worker?'

'He's all right.' He made it sound as though he wasn't. 'He usually turns up on time and enjoys a gas with the ladies.'

'But he didn't turn up today?'

'No.'

'Do you know where he is?'

'No. He doesn't often leave me in the lurch. He must be sick or something.'

'You know he's doing a tattoo traineeship?'

'If you can call it that. He mucks about at the parlour with his mates.'

'What can you tell me about his mates?'

'They're nice enough lads.'

'They haven't turned up to work either today.'

'What can I tell you, Detective Inspector? I'm not their mum.'

'Georgio Papadopoulos is diabetic,' Ely announced with a flourish the following morning. We were all in the incident room, collating evidence, seeing if we'd missed anything, sharing ideas. 'He would have had the chance, the means and the skill to terminally inject Duggins. We should bring him in for questioning.'

'His motive?' I said.

'Don't know. But I'm sure I can come up with one.'

'You're biased.'

'He owns the Extreme Body Arts parlour. That's an offence in itself.' He grinned.

'Owning a building doesn't constitute murder. Have another go.'

'Okay.' He was quiet for a moment. You could almost hear the cogs of his mind chugging away. 'Duggins was involved in tattoo art. Perhaps Gorgeous Georgio was too and he'd bought some dodgy ones off Duggins that had begun composting, which made him mad, which led to murder.'

'Killing someone for selling you dud art is a long shot.' I nibbled the end of my pen and then offered. 'Though he's into tats in a big way, so maybe there is a connection.'

'Is he now?' said Ely.

'His body is covered with them.'

'And how would you know that?' said Quinn suspiciously.

I played it down. 'He showed me. And his tattoos were featured in a tattoo magazine. He's a bit of a celebrity for his body art, according to Sweet.'

'When did Papadopoulos show you?'

I flicked Quinn a glance. He was annoyed.

'Yesterday. When I tackled him about Acropolis Holdings.'

'He was naked?'

'Shirtless.'

'Dammit, Eve, you shouldn't have met him alone.'

'It was a one-off.' *Except for that drink*. 'I had no idea who I was going to interview until I got there. Ely hadn't given me a name.'

'Shall I go and arrest him?' said Ely.

'What? For showing me his tattoos?'

'No, for murder.'

'Yes,' said Quinn with an edge. 'Bang him up.'

'No,' I said, wondering how this had escalated. 'Before we bring him in, we should do more delving into Acropolis Holdings and see what else he's involved in. It's too tenuous as it stands.'

'I've a gut feeling on this guy,' said Quinn.

What? Jealousy?

'Me too,' said Ely. 'I get bad vibes off him. I told the boss to stay clear of him and his smarmy ways.'

'You did, did you?' Quinn gave me a hard frown. 'I hoped she listened.'

I decided it was politic to leave the room. There was a downside of working with someone you lusted after. Relationships got strained when the jealousy gene was triggered.

I kicked around in my office doing some superficial tidying and decided, on a whim, to ring TJ from the American skin preservation group. I asked him if he knew Georgio Papadopoulos. He did. TJ told me he'd been one of the founding members and very keen on perfecting a full skin preservation technique.

Well, fancy that? Did Papadopoulos want his own body preserved when he died? Was he that narcissistic? My brief acquaintance with him suggested yes.

Then my opposite number from the UK gave me an unexpected call.

'This is early in the day for you, Andy,' I said.

'Hah, I'm still on yesterday. It's the middle of the night here, but I thought this was important,' said Andy Miller. 'I've been doing some cross-referencing. There have been other UK nationals missing while on backpacking holidays in Australia these past few months. They were last seen on the east coast. A good percentage of them had sizeable tattoos. I reckon that's worth keeping in mind, Eve. There maybe someone running a racket to tattoo and then murder holidaymakers for their skin art, however bonkers that sounds.'

'It's not bonkers at all. We're following that lead.'

'Let me know how you go.'

Ely checked Acropolis Holdings: Georgio Papadopoulos owned tattoo parlours in Sydney, Melbourne and Brisbane.

'So Duggins' murder might be the tip of the iceberg,' said Ely.

'You think Papadopoulos is involved with these backpacker murders?'

'Yep. Let's arrest him now,' said Ely. 'Please.'

I didn't know what to say but yes. It seemed far-fetched that the American lawyer would be bumping off backpackers for their tattoos. But there again, he wanted to perfect the art of skin preservation, so it might have been a cheap way of experimenting or funding the experiments. Who knew how people's minds worked?

'Okay, bring him in for questioning,' I said.

'You've just made my day, boss.'

Ely went off with a couple of uniforms to arrest the lawyer but came back hours later, empty-handed.

'It's crazy. Georgio Papadopoulos has disappeared into thin air,' said Ely. 'His receptionist is hysterical. Work's banking up and he's not answering his calls, which apparently constitutes the end of the world.'

'Reckon he's done a runner?' I said.

'Looks like it. We've alerted the airports and traffic cops.'

'Does he have any family? Wife? Boyfriend?' said Quinn.

'Not that we know of.'

'Eve?'

'I only know he's not married.'

'Or that's what he told you,' muttered Quinn.

I ignored the jibe. 'What about Extreme Body Arts? It's a long shot, but maybe he's there.'

Ely rang the number. There was no reply. 'Perhaps Sweet has already knocked off. It's getting late.'

'How about we swing by and check,' I said. 'You never know our luck. The other three tykes might be hiding out there even if Papadopoulos isn't.'

The sun was dipping, the day dying, but the heat was still our tangible companion. I could have done with a long cool shower and longer, colder drink instead of chasing around for missing suspects. But, hey, this was my lot in life.

The industrial estate was pretty much deserted except for the odd tradie in his ute heading home. We walked across the zig-zaggy forecourt to the door and knocked loudly.

'Dead as a dodo,' said Ely. 'We're wasting our time.'

As we turned to retrace out steps, I looked down at the pink paving. 'Is it my imagination or have these pavers been re-jigged?'

'Not that old chestnut,' said Ely.

'I'm not kidding.' The white sand looked fresh. A couple of the paving slabs rocked slightly as I tested them with my weight.

'No,' said Ely but he sounded in denial.

I bent down and brushed away the sand with my fingers and felt the concrete beneath. 'It's damp.'

'No,' he said again and scratched the back of his head. 'Hell, no.'

24

It didn't take long to cordon off the area and rig up barricades and arc lights. It didn't take much longer to find the remains, neatly butchered and laid in orderly fashion under the slabs.

'Reckon it's human remains, Rach?' I asked the pathologist.

'Yep.'

'We'll need to know who it is ASAP.'

'You've got it, Eve. I'll fast track it.'

We couldn't rouse Karl Sweet and so tried his cousin. 'Why would I know his whereabouts?' whined Jeremy. 'We don't hang out together.'

'Do you have a key for the tattoo parlour?' I asked.

'No.'

'Then we'll have to break in, but of course with your permission.'

'Do I have much of a choice?'

'Not really,' I said with my fingers mentally crossed. I didn't want the delay of getting a warrant.

'Then I should be there. As a witness.'

'Make it quick.'

Jeremy was there in ten minutes. 'Karl's not going to like this,' he said.

'Karl will have to suck it up,' said Ely.

Unless it was Karl who'd been chopped up and hidden in bits under his prissy pink forecourt, but I didn't share that thought. I didn't think my tasteless observation would be appreciated.

We rammed open the multi-coloured painted door and Ely flicked on the lights. Fox, Burton, a couple of uniforms and myself, with a mincing Jeremy, followed him in. We moved swiftly through the hot, stuffy reception area and into the oven-hot workshop.

We stopped with necessary abruptness.

The bright strip lights left nothing to the imagination.

They harshly illuminated the stretched human parchment, the animal skins and the stuffed tabby, which stared back at us in open-mouthed, mute miaow.

'This is horrible,' said Jeremy. It was. With the hard yellow light, it resembled a horror torture chamber. You could smell the blood, the *fear*.

Jeremy tugged at his bow tie, trying to get more air.

Fox swore.

So did Ely. 'Take a look at that, why don't you,' he said.

There was a full-sized mannequin that hadn't been there on our previous visits. The grotesque statue was standing in the middle of a blue tarpaulin that was awash with blood and other gunk.

The mannequin's glossy black, blood-dripping beard was the give-away.

'Oh boy. Gorgeous Georgio is no longer gorgeous, if I'm not much mistaken,' said Ely.

There was a thump behind me and Jeremy Sweet hit the ground in a dead faint. I nearly followed suit but Fox gripped me by the arm and marched me out into the fresh air.

'Breathe,' he said. 'Deeply.'

I sucked in the dark, sweet air untainted by blood until I had myself back in control. Or thought I did.

I threw up over Fox's shoes.

'Omigod, I'm so sorry.'

Fox looked down ruefully at his footwear. 'No worries. It happens,' he said.

And then I did it again.

It wasn't my finest hour.

The night stretched into a long one. Merv Turner, Tyson Pike and Louis Ragnall were arrested on the Nullabor, flooring

Papadopoulos' sports car and heading east. Karl Sweet was also found, tied to a chair, gagged, distraught with his eyes stretched wide, in the tattoo parlour's kitchen.

He was taken to the station, checked by the medics and then pronounced fit enough to be interviewed.

'What happened?' I said.

Karl cowered in his seat and turned his head away.

'We'd call your lawyer except he's busy shrink wrapping a shop dummy,' said Ely with his off-colour humour.

I tried not to shudder. I couldn't get the image out of my head.

'Come on, Karl. Get it off your chest. Just like you sliced the tats off those backpacker bodies,' said Ely, on a roll.

'I never done that. I didn't do the flaying. I just cured the kosher ones from the funeral homes.'

'So who did?'

'Tyson mainly. He had the knife skills.'

'Did he kill Georgio Papadopoulos?'

Karl slightly nodded.

'For the tape, mate,' said Ely.

'Yeah, Tyson slit his throat.'

'Run us through what happened.'

'Mr P called a meeting the night before last.'

'Who with?'

'Tyson and his mates, Louis and Merv.'

'Not you?'

'No. I wasn't part of the in-crowd. They were just using my place to meet.'

'Which actually belongs to Georgio Papadopoulos.'

'Yeah.'

'So why the meeting?'

'Mr P said things were getting out of hand and they should lay low for a bit.'

'What sort of things?'

'That this police bird,' he flicked a look at me, 'was getting a handle on our operation. He wanted them to stop till things died down.'

'What was the operation?' I said.

He squirmed and it took us time and patience to winkle the story out of him. 'The lads,' he said, 'had offered free tattoos to backpackers at the city hostel. When the time was right, they took the tattoos.'

'As in sliced them off?'

'Yeah. It wasn't good.'

'I think that's what I'd call an understatement, Sweet.'

'I didn't like it. I wasn't involved. I didn't do anything wrong.'

'You knew it was wrong yet you provided the venue,' I pointed out.

'I didn't have a choice. It was part of my contract with Mr P.'

Tyson Pike refused to co-operate so we let him stew in a cell while we interviewed his mates.

Louis Ragnall was first cab off the rank. He sat there sweating in the interview room, trying to hold it together, but nervously cracking his knuckles.

'It started off when we bodged a tattoo commissioned through the skin preservation association,' said Ragnall. 'The family had paid us a lot of money upfront. We couldn't afford to pay it back. So Tyson came up with the idea of tattooing someone else with the same design and then we could harvest it and no one would be any the wiser.'

'Harvest?'

He dropped his eyes and hunched his shoulders, trying to make himself smaller. 'Okay, we killed and skinned him.'

'Who?'

'Some guy.'

'Can you be more specific?

'Tyson had met this backpacker. He offered him free tattooing.'

'This guy?' We showed him a picture of Charlie O'Toole.

'Yeah. I guess.'

'And then what?'

'Duggins had been bragging to Merv at the funeral home about how much money could be made from the framed tattoos. We weren't getting that many jobs through the association. We wanted some of the bigger action.'

'Go on,' prompted Ely.

'Tyson reckoned we could organise our own supply after our success with the backpacker. And Merv had the opportunity of slicing off dead people's tattoos and bringing them over to us at Extreme Body Arts.'

'Do you know anything about the tongues and livers in the freezer at Cranberry Court?'

He shrunk further into his seat and swiped at his sweating upper lip.

'Louis?'

'Yeah, I wasn't keen on that. The freezer belonged to Tyson's uncle. He kept surplus stock in there. Tyson thought we could cash in on the cannibalism fetish as we were trying to work out what to do with the dead bodies.'

'How entrepreneurial,' I said drily. 'Did you sell any...er...pieces?'

'No. Tyson had put out feelers online but we hadn't made any sales.'

Thank goodness for that.

'What was Georgio Papadopoulos' role in all this?'

'He met us at Karl's and realised what we were doing.'

'He was for it?'

'Yeah. He thought we were on to something good. But he wanted us to expand our skills to cure full-on bodies. That's why we were mucking around with stuffing animals. Trying to get our heads around it.'

'Have you done any complete bodies?'

'No.'

'Except for Georgio Papadopoulos.'

'Well, yeah. Except for him.'

Merv Turner was apologetic.

'I admit it got way out of hand,' he said.

'That's perceptive of you,' I said. 'Why did Tyson kill Georgio Papadopoulos?'

'He was threatening us. He said we were out of control and that he'd deal with us like he dealt with Duggins.'

'He told you that?'

'Yeah. Duggins was going to tell you guys about the cannibalism racket but Tyson found out and threatened him.'

'By cutting off his finger?'

'Yeah, so instead of squealing to you, Duggins told Mr P.'

'So Papadopoulos didn't know about your gruesome sideline before that?'

'Not the cannibalism, no.'

'But he did know about the tattoos?'

'He found out through Karl, I think.'

'Was it you who put Charlie O'Toole's remains in Mrs Booth's casket?'

Merv hung his head. 'Yeah. We'd dug up the remains and needed to get rid of them quick. I'd done it before and thought we'd be okay.'

'But Mr Hammer had forgotten to tell you about the coffin recycling.'

'Yeah. Bummer.'

'So the murdered men's remains were cremated with other bodies?'

'Yeah. It was a sensible way of doing it. But the Hammers don't always have cremations. That's why those remains were put under the paving until a cremation was booked. With you guys digging up the garden, we had to make a diversion and get them out them quick.'

Tyson Pike was last in line. He was belligerent and arrogant, maintaining he'd done no wrong.

'Them backpackers were free-loaders. They'd never done a decent day's work, they won't be missed,' said Pike

'How do you know they weren't tradies like you?' I said. 'With family and friends who'd miss them?'

He didn't answer.

'All of them had been reported missing. So bang goes your theory, Pike.'

'Why did you do it?' said Ely.

'Money. Why else?'

'These were real people with lives and dreams and goals and you cut them down for money?' I said.

'I'm a butcher. I deal with carcasses all the time. The animals don't ask to be killed. I looked on these blokes in the same way. Supply and demand. Simple.'

'Do you like being a butcher?'

'It's a job. I don't mind it. But the money's not that good.'

He showed no remorse for his crimes. The only flash of emotion was triggered by the mention of Georgio Papadopoulos.

'That up-himself bastard,' he said. 'He tried stopping us, as if he owned us. He treated us like halfwits. He deserved everything he got.'

We needed psych reports on the three youths, but basically Operation Popsicle was in the bag. Now I needed fresh air and sleep.

The air part was easy. I wandered along the Swan River foreshore, watching the pelicans and black swans going about their birdy business while rowers burst gaskets as they propelled their boats through the smooth, dawn-kissed water.

The sleeping wasn't. For one, I had OD'd on caffeine during the night and my brain was sparking like a faulty switch. And two, I didn't fancy bedding down at the hostel. It wasn't a venue conducive to daytime sleeping – nor night-time, if the truth be known. I decided to beg my iron nun of a mother to let me bunk down at the school.

It was still early and St Immaculata's had the heavy stillness of sleep settled over it like a comfortable quilt. I wandered over the sprinkler-damp lawn. The temperature was pleasantly warm but would no doubt become intense by mid-morning. I let myself into the cool kitchen. I listened. All was quiet on the home front. I toyed with the idea of making myself a snack as I hadn't eaten since the day before. But in all reality, I couldn't stomach food. Not yet. Not until I could erase the monstrous mannequin from my mind.

Georgio would be spinning in his grave if he'd seen the hideous mutilation of his beautiful body, except he didn't have a grave yet, and probably wouldn't. Being in bits, he'd more likely be cremated once his remains were released.

Leaving the kitchen, I went into the foyer. Someone was up. I could see a sliver of light coming from under the door of my mother's study. I knocked and walked in without waiting for permission.

'Eve!' Sister Immaculata slammed shut the Bible, but it was too late. I'd clocked her stash.

'Doing a Dawn French, Mum? Clever. I would never have thought to look in your Bible. So much for it being a revered antiquity.'

Like the Bible in the Vicar of Dibley, the inner pages had been cut to make a sizeable secret compartment. It was large enough to hold several bars of chocolate – or a bag of necklaces, rings and a bracelet.

'I was forced to,' said the nun. Pink spots of annoyance arose on her cheeks. 'For survival.'

'Really? Doesn't God provide to those who ask?'

'Yes. He brought the jewellery into the school.'

'Are we talking here of God or Henry?'

'Henry was a tool of the Lord.'

I decided there and then that my mother would join Pike, Ragnall and Turner in having a psychiatric appraisal.

'Without the income generated by the jewellery, the school will have to close. It doesn't make enough money,' she said.

'Put up the fees.'

'That's not an option.'

'You can't expect me to turn a blind eye.'

She gave me a challenging stare, but I knew that if I compromised my position, I was up the proverbial. I had to hold firm to that sentiment. If I let my standards slip, I'd be done for. That meant if I suspected a fellow cop or colleague of being bent, I reported it. Even if he was a friend, a lover, or whatever, the case had to be investigated. Family members were the same. I wouldn't cut them slack or I'd lose credibility and my own self worth.

Okay, so I admit there were a few things I wasn't quite so black and white on, like taking my gun home, which was dead against regulations. But, in my defence, home, through my extensive personal experience, could be a pretty dangerous environment.

Of course, that's if one has a home: I was still working on that outcome.

'I'm sorry, Mum, but you've had a good run. It's time to face the music.'

I rang Quinn to come and arrest her.

25

Operations Popsicle and Wisteria Place had been satisfactorily put to bed. Ely had changed his pink paving and Fox his shoes. Mum was temporarily "away" and the State had seized St Immaculata's because it had been bought with the ill-gotten gains of the late Harry Shorten, AKA Henry Talbot. The school was to be closed and sold off.

On a high note, the insurance had paid out on my car.

On a low one, they hadn't paid out on the house. We were locked in mortal combat over that tricky issue.

And my country posting was looming fast.

'So where does that leave me?' said Chastity. We were packing our last few personal effects.

'We've discussed this already. You'll be coming with me and enrolling at high school.'

'Why can't I go to school here?'

'I've no one to look after you and I can't afford fees for a boarding school.'

'So I have to be buried in the country with you? That is so totally unfair.'

'Yes, Chastity, it is, for both of us. I don't want to go either but we have to get on with it.'

'But what about my boyfriend?'

'You have a boyfriend?' I blinked in surprise.

'Yes. Duh. Where did you think I've been hanging out all this time?'

'Gran said you were with a girlfriend.' And I had just accepted that. No wonder Chastity had looked so tired!

'Bless her. Gran's so unworldly.'

I disagreed. That was never something you could lay at the Iron Nun's door.

'I mean, look how she got caught up with Pops and the jewels.'

Hmm. Should I disabuse her? But I wanted to find out more about the boyfriend. There was plenty of time for her to discover her grandmother's foibles, but this was more pressing.

'So who is this boy? Will I get to meet him?'

'That depends on whether you will be nice to him or not.'

'I can be nice.'

'I'll think about it.'

And with that I had to be content.

I had a hot date. I'd bought a nifty little black number especially for the occasion. Feeling jaunty, I flicked on some mascara and lippy. I smiled at the mirror, pleased with the result.

My reflection stared back, those big brown eyes growing intense. I shivered. My smile faded. My bubbly mood popped and died.

Because look what had happened the last time I'd glammed up. I'd ended up looking like Heath Ledger's Joker; half dead and floating in the Swan.

With an effort, I brushed off the bad feeling. This time all would be good, and about time too. I deserved a bit of loving.

I tizzed my hair. And tizzed some more. It didn't do much. The tight orange curls looked as though I was wearing a dyed sheepskin. I hastily blocked the thought.

Don't think of skins.

Though it was a warm evening, I intended on wearing my new-old leather jacket. I held it up. Bullet holes perforated the heavy brown leather. What a sacrilege. But I would wear it anyway. I shrugged into it and, heart lifting, went off to meet my destiny.

He was waiting in his Holden.

He'd had it fixed up, sort of, though it was still a little crumpled in places.

'I've booked us into Jinxed. You cool with that?' he said.

I could have said no, but I didn't want to give reasons. Georgio Papadopoulos was best left out of the equation. I didn't want anything spoiling our night together.

We arrived at the restaurant and I was glad to see Jimmy the hipster was still alive. He greeted me with a knowing smile as he showed us to our table. I reckon he thought I was a player because I kept turning up with different men.

Quinn and I sat under the awning of stars with the Swan River reflecting a myriad of lights. The cyclone had finally run out of steam and a gentle breeze, scented with frangipani, caressed our cheeks. We were serenaded by a young guitarist and the muted sound of the other diners while we sampled a platter of tapas delights. It couldn't get much better.

And then Quinn dropped his bombshell.

'I've an undercover op coming up. I leave first thing tomorrow.'

There was no point asking questions. I knew he wasn't allowed to share information.

'And I'm off to the country. So this is goodbye, then.'

I took a mouthful, but the tangy lime marron turned to tasteless ash as my throat constricted. I doggedly chewed on and hoped I wasn't going to embarrass myself by choking or crying.

'Only for a while, babe.' He reached over and took my hand, stroking it with his thumb. 'You gonna be a good girl and wait for me?'

'Maybe,' I hedged. 'But I may have to use Cub Fox as a substitute. Keep it in the family, so to speak.'

'Do that, Red, and I'll kill the both of you.' He crushed my fingers in his fist, but then he raised my hand and kissed my knuckles.

'Not jealous, Quinn?' This was easier, sparring rather than giving into the sadness and disappointment.

He held my gaze over our joined hands that he still held close to his lips. 'I'd never thought I was the jealous type, but you do press my buttons, honey. Leave my boy alone and we should be just fine.'